GUIDE
STAR

A gripping and emotional rollercoaster of a novel about
love, life and not giving up

JOY ELLIS

JOFFE
BOOKS

Published 2017 by Joffe Books, London.

www.joffebooks.com

ISBN- 978-1-912106-52-3

In memory of Thomas James and Florence Mary Ellis —
Tom and Florrie — love always.

CHAPTER ONE

'Stella? Can you hear me?'

With a monumental effort, Stella North opened her eyes and a stream of figures swam in her vision. Smiling, shadowy strangers looking down upon her.

She closed her eyes again, preferring the heady confusion of her dreams to this scary, odd-smelling room filled with people she didn't know.

The voice persisted. 'Stella? Open your eyes for me.'

No. She would stay where she was, wrapped in that warm cocoon.

It's not nearly as safe as you think.

Stella's eyes snapped open.

'Hello there. Welcome back. You are in the neurosurgical ward at the Pilgrim Hospital.'

Hospital? Why? she tried to ask, but the words wouldn't come out. Her tongue lolled uselessly like a piece of damp chamois leather.

Someone squeezed her hand. 'I'm your surgeon, Dr Field-Latimer — Donald to you — and I'll be looking after you.'

So the voice had a name. And a double-barrelled one! God, I must be really ill, she thought, he said he was a surgeon.

'Do you remember what happened to you, Stella?'

Stella couldn't think of anything to say. She struggled to focus her wayward mind. Suddenly she had a picture of a brand new leather jacket. Another dream? No. Black, soft, lined in grey silk — expensive. She had just put it on and it felt like heaven, and then . . . ? She frowned. Then nothing.

'What were you thinking of? Can you tell me?'

'My new jacket,' she croaked. The words sounded odd, as if they didn't belong to her. 'Where's my bloody jacket?'

Laughter trickled around the room and Dr Double-Barrelled squeezed her hand tighter. 'Well, that's something I suppose,' he said.

Stella wanted to laugh with them, but she didn't get the joke. Then she wanted to cry, and she didn't understand that either. Oh shit! What did she know? Her panic intensified.

Then she heard another voice, gentle and cracking with emotion. 'Thank God. Oh, thank God.'

The speaker caught her breath and seemed to sob. But that couldn't be right, could it? She had recognised the voice alright, but its owner *never* cried. 'Gran?'

'Sweetheart! My darling.' Her grandmother took her other hand, and rocking backwards and forwards, held it in silence.

Warmed by the familiar touch, Stella's panic subsided and she finally let go of her dreams.

She looked around her. Banks of humming, bleeping machines flanked her bed. Most of them seemed to be connected to her own body. Oh, this was not good, this was serious. She had better do an assessment.

There was little pain, but she couldn't seem to move. Why? She tried a small wriggle and felt considerable discomfort down her right side. Something was pulling. A dressing?

Dr Double-Barrelled was watching her. 'It's a drain, Stella. You'll be sore for a while, but it will be out soon.'

'I've had an operation?'

'Several.' He smiled cautiously. 'You've been very ill.'

Anxiety began to bubble up again. 'Oh. Am I *still* very ill?'

'You are doing brilliantly.' He looked at her intently and seemed to wink. 'Partly due to my miraculous skills as a surgeon, of course, but . . .' The smile faded somewhat. 'We do need to do further tests to know what is going on.'

'Going on?' Her voice trembled.

'I think we should tell her everything, Dr Field-Latimer.' Tears gone, Stella's grandmother, Beth Cartwright, looked directly at the surgeon. 'She's a resilient and very brave young woman. My Stella doesn't like being fed half-truths.'

Right now, Stella felt far from brave, but on some level she knew that her grandmother was right.

The surgeon nodded. 'We know all about her resilience, or she wouldn't be here now.' He looked down at her. 'The thing is, Stella, you have been in an induced coma for two weeks. You have damage to your right side — a broken rib and a considerable flesh wound, all of which should heal well, and if you work on exercising the muscles, they should give you few problems in future.'

He paused while Stella absorbed what he was saying. So why a coma? Surely a busted rib and a gash to her side weren't that serious?

He sat on the edge of her bed. 'The side injury wasn't all. You also have a serious head trauma, Stella. We have had to wait for the swelling in your brain to subside. That's why we need to do the tests.'

Head trauma? 'Did I fall? Was I in an RTC?' She stopped, confused. What the hell was an RTC anyway?

'No, sweetheart.' Beth took over, and her words hung in the air like a guillotine blade. 'It was not an accident. Someone shot you.'

* * *

A while later in the relatives' room, Beth sank down onto a chair and let out a long sigh. She had expected only Edward Byrne, Stella's ex-husband, to be waiting for her, but instead three haggard faces looked up expectantly.

Edward leaned forward. 'Well, Beth? How is she?'

'She's awake.' Beth patted his knee, and allowed herself a tight smile. 'She's not only awake, but she's talking and she recognised me.'

Edward gave a little whoop and hugged the small brunette who sat beside him. 'I *knew* she would pull through!'

Lexi, wife number two, hugged him back and smiled broadly. 'We all thought she'd make it, but . . .'

Beth knew exactly what Lexi meant. Stella was a police officer, and one tough woman, but you couldn't rely on that. You didn't dare.

For a moment she saw them as an outsider might. No parents and no anxious spouse or partner, just a wiry stick of a grandmother, a divorced husband, his pretty new wife and a rather ragged work colleague. Beth looked across the room at the third occupant, a tall, lanky and uncomfortable-looking man in scuffed trainers, faded jeans and a hooded sports sweatshirt. He might have been a teenager, somebody's son, but Beth knew that he was much older than he looked.

Robbie was silent, but the relief on his face needed no words. After a while he stood up. 'I'd better be going. I guess you guys will have a lot to talk about.' As he passed Beth he lightly touched her shoulder. 'I can't tell you how pleased I am, Mrs C. Now I know what they mean when they say, "a tower of strength." I'm sure her recovery has a lot to do with your being there for her.' He smiled awkwardly. 'Er, well, give her my best. I'll be back as soon as she's well enough for visitors. Oh, and tell her the whole station is rooting for her.'

The door closed.

Lexi smiled. 'Doesn't look much like a detective, does he?'

'Nor does Stella, come to that,' Edward added. 'Still, wouldn't work if they all looked the part, would it? The criminals would spot them a mile off and have a field day.'

Beth knew that this chat concealed turbulent emotions. For the past two weeks they had been considering matters of life and death, and what sort of life might follow a severe head injury.

'So what happens next?' asked the ever-practical Edward.

'Tests. Then more tests. Assessments, reviews and then more of the same.' Beth felt drained. She had been through some truly dreadful times in her life, but nothing had been as bad as seeing her only grandchild lying in that room, a machine causing her chest to rise and fall. 'The doctors say it will take a while to evaluate the damage.' There was a catch in her voice. 'And we have to be aware that there *will* be changes in her, even if her recovery goes well. The doctor told me that no one comes back from a traumatic brain injury exactly as they were before.'

Donald Field-Latimer had sat down with her to explain that the bullet they had removed had struck an area of the brain that affected a multitude of behaviours.

'No two brain injuries are the same, Beth, but we know that there is a good chance that she will have problems with basic cognitive skills. She'll find it difficult to concentrate, and will have trouble remembering or retaining new information. And she is likely to experience exaggerated mood swings, with severe depression. And this is on top of other possible problems including seizures, loss of balance, vision, sense of smell, hearing.' He shrugged. 'The list is endless. This is just a warning that you should be prepared for anything, but some of the impairments will dissipate completely over time. Her life's course has changed, Beth, but with careful guidance, she *will* have a life.'

Beth had nodded, but knew something that the doctor didn't. Stella's career was her life. From dawn to dusk, and on through the night, Stella lived and breathed the police force. Her broken marriage was testament to that.

'Can we go in and see her?' Edward asked, breaking into Beth's musings.

'Yes, of course. We shouldn't tire her out, but the doctor thinks it will help her to know that she is surrounded and supported by friends and loved ones.'

Lexi stood up. 'I'd better get back for Ethan. I rather dumped him on Mum when we heard the news about Stella coming off the respirator.' She smiled at her husband. 'He's probably driving her mad by now. You go spend some time with Stella, Eddie. Give her my love and tell her I'll visit tomorrow.' She gathered up her bag and coat, pecked him on the cheek, and turned to Beth. 'Now, will you finally get some rest? She's going to need you so much in the coming days, and *you* need sleep and hot food. Come to us tonight. I've got a chicken casserole in the oven and there's enough for all of us *and* a small army.'

Beth knew she meant it. They certainly hadn't acted like most families following a divorce. They all got on, including Stella and Lexi. 'Thank you. I'll wait until she's settled for the evening, then I'll call in on my way home.'

'If you're not with us by eight, I'll come and get you myself,' Lexi said. Before having their baby son, she had been a teacher and every so often she slipped back into classroom mode. 'You won't be running marathons again if you neglect your body.'

'No, ma'am.' Beth gave a mock salute and tried to look contrite. Long-distance running was the last thing on her mind right now. Even the love of her life, a field spaniel called Frisbee, was "holidaying" with a neighbour.

Edward ran his fingers through his thick brown hair. 'How much does she know?'

'Just that she was shot, and that she's been in a coma. She can't be inundated with information yet. She won't be able to process it,' Beth replied.

'But no memory of what happened?'

'Not yet, possibly never.'

'Maybe for the best?' He looked at her.

Beth shrugged. 'Maybe. I think she'd cope with knowing about what happened to her. It's the fact that she'll never be able to go back into the police force that's worrying me.'

'With very good reason.' Edward's forehead creased. 'I certainly wouldn't want to be the one to drop that little bombshell into her lap.'

'Nor me,' Beth said glumly. 'Although I'm pretty certain who will finish up with that delightful task, what do you reckon?'

Edward gave a rueful smile. 'Good luck with that.'

* * *

Robbie Melton sat in his car, gripping the steering wheel until his knuckles turned white. He stared through the windscreen. His earlier euphoria at Stella's re-awakening had quickly turned to anxiety. His grandfather had suffered brain damage in the Falklands War, and Robbie would never forget the vague, absent shell that he became.

He exhaled and made himself relax. Whatever happened from now on, she had made a good start. If ever there was a woman who would fight back, it was Stella. A small smile spread across his face. In the five years they'd worked as a team, she had outshone him by far — faster, stronger and brighter. Sure, he had his qualities too, but he knew that Stella could get to the very top. She had made detective sergeant at thirty, while he was still a constable. The smile widened, because that was fine by him. He loved his work with a vengeance and had no aspirations for gold braid and pockets full of pips.

He sat back and watched figures huddled in warm coats and jackets, fight the biting east wind as they hurried across the car park. He and Stella had gelled from the start. Now, without her, he was adrift, working by rote and finding little excitement or pleasure in his life. If she knew how much he was suffering, Stella would give him a bollocking and tell him to get a bloody grip. But somehow he couldn't. She had got him out of several tight corners, and once had actually saved his life, even if she denied it vehemently. But he hadn't been there for her when she needed him. He knew it was irrational to feel guilty, because he had been miles away. She was off duty and simply in the wrong place at the wrong time.

Two drug-fuelled kids, a bungled robbery, and a gun.

Stella had done what came naturally. She had protected those around her, and taken a bullet for her troubles. Two bullets, actually.

Robbie smashed both his palms hard onto the steering wheel and let out a stifled cry. It wasn't fair! She had been the most alive person he had ever met. He never tired of working with her, despite the teasing he received from some of his colleagues. Some of them had suggested that it would be a relief for him not to be working in her shadow, and that his career would progress further in a different crew. What rot! It had never been cold in her shadow. She needed him as much as he needed her. He had always seen himself as an important component in a well-oiled machine.

Robbie turned the key in the ignition and slowly released the handbrake. Now he was just a spare part.

CHAPTER TWO

Six months later

Stella looked up at the clock. Two more minutes on the cross trainer, and she would have done more than yesterday.

Donald Field-Latimer, her neurosurgeon, had said she was his only patient ever to actually enjoy physiotherapy. Certainly, few begged him to be let *into* the gym, rather than out of it. Luckily he was a great believer in physical exercise and as soon as her side had healed he, her physiotherapist and her grandmother had got together and worked out a programme for her.

In the six months since she had left the hospital, Beth's gentle encouragement had turned into a punishing fitness regime that stretched Stella's body further with every session. The wounds had healed well, the scarring on her side was not exactly pretty but she could handle that, and her hair covered the site of the surgery to remove the bullet to her head. Her mind, on the other hand, was proving trickier to mend.

She stood down from the cross trainer and steadied herself against a wave of dizziness. Her grandmother appeared, holding out a water bottle. 'Okay, kiddo, take in some fluids, have a quick shower, then I'll see you in the pool for a wind down.'

Stella watched her grandmother stride between the pieces of equipment towards the changing rooms. She was now seventy, but still wiry and as fit as a much younger woman. Before Stella's injury, Beth had not only trained to run marathons, but was also an aerobics instructor. 'I sure hope I've got your genes,' muttered Stella, 'because if I haven't, this will probably kill me!'

Like her grandmother, Stella swam like a fish. The pool was the place where all her problems left her and she could be herself again. Sometimes she was even able to smile.

Beth swam up to her, flipped over and floated on her back. 'Today was good in there.' She nodded towards the gym. 'Tomorrow will be even better.'

Stella felt a rush of emotion, and dived before her grandmother saw her tears. She knew that without Gran, she would have given up by now. But the need to meet her expectations was sometimes almost too much to bear.

Under the water, she had a sudden memory of waking up in the Intensive Care Unit and realising that her grandmother was by her side. In those confusing moments she had felt Gran's outpouring of love covering her like a warm duvet on a cold night. She was grateful to the surgeon, but it was her wise grandmother who had brought her back from the banks of the Styx.

She had to fight back and get well, for Gran's sake. Before the shooting, Stella had climbed sheer rock-faces, leapt over roaring torrents suspended on a slim bungee cord, and had run several marathons. But nothing had been as hard as this.

Stella swam harder, trying to fight the misery that threatened to engulf her. The problem wasn't her body. Okay, her coordination was rubbish, her balance was shot and her hand had an occasional tremor, but basically she was really getting strong. She had miraculously avoided seizures and her sight was unimpaired, so she would soon be allowed to drive. She knew she was incredibly lucky, but it didn't help. No, it was her mind that wasn't responding properly, from some subtle but irritating little quirks to full blown dysfunctions that terrified her. And despite numerous therapy sessions, she still had no idea how to confront them. She wasn't fighting the psychologists, in fact she readily embraced all the help they could offer, but the underpinning of her whole life had been knocked away from under her. She hardly recognised the woman she had become.

Stella powered up and down the pool, trying hard to count her blessings. At first, the simple fact that she was still alive had been enough. She was a survivor! She had taken two bullets and was still standing! She had been surrounded by friends and well-wishers, all amazed at her strength and courage. Not that she thought of herself as brave — actually she thought she'd been a total prat to get in the line of fire in the first place. But then what did she know? She still couldn't remember anything about it. Now the friends were distancing themselves, and she knew it was because she was pushing them away. Even Edward and Lexi sometimes seemed guarded, as if afraid of setting off an angry outburst. Last week she had snapped poor Robbie's head off. His hurt look still haunted her.

'Listen, I don't give a damn about what a blinding good result the team had on the Godwin case! And I don't care about the new arrest stats! If all you can talk about is force stuff, then don't visit. Can't you understand? It's nothing to do with me anymore,' she had told him.

Later she had rung him and apologised, but his tone was reserved and she sensed that a barrier had come up. If it had been the other way around, she would have had nothing else to talk about either. They were both dedicated police officers, living alone with no partners. Their work was everything. What else would he talk to her about? God, she could be such an idiot sometimes.

Stella turned and swam backstroke. She should never have been so harsh on Robbie, who was hoping she would accept the offer of a desk job.

One day a high-ranking officer, someone she only knew by name and reputation, had appeared by her hospital bed and assured her that there would always be a place for her. She had held onto that like a drowning person clinging to a spar. Then, as the weeks wore on and the extent of her injuries became clear, the offer had subtly changed. She heard words like "limited" and "reduced," and finally she realised that the "place" for her would be behind a desk.

After all she had been through as a serving officer. She couldn't even bring herself to think about it. She imagined watching all her old mates pulling on their stab-proof vests and adjusting their equipment belts ready for the next shout, and it reduced her to tears. There was no way she could sit behind a desk and stare at a monitor all day. Best to be well out of it. If being a glorified clerk was her only prospect, perhaps it would have been better for everyone if she had not surv—

'Are you done?' Her gran appeared at her side. 'Fancy a few minutes in the Jacuzzi?'

'Okay, a couple more lengths and I'll join you.' Stella dived under the water to wash away the tears.

* * *

Beth laid the table for lunch, thankful that she had not sold her lovely home. Her friends had all insisted that she needed to downsize: the place was far too big for a woman living alone. Beth thought the old green eye might have something to do with their words. Most of her small circle of contemporaries lived in compact bungalows or two-bedroomed houses in the village, whereas Coggles Barn was a beautiful conversion with views over the

Lincolnshire fields. It probably was too big for one, and it did take a lot of upkeep, but she loved it. Now that she had Stella staying with her, she was pleased that she'd stuck to her guns. One day she might consider moving, when Stella was settled back in her own house. Or maybe she'd only leave feet first! She didn't want change, not at this stage in her life. She'd had enough of that as a young woman. She recalled the frenetic and exciting time when she had lived and worked in London, travelling extensively and dreaming of a place of her own. Well, now she had it, and she wasn't going to let it go until she really had to.

Beth wondered when her granddaughter would decide to move back to her own house. It would be a wrench for both of them, but Beth had a feeling that, as soon as she was able to drive again, Stella would go. Physically she was doing amazingly well. If they could just get on top of the mood swings and bouts of depression, then Beth would be happy to let her move on. After all, Stella's house was only half a mile away, just a gentle stroll from Coggles Barn.

A noise at the front door made her look around. Her dog Frisbee, with a mouthful of letters, padded towards her from the hall. 'Thank you, Jeeves. Can I have those?'

The spaniel obediently released the envelopes onto the floor and sat staring at them hopefully.

Two of the letters were for Stella. It was handy living in a village, as the postman knew everyone and redirected Stella's post to Coggles Barn. 'Sorry, nothing for you today, Fris, unless you'd like to read the Dog's Trust newsletter?'

The dog strode off to his bed, where he scuffed the carefully folded blankets into an untidy heap and threw himself huffily onto them.

Beth placed the letters on the table and called out to Stella. 'Post's here and lunch will be in five minutes!'

Stella appeared a few moments later. Her pale face was drawn and the darkness beneath her eyes was more pronounced.

13

A feeling of total helplessness engulfed Beth. It wasn't working. None of it. Not the therapy sessions and now even the exercise routines were not enough. Stella needed help of a different kind, but Beth had no idea where to find it.

Stella dropped into a chair, picked up the post and slowly opened one of the envelopes. Beth saw an official-looking document.

'Another invitation to apply for a job.' Stella's voice was flat.

'Surely that's no surprise?'

'No, I suppose not, even though I told them I wouldn't be accepting it. They don't seem to get the message. If I can't do detective work, then . . .' Stella left the sentence unfinished.

'They don't want to lose you, sweetheart. You're too valuable.'

'I'm about as useful as a chocolate fireguard, and you know it.' She stood up and threw the second letter down unopened. 'Sorry, Gran, I'm really not hungry. I'm going to lie down for a while.'

* * *

In her room, Stella closed the curtains, lay on the bed and shut her eyes. All she wanted to do was curl up in a tight ball, sleep, and not have to face the world. No decisions, no confusion, no frustrations, no anxiety attacks, just deep, deep sleep.

She knew she wasn't being fair on her gran and she hated herself for it. The terrible emotional upheaval inside her allowed no room for others. She had no control anymore, and it wasn't her at all!

Stella pulled the duvet over her face. She knew she had to fight the black depression that threatened to overwhelm her, but sometimes the sense of failure and despair was just too much to bear. Her reason for being had gone, stolen in the blink of an eye. The rising star of the Fenland constabulary had plummeted to earth, brought down by a gun. She had only ever wanted to be a good police officer.

* * *

Downstairs in the kitchen, Beth bit her lip hard. There must be something she could do, another avenue to try. If only . . . Beth drew in a sharp breath. Where were her brains? Of course!

She turned and almost ran to the small room that she used as an office. She pulled open her desk drawer and began to rifle through the old diaries and notebooks it contained. Finally she found what she was looking for. The pages of the old address book were creased and faded, and many of the names were crossed out.

'Bugger old age,' she muttered angrily.

She leafed through to the letter 'L.' It was a long shot, but worth trying. It had been years, decades, but . . . 'Ah, here you are.' She stared at the name, overwhelmed by an avalanche of memories and emotions. Perhaps this was not such a good idea after all.

Beth eased herself down onto a chair and exhaled loudly. 'Get a grip, woman! Time for all that later. Right now, if anyone can help my girl, it's you, Michael. Just please, please be still there!'

Her hand shook as she began to dial, and her finger remained poised above the last digit for some time.

'Michael Lindenfeld,' he answered.

The voice was exactly the same. It took Beth's breath away.

'Michael?' Her voice was hoarse. 'I'm so sorry to bother you. It's . . .'

'Beth?'

For a moment there was silence, the connection as charged as a high-voltage power line.

'Beth? Is that really you?'

For a while Beth couldn't answer. Memories crashed around her like waves over rocks.

'Is something wrong? Are you alright?'

'No, Michael. Well . . .' The dam burst. 'Yes! Yes, something *is* wrong. Terribly wrong. I would never have asked this of you, but I need your help.'

It took almost fifteen minutes to pour out the story. When it was done she exhaled and added, 'Please tell me if I'm being unfair to call you after all this time, but I didn't know who else to turn to.'

'I would have been devastated if I'd found out about this and you hadn't contacted me.' The hint of an accent was still there. 'And this is now my field of expertise. A lot has happened in recent years and I'm no longer a neurosurgeon, Beth. I am a neuropsychologist. I practise here in Bad Harzburg, but I lecture all over the country — well, all over the world actually.'

'Then could you recommend someone, someone you trust, who might be able to help my Stella?' Beth hated her pleading tone, but right now, she'd crawl over broken glass for her granddaughter.

'Oh yes. As it happens he's the very best.' There was a hint of a chuckle in his voice. 'Depending on flights, I should be with you by tomorrow afternoon.'

Beth let out a small cry. 'But—'

'No protestations, Beth Cartright. I am due to give a talk on cognitive neuropsychology at the University of Essex in Colchester next week, so it will be no hardship to fly in earlier. I'll hire a car at Heathrow and drive up. Could you book me in somewhere local? Just a B&B would do nicely.'

'Of course. We have a very nice place right here in the village. I'll ring right away.'

'Give me your mobile number and email address and I'll let you know my flights and times.'

Beth rattled off her contact details and stammered some words of thanks.

'Forget it. It's my pleasure, and I can't wait to see you again.' His voice became gentle. 'How have you been?'

She didn't know where to start. 'Apart from my desperate worry about Stella, I guess I'm fine, Michael.'

'Still married?'

Beth drew in a breath. 'Widowed. Years ago. And you?'

There was a pause. 'I'm still with Frida.'

In the ensuing silence, Beth felt a sudden twinge of discomfort. 'Have I done the wrong thing, Michael? Perhaps I shouldn't have called you. Will this cause a problem for you? I'd hate it if—'

'Stop! There's no problem, I promise. Frida is staying up in the mountains, helping our youngest son and his wife with their new baby. She could be gone for weeks. And I, well, I spend more time away from home than ever, with my lectures and my patients.'

'I wish we'd stayed in touch.' There, it was said.

'We couldn't. We agreed.'

Was that sadness or regret in his voice? Beth wasn't sure, but there was certainly something.

'But there's barely been a day gone by when I haven't thought about you,' Michael added.

'After all these years?'

'Too many years.'

'We'll talk, when you get here.'

'Yes, Beth. We will.'

'And, Michael? I'm not sure how to tell Stella about your coming to see her. Her emotional state is so unpredictable at present that I don't know how she will react.'

'Then tell her nothing. We'll cross that bridge when we come to it. I'm used to reluctant patients. Sometimes they are hostile and aggressive. It comes with the territory. Maybe, if I could impose on you for dinner tomorrow night, you could just mention that an old friend, a former colleague, is in the country for a while?'

'And do you still like your steak rare?'

He laughed. 'What a memory! Now I need to get online and book a flight. I'll see you tomorrow.'

Beth replaced the phone with a sigh of relief. Then a river of excitement coursed through her. She was going to see Michael again, and he would help them. The hospital doctors and therapy groups had done their best, but Michael would not treat Stella as just another patient. She would be Beth's beloved granddaughter. They just needed to get Stella on side, and that could be a nightmare, given her frame of mind. Stella had refused all further counselling. But then she hadn't met Michael, who was one of the most charismatic men Beth had ever met. She hoped his old charm was still working.

Beth returned to the kitchen and finished preparing their lunch. She'd take Stella something on a tray.

She knocked softly, told the girl that there was food and a hot drink outside her door, and then tiptoed away without waiting for an answer. She took her own lunch to the table. For the first time in many months she didn't feel alone. There would be someone else fighting in her corner.

She glanced up at a framed photograph that stood on her bookcase. It was a picture of her crossing the finish line of the GrimReaper ultramarathon. Stella had taken it. She was a brilliant photographer, and had managed to capture all Beth's emotions in a single shot. There was pain, relief, and most of all the jubilation of completing that gruelling challenge. Beth desperately wanted to be that woman again, powerful and successful, taking every trial in her stride. Maybe she could, with someone to support her.

She took a forkful of pasta and tried not to let memories of Michael Lindenfeld overwhelm her. Her past, and all its complicated emotions, was bubbling to the surface. There had been so much between them, but circumstance had forced them to take different paths.

'What if?' Even then she had never permitted herself to whisper the words aloud. 'Don't even go there, Beth!

Oh God, I need a distraction.' She pushed her chair back and picked up her plate. Then she noticed the unopened letter that Stella had discarded on the table. The crest on the envelope was clear to see.

Buckingham Palace.

Beth gave a little gasp. It could only be one thing. She'd seen one of these before. A letter asking the recipient not to mention the contents to anyone, but the news of her Queen's Commendation for Bravery would be printed in the *London Gazette*.

'Oh, Stella,' she whispered to herself. 'I know you won't believe you deserve this, but you have no idea what you really did. Your selfless action saved several lives.' Beth placed both the letters on the dresser and went to dispose of her plate in the dishwasher. They'd talk about the award later. Well, Beth hoped they would.

She stared out of the window and surveyed her garden. Once it had been perfect. Now, the sight of the ragged weeds and uncut grass brought home to her just how much of her life she'd let slip since Stella had been shot. She didn't begrudge a second of it, but as time went on she would need to find a balance, or they would both fall apart.

CHAPTER THREE

Edward Byrne sat at the kitchen table and watched Lexi empty the dishwasher and stack the crockery in the appropriate cupboards. Her slender back was towards him. Everything about Lexi was neat, from her delicate, elfin face to her crisply ironed denim shirt.

He shouldn't, he knew, but even after all these years, he still found himself comparing her to Stella. He blamed the fact that he still lived in the house where he and Stella had begun their ill-fated marriage. Her presence still haunted the house. He could almost see her sitting on the sofa in the front of the big open fire.

Lexi closed a cupboard door and smiled at him. 'We had another milestone today. Our son strung two separate four-word sentences together!'

Edward forced a smile. 'Were they repeatable?'

Lexi shrugged. 'I'm still not totally fluent in Toddler, but the first was a definite recommendation to remove carrots from the luncheon menu, and the second was an observation as to the clinical obesity of next door's Labrador.'

'Not bad for a two-year-old. And what else has he achieved today? A little origami? Algebra? The Russian alphabet?'

'Give him time, Ed. He's still working hard at A-level potty training.' Lexi kissed the back of his neck and ruffled his hair as she passed him. 'Heard from Stella today?'

Edward tensed. 'No. Maybe I should ring her, though I know she hates talking on the phone, especially in the evening. She still gets confused and dead ratty when she's tired.'

'Then call in tomorrow on your way home from work. You know she'd love to see you.'

'Maybe. If I have time.' Edward refilled his coffee cup. 'Top up?'

She shook her head. 'I'll be dancing on the ceiling if I have another.' She went into the utility room and returned with a basket of freshly washed laundry. 'I'll just get this ironing out of the way and then maybe we could watch a film together?'

After a moment's silence, Edward said, 'I really need to get some emails dealt with.' He gave an apologetic shrug. 'And frankly, I'm exhausted. We have more orders coming in than manpower to fulfil them. Not that I should complain, seeing the way things are for most companies these days. How about we turn in early and try to grab some sleep before His Lordship begins another of his two o'clock yodelling masterclasses?'

Lexi pulled the ironing board out of the cupboard. She nodded.

'Oh dear. Am I turning into a boring old fart?'

Lexi gave a little snort. 'What do you mean "turning?"'

'That bad, huh?' He put his arms around her narrow waist. 'I blame the demon child.'

'Don't worry. One day he'll learn what a bed is for.'

'And then our worries will really begin!'

Lexi gave him a playful slap. 'Go sort out your computer.'

Edward closed the door to his study and sank down into his chair. He was worried sick. And he could not afford to share those worries with his wife. He closed his eyes and sighed. He loved Lexi, he did, but this was something he had to shoulder alone, and he wasn't sure how. The only person he could have talked to was Stella, and now that was out of the question. She had enough on her plate, and from the look of her, just getting through a day was a battle. The best he could do was to keep up a front, fool Lexi for as long as possible, distance himself from his darling son, and pray for a miracle.

* * *

Lexi carefully folded the last T-shirt and unplugged the iron. She was worn-out too, but it wasn't little Ethan's fault. She was worried about Edward.

Something had changed when Stella was shot, something deep. And it was affecting their little extended family. She knew he hadn't stopped loving her, that wasn't it. But there was a part of Edward that would always belong to Stella.

Lexi had known it from the outset. If she was to have him, the love of her life, she would have to make a space in their relationship for Stella. It had taken time and anguish, but as she'd never had a sister of her own, Lexi had decided to give that vacant position to Stella.

Somehow it had worked. After all, Edward and Stella were more like siblings than ex-partners. She could only think that that was why her injury had hit him so hard.

She carried the pile of ironing to the airing cupboard and carefully laid the clothes on the wide shelves. Lexi kept everything in order, neat and tidy. She was good at organising things. She'd once overheard Eddie telling his mother that Lexi had turned housekeeping into an art form, and it wasn't far from the truth. She loved looking after her husband, her son and her home, but emotions were another thing. They couldn't just be tidied away. He was slowly changing from the perfect husband and doting father to a distant stranger. In fact, Edward Byrne was a mess, and she didn't know how to put him back together again. But for the sake of their marriage, she *had* to find a way.

* * *

Beth glanced at the kitchen clock. It was after seven and Stella was still in her room. Earlier she had removed the untouched lunch tray and now Beth wondered if she would be cooking another meal that only she would eat.

She opened the fridge and peered inside, hoping for inspiration. She took out two salmon fillets, some new potatoes, asparagus and the makings of a salad. This was usually one of Stella's favourites. Beth sighed. The salmon could be eaten cold the next day if her granddaughter was still on hunger strike.

She prepared the meal and just as she was lifting the fish from the pan, Stella walked in and sat down at the table.

'Sorry about lunch, Gran. It's not your fault, but you're the nearest person to take it out on. You must think I'm an ungrateful cow.'

'Oh, all the time.' Beth gave her a warm smile. 'You must be famished. Let's eat.' She passed a plate to Stella. 'Fancy a glass of wine?'

'Are we celebrating?'

'Since when have we needed an excuse to crack open a bottle?' Beth pulled a chilled Chablis from the fridge.

Stella raised her eyebrows. 'True, although my tablets still limit me to one glass.'

'Then enjoy that one glass, hey? And actually, we do have something to celebrate.' She walked over to the dresser and picked up the sealed letter. 'I wasn't prying, but that seal on the back can mean only one thing. Congratulations, darling. It's absolutely wonderful.'

Stella took the envelope and opened it. '*The London Gazette*, huh? How very British.'

'Certain things must be done properly, you know.' Beth hugged her granddaughter. 'I'm *so* proud of you, Stella, and your mother would be over the moon.'

'I'd rather not have been shot, and have no medal.'

'I'm sure you would, sweetheart, but at least they have recognised your sacrifice. Like it or not, you're a hero.'

Stella stared at her plate, then picked up her knife and fork. 'I feel like a fraud, Gran.' She ate a mouthful of food. 'In fact there's something I've been meaning to talk to you about. I want to see the CCTV footage of the shooting. I'm never going to remember it for myself, but I need to know what happened. Can you understand that?'

Beth shivered. 'Yes, I understand, but I'm not sure it's a good idea.' *Watching yourself get shot? Stuff of nightmares, surely?*

'Nor am I, but I think it's something I have to do.'

'Would they allow it? Surely the tape is evidence?'

'You're right, Sherlock, but I asked Robbie if they'd made a copy and they had. I want to see it if I can.'

Beth frowned. 'What did Robbie think of the idea?'

'He said my brain damage must be worse than he thought.' Stella gave a rueful smile.

'Shouldn't we run it past your psychologist first?'

'I've had it with the shrinks, Gran. I want to make this decision for myself.'

Beth decided not to argue. Michael would be here tomorrow. 'Okay, well, don't rush into it. You really need to do it when you feel strong.'

They ate in silence until Stella said, 'I thought I'd see if Lexi is free for lunch tomorrow. I really need to hand her an olive branch. The last time we talked my mouth ran away with me. I don't know. I don't seem to have any tact or consideration for other people's feelings.' She took a small sip of wine. 'Would you ring her for me, Gran? I'm feeling a bit fuzzy and if she puts Edward on, I'll just say all the wrong things. Tell her I'll treat her to a baguette at the Café des Amis.'

After they finished the meal, Beth made the call. 'She said that would be lovely and she'll pick you up at the gym around noon. Which actually suits me too. Our Frisbee is down to his last Bonio and I need to get to the shops and stock up. And I know how you hate supermarkets.' Whether it was the lighting, their size, or maybe just the general hubbub, but the supermarket had triggered more than one panic attack and several spells of faintness. 'So I'll take you to the sports centre, then when we've finished I'll go shopping, if Lexi wouldn't mind dropping you home afterwards?'

'I'm sure she won't mind at all.'

'Oh, I forgot, Edward sends his love, and so does little Ethan.'

'Ah, sweet.'

But Stella's smile had faded. Once again she wore that grey mask of sadness. Beth was sure Stella missed Edward, even though the marriage hadn't worked out. It *had* to hurt, seeing him so happy with Lexi and their little son.

Beth's heart went out to her granddaughter. Until Stella found someone else to share her life with, all Beth could do was be there for her and give her as much support as she could.

* * *

That night, as the wind continued to howl in off the fen, Beth lay in bed, thinking of the past.

Beth watched the clock, nervous as a teenager before her first date. She could hardly believe that she would be seeing Michael Lindenfeld again. She felt guilty that she hadn't told Stella about his visit, but she believed it was for the best. Sometimes it was necessary to adjust the truth a little.

As soon as Stella turned in for the night, Beth sent a text to Lexi telling her that she had found some specialist help for Stella, but wanted to keep it a secret for now. Lexi replied immediately, saying that she understood perfectly and thought she was doing the right thing. Beth's thoughts returned to Michael. What should she tell Stella about him? She had never told anyone about her relationship with Michael. Their parting had torn her to shreds. How would she feel when she saw him again?

Beth sat up, rearranged her pillows and glanced at her clock. Well, she'd soon know.

* * *

Stella's mind was buzzing. She couldn't sleep either. There had been something different about her grandmother this evening. Maybe she was just excited about the Queen's Commendation. It was a great honour, after all. But somehow Stella didn't think that was the reason.

She turned over and tried to sleep, but she was haunted by thoughts of that CCTV footage. How would she react? Beth was probably right, she could be doing herself considerable harm. But she *needed* to do it. She'd ring Robbie tomorrow and organise it.

Stella sighed in the darkness of her room. It didn't help that they had never caught the men who'd hurt her. It was an ongoing investigation and detectives were still working on it as a priority case, but as more and more time went by, Stella knew the chances of an arrest were very slim. It wouldn't make any difference to what had happened to her, but just maybe she would feel better if someone was finally held accountable.

Then her rambling thoughts took her back to the days when she and Edward were together. Another place she didn't want to go. Who wanted to dwell on a failed marriage?

For a moment Stella couldn't remember which of them had had the courage to say it first.

'It's not working, is it?'

Edward stared at the floor, avoiding eye contact. 'No, I suppose not,' he mumbled.

The heavy silence seemed to last forever, until she broke it. 'I know it's my fault, Eddie. My career is so important to me that I can't be a proper wife to you.'

'It's not just you, Stel, it's both of us. We are both too committed to our work. You are dedicated to your job with the police and I have the family business. We knew this, but I don't think we really understood the implications for our marriage.'

Stella sighed. 'I thought, I really thought . . .'

Edward flopped down on the sofa next to her. All their earlier anger at each other had dissipated. He drew her to him and she let her head fall on his shoulder. 'So what do we do now?'

Edward spoke slowly. Had he rehearsed his next words? It sounded like it. 'You're my best friend, Stella. You have been my closest mate since schooldays — my climbing partner, my diving instructor, my everything, and I don't want to lose you.'

'But?'

'But even I know we make a crap husband and wife. For a start, neither of us are ever here. The housework builds up, then we let fly at each other over the smallest things. Like just now. Okay, neither of us remembered to put out the rubbish, but it was hardly grounds for a major fight, was it? I think we resent all that stuff because it keeps us from our precious jobs.'

Stella sighed. 'And when we are together we both just want to chill, not clean the windows or defrost the fridge. So. What? We cut our losses?'

Edward nodded, but when she looked at him his eyes were full of tears. 'I'm so sorry, Stel. We did best mates so well that I really believed we'd be the dream couple. Everyone did, our friends, family, everyone.'

'I think Beth knew we were making a mistake,' said Stella.

'Why do you say that? She supported us from day one.' Edward sniffed.

'She would. She's always supportive. But there were little things that told me she had her doubts. She's very perceptive.'

'It just seemed perfectly normal to me, a natural progression.' He wiped his eyes with the back of his hand. 'I do love you, Stella. I always will.'

'And I love you too, Eddie, but we are going to crucify each other if we continue like this.' She looked up at his handsome face. 'There's no one else. You do know that, don't you?'

'As if either of us have the time to be unfaithful.' He placed a light kiss on her forehead. 'Of course I know, and it's the same for me.'

'So where do we go from here?' she asked. He still held her tightly.

'Solicitors, I guess. Then tell the families.' He exhaled. 'I won't be looking forward to that.'

Stella was shocked at the relief she felt. It was as if someone had drawn a line.

Stella pulled the duvet closer to her. By abandoning their marriage they had salvaged their friendship. The whole process had been remarkably simple. The house had belonged to Edward's father, and she had sold her old family home when they married. She hated the place anyway. The money from the sale had sat in the bank ever since, so buying again was a breeze. Easy-peasy.

They had moved on. She had risen through the ranks, made detective sergeant, and spent every waking hour working or doing extreme sports. Edward had made remarkable strides in expanding his business. He'd even managed to get it to a point where he could indulge in a private life again, and then he met Lexi, the perfect little *hausfrau*.

Under the covers, Stella pulled a face. That was so unkind! She really liked Lexi, there was no way you could *not* like her, and she was a far better wife to Edward than Stella had ever been.

She thought of all the things she had aspired to just six months ago. All gone.

She didn't have a job or a partner to help her through the confusing world that she found herself in.

A wave of sadness, blacker than the night, swept over her. Was it really only six months? It felt like forever, and she wasn't sure she had the heart to go on. But the alternative was unthinkable. After her mother died, Stella's father had committed suicide. At first, she'd hated him for that. He had abandoned her, hadn't loved her enough to stay and face his demons. Could she really do that to her grandmother? Edward? Or Robbie? In her job she had seen the devastating ripple effect of a suicide on those close to the deceased. The act often destroyed more than one life. No, she had to beat this. She needed something new, something to fill the void in her life before it swallowed her up. But what?

Stella yawned. If only sleep would come.

* * *

Lexi felt Edward's weight on top of her. With a little moan of pleasure, she lifted her hips and began to move rhythmically against him. She whispered that she loved him and wanted him inside her, but tonight he didn't answer. There had been no joyful, teasing foreplay. Edward was merely going through the motions, and it was breaking Lexi's heart.

Until six months ago, their sex had been wildly exciting, fulfilling beyond words. They both agreed that they were second-time-around virgins, learning about each other's bodies and all the things that made those bodies come alive. Lexi's previous partner had been so unadventurous that he made the missionary position seem depraved. Edward had told her that sleeping with Stella had been "cosy," and he had never felt such glorious sexual freedom before Lexi.

Lexi didn't know how to rekindle that wonderful fire.

After a few minutes, Edward grunted and pulled away from her.

Job done, she thought sadly.

After he turned on his side, she nestled into his back and held him tightly. Once, they would have lain side by side in the darkness just holding each other's hands, and sometimes when Ethan's crying woke them hours later, they were still tightly clasped. Now, while Edward softly snored, Lexi felt terribly alone.

CHAPTER FOUR

Stella turned up her collar against the wind and hurried across the sports arena car park to Lexi's white Honda.

She had struggled through her morning session, and while they were in the changing room her grandmother had received a phone call. A very old friend, she said, a former work colleague, over here from Germany for a few days and eager to meet. She added that she'd invited him to dinner. Almost brusque, she had hurried off before their usual swim. Stella felt tired and stressed. She was pleased for her gran, but afraid this visitor would upset her routine. Stella liked this routine. It was safe. She just hoped that a stranger in the house, even just for one meal, wouldn't set her back. Maybe she should go out for the evening.

She waved to Lexi, and then her heart sank. Two other figures were seated in the back, clearly having a big laugh about something.

Oh no! This was not what she had planned! She should have got a cab home or tried to go shopping with Gran. She had made a major effort to even get here. This coffee was meant to be an apology to Lexi for being such a bitch of late, just a quiet natter in the Café des Amis, not a bloody girlie bunfight!

She took a deep breath and forced a smile. She *had* to get a hold on these damned moods of hers. She needed to build bridges, not cock things up even more.

Lexi leaned across and opened the passenger door for her. 'Hi, Stella! Don't worry about these two! I'm only giving them a lift into town. There's a sale on at Oldrids. They *need* shoes desperately and they have money burning a hole in their pockets.'

'Actually I have my Keith's credit card. Not that he knows it, poor sod.' Amy Briggs grinned maliciously from the back seat.

The other woman was Jenny Rose, whom Stella had known since Girl Guides. She leaned forward and gave her shoulder a friendly squeeze. 'How are you doing, Stella? Lexi says you've already worn out two cross trainers in the gym.'

Stella's apprehension melted away. She even managed a laugh. 'Not quite, but with a personal trainer like my grandmother, you toe the line, or else.'

'Oh yes, that's the famous Beth Cartright, isn't it? She's a miracle worker! She helped to get my chubby Paul fit for a charity run. He reckoned that she was a right ball-breaker! Tougher than most of the blokes, and a wrinklie, to boot!'

Stella nodded. 'That's the one. Even *she'd* agree about the balls, but for heaven's sake, don't let her hear you call her a wrinklie!'

The women all laughed, and the short trip into town turned out to be a quite bearable ten minutes.

'How about we meet up and go out for a meal one evening?' suggested Jenny, opening the back door. 'Leave the men at home with the kids and have a girls' night out?'

'I'm in,' Amy said immediately.

Stella felt panic rising. She couldn't think of anything worse.

Lexi came to her rescue. 'Ah, well, that's a bit difficult for me right now. Eddie's heading up a new project that keeps him at work all hours. Ethan is teething, and I'd hate to have to cancel at the last minute.' She looked across to Stella and gave her a discreet wink. 'How about we take a rain check?'

'Shame, but still. Ring us as soon as you're free, huh?' Amy gathered up her handbag and waved to Stella. 'Keep up the good work. See ya!'

As the two women walked away, Stella let out a sigh of relief. 'Phew! My hero!'

Lexi chuckled. 'I saw your face. Not quite your cup of tea, I guess.'

'Too right. Jenny's okay, but I could only ever take Amy Briggs in very small doses. A whole evening with her and I'd need Valium.'

'You're right. She's got a good heart, but she is full on.'

In the café they went to the counter and ordered, then took a table by a window and looked out at the busy street.

'Gran has a friend coming round for dinner tonight. Someone from the old days, she said.'

Lexi smiled warmly. 'Oh that's nice for her. It'll do her a power of good.'

'Mmm. I just hope I don't let the side down.' Stella's anxiety about the coming evening was mounting. 'I'm flaky as hell, and it's very hard trying to explain it to others, especially strangers. They either look at you with pity, as if you're some kind of hopeless victim, or with total horror at being stuck with a basket case. Either way, it's pretty shitty.'

Lexi smiled at Stella. 'You'll do just fine, I know. If it does get too heavy, you can always hightail it over to our place, okay? I know Edward would tell you exactly the same thing. He's still fretting over your health.'

At the mention of Edward, a shadow passed across Lexi's face. Stella wondered what was troubling her. Maybe the time had come to back away and let them get on with their lives. 'I'm really sorry, Lexi, it must be a right pain for you. You have enough to worry about with a rampant two-year-old and a workaholic husband without having his ex always lurking in the background.'

'Wash your mouth out immediately! You're my friend and what bothers you bothers me.'

The waiter placed two delicious looking tuna niçoise baguettes on the table. When he'd gone, Lexi dropped the smile and said, 'You seem pretty cool right now, Stella, but I'm guessing it's a show. How are you really? Eddie is worried sick about you. So am I.'

Stella fiddled with her napkin. It was difficult to lie to Lexi. 'I've been better.'

'You can always call. Day or night. You know that, don't you?'

Stella swallowed hard and nodded. Lexi's kindness made her feel even worse, and she didn't want to keep going on about her problems. Edward and Lexi had their own lives, and they'd soon get sick of her if all she did was moan.

'We can't begin to understand what you're going through, but we are here for you.' Lexi leaned across the table and covered Stella's hand with hers. 'I mean it.'

Stella didn't take her hand away. 'I feel like a ghost, Lexi. I've lost myself. I'm acting a part and I'm not real anymore.'

'You *are* real, Stella. As real as when you took on all those challenges, like rock climbing and all the other wacky adrenaline-fuelled sports that you and Edward used to do.' She squeezed Stella's hand. 'Getting yourself back together again after what happened to you is another of those challenges. You'll come out on top, I know you will.'

Stella could almost believe she was right.

The smile was back. 'And don't worry about tonight. Beth deserves a bit of a lift, doesn't she? Make the effort for her sake, huh?'

'I will. Actually, I'm rather curious. My gran never talks about her past, only that she was a civil servant and travelled abroad a lot.'

'Maybe he's a spy! Wait! Even better, maybe he's an old flame!' Lexi's eyes lit up. 'It's up to you to dig the dirt, Stel! I'm relying on you to give me all the sordid details.'

'Oh, I hadn't thought of that.' Stella cut into her baguette. 'More likely he's just some boring old fart of a retired pen-pusher. Still, even if he is, I suppose I can try to prize a few skeletons out of my grandmother's cupboard, can't I?'

Lexi nodded. 'Absolutely. Waste not, want not. My mum always says you should make sure to get something out of every situation, even if it's not what you planned.'

'Wise words.'

'Mum's a regular Gandhi sometimes.'

'But she does wear shoes?'

'Well, she'd look a bit of a wally pushing her trolley around Aldi in bare feet.'

They both laughed. Stella looked across the table at Lexi's pretty elfin face and perfectly styled hair. 'How come we are such good friends?'

'Whatever the reason, it really doesn't matter; I'm just really glad that we are.' Lexi laid down her pastry knife. 'Oh yes, and I'm quite fond of you too.'

Stella nodded. 'You know what, Lexi, I think your mother is not the only wise woman in your family.'

* * *

Stella had just got home when the bell rang. Frisbee charged past Stella, his eager bark announcing a friend.

'Robbie! Shouldn't you be working?'

He grinned at her. 'I am. I had an interview in Park Close, and since you are just round the corner, I brought you these.' He held out a bunch of flowers wrapped in cellophane that had "garage" stamped all over them.

Stella took them and sniffed the slightly drooping pink carnations.

'How sweet of you! But I think I'm past get well bouquets by now.'

'They aren't saying "Get Well." They are saying "Can You Forgive a Total Prat for Being So Bloody Insensitive?"'

Stella held the door open. 'Come in and have a coffee.'

They went into the kitchen, and Stella said, 'It's me that needs to apologise, Robbie. I never should have said what I did. I've been a real bitch lately and I'm truly sorry.'

'We're quits, then?'

'Absolutely.' She spooned the coffee into two mugs. 'And before you say anything else, it's okay to talk about work. I promise not to scream at you again. Well, I'll try not to anyway.'

Robbie smiled and brushed his fringe from his eyes. 'There's not much to tell anyway. It's all pretty quiet at present, quiet and boring.'

'Well, you've just put a jinx on that. Fancy using the 'Q' word, and out loud!'

'It's better when it's busy, although it's not the same without you, Stel. I don't seem to be able to enjoy my work like I used to.'

'Have you got a new partner yet?'

'No. I'm still filling in on DI Cash's team. Looks like I'll be there until Smithy and Joe Dalton are back from secondment. Cash is okay, but he's not exactly dynamic.'

'You can say that again. Cash wouldn't break into a run if his pants were on fire.' Stella poured hot water into the mugs and stirred in two sugars for Robbie. 'Here. Just the way you like it.'

'Thanks, Stel.' He took the drink and stared into it. 'I was wondering if you'd had any more thoughts about coming back to work? Only there's a couple of new jobs coming up, both suitable for retired detectives.'

Why did he have to say that? 'Put yourself in my shoes, Robbie. Would you be able to do a job that a civilian could do? It would be purgatory.'

'They aren't rubbish positions. They both need a lot of expertise and . . .' He looked at her stony face. 'Oh well, it was worth a mention. But don't think I'll give up asking, because I want you back and I don't care how. The place is like a bloody morgue without you.'

'I'm sure things will get better once you have a regular partner. You need the stability of a close-knit team, not moving from this one to that one. Tough it out, Robbie! You're a good copper. You'll do just fine without me.'

'Thank you for that vote of confidence. Now I'd better drink this up and go before they send out a squad car to look for me.' He gave her a rueful smile. 'You will keep in touch, won't you?'

'Of course I will, you muppet! But before you go, I've decided that I want to see that CCTV footage. Can you arrange it for me?'

He pulled a face. 'I can, but I really think you should reconsider.'

'I need to see it, Robbie. A chunk of my life has been wiped out and I want it back.'

'It could have been wiped out for a reason, Stel. But if you're adamant . . .' He shrugged. 'I'll have a word with my boss and set it up. It will probably be the end of the week, okay?'

Stella gave him a big smile. 'Thank you. I appreciate it.'

They talked for a few more minutes and then Robbie stood up. 'You know where I am if you need someone to talk to. And don't dismiss the idea of coming back to work when you are ready. You are too good a detective to stay at home and watch re-runs of *Murder She Wrote*.'

'Go! Now! Before I shout at you again! I'll ring you soon, Robbie, and thanks again for the flowers.'

Stella arranged the carnations in a vase, deciding that she was not only a bitch but a hypocrite as well. Listen to me, she thought. "Tough it out, Robbie!" I'm a fine one to dish out advice.

Robbie was also suffering. The shooting had put an end to his world too. Robbie was a great right-hand man, but he wasn't good at flying solo, and he didn't adapt easily to change.

It was time she started considering all the other people who had been affected by her injury, instead of wallowing in self-pity. A great idea — if only someone could tell her how to stop the waves of black depression that came crashing over her out of nowhere. She could not rationalise those away.

She straightened up. 'Enough, Stella North! Go find something to wear for this evening. Whoever this mystery guy is, even I don't think joggers and a hoodie are the right clothes for entertaining a dinner guest.'

CHAPTER FIVE

The bell rang. He was here. Beth took a long, shaky breath.

Even though travel-weary, Michael Lindenfeld radiated charisma. He was still tall. His hair, now grey, was as thick as ever, and his brown eyes behind the new glasses were intelligent and shrewd.

'Beth! You haven't changed one iota!'

She had pictured this meeting so many times, but the bear hug took her by surprise.

'Come in, come in.' She knew she sounded flustered, but seeing him again, after all those years, was almost too much for her.

'It's wonderful to see you again. You look amazing!'

Beth blushed. 'Hardly. No need to be kind to an old woman, you know.'

'Far from it.'

Beth took his coat and tried to fend off an excited, barking Frisbee, who was clearly delighted to meet a new friend.

'Stella! Michael is here!'

'I know. Frisbee told me'

Stella stood on the bottom stair.

She's made an effort, Beth thought. Stella was in a grey-blue mohair sweater and smart navy chinos.

Michael walked towards her, his hand outstretched. 'I'm Michael Lindenfeld. I'm so pleased to meet you.'

Stella took his hand. 'Stella North. I'm Beth's granddaughter.'

'I can see the resemblance. Are you an athlete too?'

'I try, but Gran takes some beating.' She looked at her grandmother with pride. 'I don't know what she got up to when you two worked together, but she's now a marathon runner. She competes in the 65+ category — they are called veterans. And she actually wins races.'

'Now why doesn't that surprise me?' He looked around. 'You have a beautiful home here, Beth. Did you have it built to your own design?'

'No, although I suppose I've put my mark on it over the years.' Beth took her time hanging up his jacket, willing her heart to stop pounding and reminding herself that he was here for Stella's sake, not hers. 'Stella, take Michael through to the lounge, and maybe we should put Frisbee in his bed in the kitchen? He seems to think everyone who comes here has come to visit him.'

'He's a great little chap. I had a field spaniel as a boy. They are full of life and really plucky. Don't put him in the kitchen on my account. It's his home too, after all.'

Frisbee gave Beth a supercilious look, and gazed adoringly up at Michael.

'I think you have a fan there.' It was surreal seeing Michael here, in her home. And Stella seemed remarkably relaxed. Maybe things would go smoothly.

'So, you worked together?' Stella sat opposite Michael, looking at him with interest.

Beth wondered what he would say.

'Oh yes, in Germany. Your grandmother came to Mannheim to sort out some legal problems with the British staff at one of the military bases.'

'But my German wasn't quite up to the job.' Beth smiled.

'Enter Michael Lindenfeld — poor, starving university student and part-time interpreter.'

'Michael became my tour guide and guardian angel.'

'And a very good friend,' he added. 'I even came over to England later, to visit her.'

Stella smiled. 'Your English is very good, you've hardly a trace of an accent. Where were you born, if that's not a rude question?'

His eyes sparkled. 'Somewhere between Heidelberg and Northallerton. I was born to a Yorkshire woman and a German father who travelled around a lot. I am told that I arrived in a stable!'

'I never knew that!' laughed Beth. 'How come?'

'My father was an architect, drawing up plans for a big project at a massive country house. My mother travelled with him, and I arrived prematurely and unexpectedly. Hence my bilingualism, although the people say my German has a hint of a British accent about it.'

Beth poured them three glasses of wine, and stood up. 'Time I got on with the dinner. Will you excuse me? It won't take long, it's very simple.'

'Want some help?' asked Stella.

'If you could just make up one of your wonderful dressings for the salad, I have the rest in hand.'

And so they all migrated to the kitchen, chatting about the village and Bad Harzburg, where Michael lived.

'How come you lost touch? You obviously got on really well,' Stella asked.

Beth glanced at Michael and saw him give a slight intake of breath.

'These things happen, I suppose. Life gets in the way, and before you know it, years have gone past.'

Nicely put, thought Beth.

She served up thick sirloin steaks and matchstick fried potatoes, green beans, tomatoes and the salad. The meal was good — even Beth was pleased. Between mouthfuls, Michael entertained Stella with stories of their time together in Germany, keeping the conversation to the past.

But Beth knew that Stella was born inquisitive, and she had been a fine detective. It wouldn't be long before she asked some awkward questions.

* * *

Stella was fascinated by Gran's "old friend," and was soon certain that there had been something between them. Not wishing to embarrass her gran — or the visitor — she didn't ask pointed questions. There was something about him that drew you in. He must have been absolutely gorgeous when he was young. She tried to work out when they'd met. She knew that Gran had known Archie, Stella's grandfather, for many years before she married him, but when exactly had she gone to Germany? Her muddled brain couldn't work it out, and she gave up.

She watched them over the rim of her wine glass. Michael was reminding Beth of some massive faux pas she had made with her bad German, and they were both laughing.

Back in police interview mode, Stella observed their body language. They were very comfortable with each other. There were those little gestures that come only from being close to someone. Great friends? Certainly that, but there was something more.

Beth hadn't asked Michael how he wanted his steak cooked, had she? And how did this old acquaintance from so long ago have Beth's mobile number? She'd only owned that phone for a year or so.

Stella sat back and sipped her wine. Something was up.

'Are you still an interpreter, Michael?' she asked casually.

'I still use my linguistic skills, but no, I didn't choose that career.'

Something in the room subtly changed, like a breath held.

'So what did — or do you do?' Her words were clipped.

'I'm a doctor, Stella. I met Beth when I was a medical student. I was a neurosurgeon for many years, and then I moved to neuropsychology. And, yes, I *do* know about what happened to you.'

At first she didn't know what to say. She had been so caught up in speculating about an old love affair that she had been blind to what was really going on. He was another damned shrink! Gran had sneaked him in, disguised as a friend.

A wave of white hot anger burned through Stella. 'How could you, Gran? After all I said about bloody therapy!' She slammed down her glass and the slender stem snapped, sending wine spilling over the table. 'How could you!' Stella pushed back her chair and stormed out, up the stairs to her room.

She flung herself onto her bed, her body racked with sobs. She had been betrayed, by the one person she had trusted. She pulled the duvet around her in a tight cocoon.

It was the final straw.

* * *

Beth sat staring bleakly at the wine-soaked table. 'I'm so sorry,' she whispered.

Michael squeezed her hand. 'Don't be. It was a classic reaction. There was a little added drama with the glass, but I expected no less.'

'I didn't.'

Beth looked exhausted, and Michael's heart gave a lurch. 'My old friend, you need to hang on for a little while longer. This is just the beginning. Try to imagine this as a horse race. Stella, our skittish filly, has just been spooked by the starting gate. She's kicked up and tried to throw the jockey. So we back her out, calm her down, lead her around, and try again. With patience and care she'll soon be out there on the flat, enjoying the race and hurtling towards the winning post.'

He stood up, went to the kitchen and returned with a damp cloth. 'Let's mop this up and clear away the debris, shall we? No harm done.'

'Should I go to her?'

Beth sounded more like a small child than the forceful woman he knew she was. 'No. We'll give her a few minutes, and then I'll go. I can help her, Beth. I know I can.'

She nodded, but there was no conviction in it.

'Maybe you should have a word with your boy.' He nodded at the forlorn dog. Huddled in his bed, he was watching them warily.

'He hates arguments. Come on, lad.' She held out her arms to him, but he stayed where he was.

'Dogs can often sense something like this before it actually happens. Did you notice that he slunk off just before Stella's outburst?' Michael walked over to the cowering animal and ruffled his ears. 'No worries, little man. She'll be good again in no time.'

Frisbee gave a feeble wag of the tail. Although he remained in his bed, he stretched.

They cleared the table and Michael refilled Beth's glass. 'Go sit in the lounge and enjoy that lovely Malbec.' He hesitated, wanting to go to her and hold her, but instead he touched her shoulder and said, 'If I cannot get that girl back down here within the hour, I will go and dance in the middle of Piccadilly Circus — in lederhosen.'

'Now that would be something to see!'

'And it's not going to happen, believe me!' He smiled and headed for the stairs. 'Her room?'

'Right at the top of the stairs, last door, straight ahead.' Beth raised her eyebrows. 'Should I wish you luck?'

'Every little helps.'

Michael stopped outside Stella's door and sank down onto his haunches. This could take a while. He knocked gently. 'Stella? Please don't be angry at Beth. It took a lot of courage for her to contact me. I'm sure she'll explain but it wasn't done lightly. She loves you and cannot bear to see you so unhappy.' He waited but no answer came. He hadn't expected one. Not yet.

'She told me that you needed help, and I think we both know she's right, don't we?' He breathed in and counted to ten before continuing. 'The thing is I *can* help you. It's what I do. Every human being that comes to me has been damaged and is looking for a way back to normality. And that's what they are, Stella, human beings. I do not think of them as case studies or lists of neuroses and defects. They are real people, who are hurting because they are not as they were and they don't understand why. Stella, I have all the time in the world, so why don't you let me help you? It can't hurt, and it could be the beginning of a new day for you.'

He said no more for a while, listening to the silence in the house. Finally he said, 'And this is something I do not generally share. If I told you that I know a little of what you are going through, it would not be a platitude. I'm not some patronising old professional who thinks he's seen it all before. I can empathise with you from personal experience.'

'How can you?'

Well done, he thought. He eased a cramped leg. 'I told you that I was a surgeon before, didn't I? Well, I didn't choose to end that career. I loved my work more than anything. It was my life, like you and the police force.' He drew in a breath. 'I was working in a teaching hospital in Mannheim. Then, also like you, I was involved in a purely wrong-place, wrong-time incident. A young patient, brought in after a road traffic accident, went on a rampage. He had been unable to tell the staff his name and he had no ID on him. So no one knew that he was dangerous.

Poor kid suffered from a whole assortment of psychoses and delusions. He'd been off his antipsychotic drugs and, to cut a long story short, he flipped. He badly injured a trainee nurse and came at me with a scalpel.'

He paused. The door slowly opened. Stella walked back and sat on the bed.

'I suppose you'd like to come in.'

He eased himself up from the floor and entered the room. 'Thank you.' He sat next to her and held out his hand.

In the dim light from her table lamp, the ridges of old scarring on the palm stood out clearly.

'He damaged nerves, mainly the median nerve, and enough blood vessels to put an end to me performing brain surgery.' He gave a bitter laugh. 'It's ironic. When I saw the blade coming towards my face, I was terrified that if my sight were damaged I'd never be able to operate again. So I held up my hands to protect my eyes.'

Michael looked deep into her eyes and said, 'It took me a *very* long time to realise that my world had not ended when my work was taken away from me, and that the brain is more than just matter, blood and tissue. I now know that as a surgeon, I was only a mechanic. As a psychologist I'm a teacher, a guide and a healer. It didn't happen overnight, and it took a string of very patient therapists to get me to where I am.'

'I'm sorry.'

'Nothing to be sorry for, not now.'

'I'm sorry you had to suffer so much to get to that point.'

'When something doesn't come easily, it's really worth having.'

'You honestly think you can help me?'

'That's why I'm here.' He stood up. 'And by the way, you frightened the dog.'

'I scared myself.'

'Well, I suggest we start with sorting out Mr Frisbee.' He walked to the door. '*You* might take a little longer.'

* * *

Back in the lounge, Stella threw herself into her grandmother's arms. 'I'm so, so sorry, Gran. Please forgive me. I was way out of line, *and* I broke your glass.'

'Hardly an heirloom, sweetheart. In fact I'm pretty sure they were on sale.'

'Michael says he could help me,' Stella blurted out.

'I'm banking on it.' Beth looked over the top of Stella's head to Michael.

'Do we start soon? Like tomorrow?' Stella felt a sudden urgency to begin. For the first time in months she had a glimmer of hope about the future.

He smiled at her. 'We've already started. And now that we all know where we stand, there will be no more secrets. Which is a huge relief, I can tell you! Now, you go get Mr Frisbee and tell him that the world is a happy place once more, and I'll get you a new glass. We should toast tomorrow and all that it holds for you, Stella.'

She felt a lump in her throat, but this time the tears were of pure relief. 'Just a very small one, please. I shouldn't have any more, but that's one toast I need to raise a glass to,' she whispered.

'Me too.' There was a catch in Beth's voice.

They sat and talked for over an hour, until Michael said that his long day was catching up on him. 'I'm going to give you some homework. I want you to think about the things that you did years ago that made your heart leap. And I don't mean jumping off high buildings. Simple things, those that were really special. Then when we meet tomorrow, tell me about one of them in great detail. Okay? One moment in your life that stirs deep, memorable feelings. Can you do that?'

Stella nodded, although the first memories that came to her all involved acute danger or adrenaline rushes. Still, she would do as he asked. She was pinning all her hopes on this man.

'And lastly, may I have your permission to talk to your surgeon? I know it was Donald Field-Latimer, and he's one of the best.' He looked at her with raised eyebrows. 'You were lucky to have found yourself in his care.'

Stella readily agreed. 'Speak to anyone you want, Michael, anyone at all. I'll ring Donald tomorrow and confirm.'

Beth saw him out, and then flopped down onto the sofa. She looked elated and exhausted at once.

'Did you love him very much?' asked Stella, the words tumbling out before could stop them.

Beth was silent for a moment. Then she sighed. 'I loved him with every fibre of my being.'

'But you married Granddad?'

'And Michael married Frida.'

'But why?'

Beth stood up. 'I'm going to let the dog out and make a cup of tea. Then, if you want, I'll tell you.'

* * *

'I realised that I was rather out of my depth with the legal jargon, and asked one of the secretaries for the name of an accredited translator. Apparently the man they normally used was working out of town, so she gave me Michael's contact details. She told me that he had been thoroughly vetted, so I could safely use him if he was free.' Beth's eyes grew misty. 'I think the seeds were sown before I even hung up the telephone. His voice was spellbinding.'

Stella listened intently.

'I'd never seen such an attractive man. He took my breath away, and from the first moment, I knew we had an unspoken connection. I couldn't explain it then, and I can't now. It happened in an instant.'

Stella knew exactly what she meant. It had happened to her once.

'I should tell you that I had become engaged to Archie before I left for Germany. Archie was the sweetest of souls. He was my friend, my confidante, and above all, he was safe. My job was sometimes dangerous, and Archie was the perfect haven.'

Stella frowned. 'But you said you were a civil servant.'

'I was. I worked for the government during the Cold War.' She drew in a breath. 'You and I, my darling, have both signed the Official Secrets Act. So much time has passed that I can now tell you that I worked on decryption.'

'You were a codebreaker?' Stella's voice rose an octave.

'I was gifted with an analytical and rather quirky mind, and was able to make links that others didn't immediately see. My teachers spotted it immediately and after rigorous background checks, my parents were asked if I could be sent to London for special training.'

'Gran! You've never mentioned anything about this before.' Stella's eyes were wide. 'You led us to believe that you sat in an office all day, typing and filing.'

'A necessary deception, I'm afraid.'

'And did you work in the field?'

'Nothing as exciting as an agent, but I did liaise with our counterparts in Europe, hence all my travelling.'

Stella's jaw dropped. 'No wonder you are so bloody good at cryptic crosswords! And is that why you kept so fit?'

'You're too young to know about the horrible fear that the Cold War generated, the constant threat of some maniac pressing a button and unleashing a nuclear strike. It was a worrying time for everyone, but for those of us actually involved, who knew what was really going on between the two superpowers, it was terrifying. I was caught up in several "near misses," dangerous situations that could have turned very nasty indeed. So, yes, I kept fit. I didn't want to let myself or anyone else down because I wasn't in top physical condition.'

'My own gran!' Stella shook her head. 'I'm gobsmacked.'

Beth laughed. 'But I'm digressing. You wanted to know about something very different, didn't you?'

'My head is spinning. I'm not sure I can take many more revelations!' Stella drank a mouthful of tea. 'But please, don't stop there!'

'I don't know how to describe those weeks in Mannheim with Michael. They were something outside of real life.' Beth shook her head slowly. 'We both knew that to take it further would cause damage and pain to those closest to us. Archie didn't deserve that, and neither did Frida. From what Michael told me about her, she was a naïve girl with a heart of gold, and he couldn't deliberately break that heart.'

'Even if it meant breaking yours?'

'I felt the same about Archie. I didn't have it in me to hurt him that deeply.' Beth sighed. 'Neither Archie nor Frida would ever find out about our affair. They were hundreds of miles away, Archie in England and Frida on a course in Leipzig. We had been discreet.' She paused. 'And to be honest, it had been so perfect that I wondered, we both did, if it was too good to be true. Would we destroy our other relationships, only to find that it had all been a fantasy?'

'So you parted?'

'Never to meet again. Or that was the plan.'

Stella frowned. 'But I thought Michael said he came to England to see you?'

She nodded. 'He was on his way to Yorkshire. He had a family funeral to attend, and although we had sworn not to contact each other again, he arrived one day at my office.' Beth glared into her empty mug. 'I need more tea. Would you do the honours?'

Stella set aside the sleeping dog and stood up. 'If this is too much for you, we can talk tomorrow.'

'No, I need to explain. I really do.'

* * *

Beth watched Stella put down the two steaming mugs. Time often erased or distorted memories, but she remembered every second of that period of her life

'My God! Michael?'

When the message arrived that someone was asking for her in the reception foyer, she assumed it was a courier or someone from another department. Michael Lindenfeld was the last person on earth she expected to see.

'I'm sorry to bother you at work.'

She stared at him, dumbfounded. His words were almost inaudible, and he seemed to have aged beyond belief in the last six months. His face was drawn and his eyes were dull.

'Is there somewhere we could talk?'

'Is something wrong?' Beth finally found her voice.

'I, I needed to talk to you . . . something I couldn't put in a letter, or speak about on the phone.' He stared at the floor. 'I'm leaving for Yorkshire this evening, and I've booked into a small hotel near Kings Cross. I suppose we could go there? Forgive me, I know what we promised, but it had to be face to face, and it had to be before . . .' He stopped abruptly.

Before what? Beth wondered. She couldn't go to his hotel with him, she couldn't trust herself. So she said, 'The park. Let's walk down to Hyde Park. I'm almost finished for today. No one will mind if I leave early.'

The park was never quiet, but it was late afternoon and cold, and they soon found an empty seat close to the lake.

Beth wanted to be angry with him. She had spent the last six months distilling what had happened in Mannheim into a beautiful memory. And now here he was, just a touch away. Why had he come?

They watched the rowing boats scattered on the Serpentine. Michael said, 'I love rowing. I row a lot in Germany.'

There was so much that she didn't know about this man, so much to discover. If only . . . Beth swallowed. 'I prefer canoeing or kayaking.'

He gave a little laugh. 'I can believe that. The thrill of the white water. Whereas the German in me likes the discipline of the oars.'

'Why are you here, Michael?'

He gazed out across the lake.

'Because the date is set for my wedding to Frida. It is two months from now.' There was such heaviness in his tone that he could have been talking of the funeral he was due to attend the following day.

'And I marry Archie just after Christmas.' Anguish began to well up inside her. 'But we knew this. It was always going to happen.' Tears threatened to spill from her eyes but she forced them back. 'I ask you again, why are you here?'

He turned to her so quickly that she jumped.

'Because I need to be sure that we have not made a terrible mistake!' He grasped her hand in his. 'Because I know now that it wasn't some fling, some holiday romance. It was real, Beth.'

She hadn't needed to be told, and she didn't need to answer him. He would read it in her eyes.

'Does this make a difference, Beth? Should we just think of ourselves and to hell with everyone else?'

He held her hand more tightly, and Beth wanted to shout, "Yes! Yes! I want to spend every second of my life with you!" But she gently pulled her hand from his and sighed. 'We can't, Michael. We simply can't. We couldn't hurt them then and we can't do it now. We always knew it was real. It's just that it comes along so rarely that we couldn't believe it.' She touched his face gently, stroking his cheek with her fingers. 'I love you, Michael, and nothing will ever alter that, but I can't see you again.' The last words were torn from her throat.

Michael slowly stood up. Tears clouded his eyes. 'So this time it really is goodbye?'

Beth leapt up and threw her arms around him, clinging to him like a drowning woman. 'Have a wonderful life, my darling. Do amazing things, and always know that you are loved.'

His body shook with sobs. 'You too. But I'm still not sure that we are doing the right thing.' He held her at arms' length and then pulled her to him and kissed her, long and tenderly.

A single kiss. The saddest of goodbyes. Beth reached into her pocket for a tissue and decided that they were wrong. Age didn't dull pain.

Stella sat still, crying too. After a while she said, 'After all that, you brought him back into your life, for *my* sake?'

'I'd do absolutely anything to help you, sweetheart.'

Stella shook her head and rubbed at her damp eyes. 'I don't deserve it.'

'Don't talk rubbish.' Beth balled up the tissue in her hand. 'And don't for one minute think that I mooned around like a pathetic schoolgirl after he left. I drew a firm line underneath what had happened, worked hard and had a successful marriage. Archie was a good man and I did love him.'

'But not like you loved Michael.'

Beth thought for a while, and then said, 'It was different, that's all. Archie was my dearest friend. Frida was Michael's. They had been friends from their schooldays, and I hope they still are.'

She did hope that, but she wasn't certain it was true. Michael had sounded almost cold when he'd said, "I'm still with Frida."

'And my marriage gave me my wonderful daughter, bless her. Your mother was my world, and then, joy of joys, she had you.' She smiled warmly at her granddaughter. 'And from the word go, you were *me* all over again! Full of life, with a love of sports and dangerous activities that stretched you to the limit!' The smile widened. 'I wouldn't have changed a thing about that, believe me.'

'Even when mum died and you became my guardian?'

'That was a privilege. Your father couldn't cope alone.'

'He never coped at all.'

'He tried, Stella, really he did, but he didn't have our survival gene.'

Stella sat drinking her tea. 'I've just realised something. You were the only person who wasn't surprised when Edward and I split up. And you were also the only one who didn't push us into getting married.' She narrowed her eyes. 'You knew it wouldn't work, didn't you?'

'I didn't know which way it would go, Stella. A marriage between good friends can work for many people. For some it's a soft option and the safest route through life. But you've never chosen safety, have you?'

'I guess not.' Stella grinned ruefully. 'But there must have been times when you regretted not making a life with Michael?'

Beth placed her mug on the coffee table. 'After Archie died, I wondered, of course I did. I followed Michael's progress from a distance. I still cared about him and I desperately wanted him to be a success — and most of all to be happy. When he became a neurosurgeon, I was thrilled for him.'

'I *will* do my very best, Gran.' Stella stared at her with determination, something Beth hadn't seen for years. 'I detest being the way I am and, okay, I've only just met him but I think I can trust him, so that's a great start, isn't it?'

'You *can* trust him, darling. I'm sure of that.' She stretched. 'I think that's enough emotional outpouring for one night. I'm drained!'

'Me too. My little grey cells, or what's left of them, are totally scrambled!'

'You get to bed. I'll lock up and see to things down here. Sleep tight, sweetheart.'

'And you, Gran.' Stella paused at the bottom at the stairs. 'And thank you . . . for everything. I won't let you down this time.'

'You wouldn't know how.'

CHAPTER SIX

Stella woke up at 6 a.m., after a night with no dreams or terrifying nightmares. She felt rested for once, and she languished beneath her duvet, enjoying the sensation.

She heard Gran up and about in the kitchen, so she reluctantly left her bed and went downstairs.

She was greeted by a delighted Frisbee, who insisted on presenting her with his favourite toy, a shaggy pink hedgehog that wolf-whistled when Frisbee bit on it.

'He really has got the knack of doing that at the most inappropriate moments.'

Beth was filling the kettle. 'Good night?'

'A very good night, thanks, Gran. And you?'

Beth shrugged. 'Sleep was a long time coming. I still find it hard to believe that after all these years, Michael is right here in Sutterthorpe.' She shook her head. 'But he is, and it's wonderful. I'm just going to make some scrambled eggs on toast. Can I tempt you?'

'Lovely.' Stella pulled out a kitchen chair and sat and watched her grandmother. 'So what's on the cards for today?'

'Well, you are excused training this morning,' Beth threw her a grin, 'but don't get used to it. It's a one-off. I think it would be good for you and Michael to spend some time together without me. Get to know each other and then he can decide how to proceed. He's going to ring us when he leaves the B&B.'

'You don't have to back off, Gran. Maybe it would be easier with you there.'

'No, this is something for the two of you to work on.' She added pepper to the eggs. 'This morning I'm going to run.'

Stella raised her eyebrows. Beth hadn't run for weeks, not properly. 'Where are you going?'

'I thought I'd warm up with some circuits on the track at the sports centre, then go out to the marsh lanes for a while. I can't train too hard after such a long break, but if I know that you are safe with Michael, I can start to get the old body back into shape.'

'Use it or lose it, as they say. But you'll never lose it. You are a born runner.'

'This ageing body can only go on for so long, kid.' Beth added the eggs to the pan and stirred them. 'But as long as I can, I will.'

'Good for you.'

Stella realised that she was not at all worried about beginning therapy with Michael. He was nothing like the people she had seen before. No matter how well-meaning the other doctors and therapists were, they had never managed to really get through to her and put her at her ease.

She sipped her tea. 'Do you know, Gran, I'm actually looking forward to today. Will he come here, do you think?'

'If I know Michael, he won't want you lying on a couch like a patient. It's much more likely that he'll suggest a good, long dog walk.'

'Well, that'll please Frisbee.' Stella smiled. 'And me. I just hope he's brought some waterproofs and enjoys sloshing through mud.'

'Why not take him to Fosdyke?' Beth said. 'You can walk for miles along the river towards the estuary, and you rarely see anyone up there on the high path other than the occasional dog-walker or seal.'

'And the wind has dropped this morning, so there's a good chance we won't get blown into the Welland.' That spot was flat, with a wide tidal river that cut through acres of marshland that merged into an immense sky. It would be very different to Michael's home in the mountains.

Michael's presence could have a twofold benefit. Stella had begun to feel horribly guilty about Gran giving up her running. Recently Stella had noticed subtle changes in her grandmother, and they weren't good. She still worked out in the gym and kept a close eye on Stella's progress, but sometimes she seemed more tired and stiff than before. Her grandmother was extremely fit for her age, but Stella was certain that if she continued to interfere with her brutal exercise regime, her gran would go downhill fast.

Stella would *not* be responsible for her grandmother giving up the life she loved.

She pulled some thick walking trousers and a warm shirt from her cupboard and hoped that Beth had been right about Michael liking the great outdoors. She sighed. She wasn't stupid enough to think that her new found sense of well-being would last. She knew that any journey into healing would be a tough one, even if your mentor was some kind of miracle worker. There would be black days. But maybe she would learn to master her depressions and make the most of the upbeat moments when they happened.

She looked hard at herself in the mirror. 'Okay, Michael Lindenfeld, I'm ready if you are! Let's do this!'

* * *

Robbie was standing uncomfortably in the superintendent's office.

'DI Cash tells me that you're not settling in too well with his team. Is that correct, Melton?' The super was a tough-looking woman with a deeply lined face and greying hair scraped back into a severe, no-nonsense pleat. Robbie guessed that she was around forty-five, but he was rubbish with ages and she was hard to read. One thing was for sure, you didn't mess with Superintendent Andrea Croxforth.

Robbie shifted his weight and muttered, 'I suppose it's because I'm floating at present, ma'am. I'm used to having a permanent partner.'

'Sit down.'

Robbie sat.

'I know that losing DS North hit you hard, Melton, but you really need to buckle down and find your place.' Her voice lacked any trace of compassion. 'We all have to cover other positions sometimes. I know it's not easy, but it's part of being a good team player.'

'Yes, ma'am. Sorry, ma'am.' Robbie looked down, half-expecting to see short trousers, baggy socks and scuffed school shoes.

'Are you in touch with DS North?'

Robbie brightened. 'Yes, ma'am, I saw her yesterday. I've been trying to get her to consider one of the new civvy posts that are coming up.'

Superintendent Croxforth frowned. 'Don't push her, Melton. I'm sure you'd hate her to get yet another knock if she applied and was refused.'

'But surely that wouldn't happen?' Robbie said quickly. 'Stella's a brilliant detective. She'd be an asset to us no matter what post she took on.'

'She *was* a brilliant detective, DC Melton. Her current medical reports indicate otherwise.'

Her eyes bored into him, making him feel confused and not a little worried.

'Brain damage, Melton, is not the greatest foundation on which to build a new career. I'm not sure what, if anything, she would be able to do to be of service to us.'

Robbie felt his concern turn to anger. 'The chief superintendent promised Stella North a place here, just as soon as she was ready to come back. She's a hero, Superintendent Croxforth. She doesn't deserve to be left out in the cold, not by the people she trusts most.'

'And does she *want* to come back? I certainly haven't seen any application of hers on my desk.'

Robbie swallowed. 'Okay, I admit that she's not ready yet, but can't you see that she needs to know that we are here for her when she is?'

'I suggest that you let Stella decide what's good for her, Detective. And in the meantime, leave well alone, because there's a very good chance that you aren't helping her.' She glanced down at some reports on her desk. 'She's not coming back, Melton. You need to sort yourself out, and quickly.' She looked up at him. 'You have a very good record. Don't throw it away by holding a candle to a ghost. Shape up and move forward. That's all.'

She didn't look up as he left.

All Robbie heard were the four words, "She's not coming back," and a dull heaviness settled on his heart.

* * *

'Are you sure you are up for this?' Stella looked doubtfully at Michael. 'The marsh in winter isn't the friendliest of places.'

Michael smiled. 'No matter. I've brought stout walking boots, and I'm tired of the mountains. This magnificent sky of yours is breathtaking.'

'It's usually the other way around,' said Stella. 'Most people think the flatlands are dead boring. Surely your mountains are spectacular?'

'Of course they are, but when you live with something all the time, even if it is stunningly beautiful, you get used to it and take it for granted.'

Stella thought of Edward and Lexi. Lexi was beautiful. Stella hoped that Edward never took her for granted. She pushed the thought away. 'You're right. I sometimes forget just how awe-inspiring our big skies are.' She smiled at him. 'Okay then, a fortifying walk it is! I've already warned the dog. I'm afraid I'll have to ask you to drive, but we can take my car. It has towels and blankets in the back for Frisbee. I don't think your hire company would be too happy about a damp field spaniel on their back seat.'

'Probably not.' Michael took the keys from her. 'Just tell me where to go, and remind me I'm not in Germany if you see me heading for the wrong side of the road.'

'The way some people drive on these roads, they might not notice the difference.'

'That's reassuring.' He eased into the driving seat. 'When is your assessment for getting back behind the wheel?'

'Friday. And I can't wait to be able to get out and about again without bothering poor Gran.'

'It will make a big difference. You need your freedom, and then your confidence will quickly return.'

They left the village and soon turned off the main road onto a long straight *drove* that seemed to have no end. 'There's a hairpin bend at the bottom, turn left and drive down to a copse of trees. There is a car park there and a footpath to the bird reserve. We'll leave the car there, but walk the other way along the river, if that's okay with you?'

'Perfect.'

Michael reversed her bright red Nissan Juke into a space and turned off the ignition. There was only one other car there. 'Is it busy in the tourist season?' he enquired.

'The birdwatchers and dog walkers sometimes come at weekends, but generally, this is it. It's no competition for Skegness, that's for sure.'

They pulled on their walking boots and Stella hooked a light rucksack over her shoulder. 'All the equipment you need for a hike with Frisbee.'

'And us?'

'Well, it's not exactly a Kendal mint cake kind of walk, but there is a flask of hot coffee in the car for when we get back.'

'Then lead on, my friend.'

Barking excitedly, Frisbee raced ahead of them down the access road to the river. To the right, the fields stretched out for miles in a giant flat patchwork of browns and greens, and to the left a high barrier of shrubs and trees hid the nature reserve from sight. Although the wind had calmed and a watery sun had made an appearance, it was still pretty chilly. Stella knew that as soon as they got up onto the high bank that divided the river and the marsh from the farmland, it would be very cold indeed.

They turned onto the river bank, and Michael gasped. 'What a strange landscape! I had no idea! I've never seen anything quite like this.' He stared ahead. 'I'm trying to find the horizon. The river and this long, straight path seem to disappear into infinity. It's most disorienting!'

Stella nodded. 'It certainly throws your sense of perspective.'

'How far is it to the sea?'

'About three miles to the Wash, I guess.'

'And there are no landmarks, just endless grass, marsh, water and sky.' Michael looked around.

'You can just make out the Port of Boston and the tower of St Botolph's church across the river.' She pointed to her left. 'We have no high rise buildings here in the Fens, other than the hospital. The only things you see on the skyline, apart from wind turbines, are church spires. They were used as markers for travellers making their way across the marshes. I used to come here sometimes when I had a particularly difficult case to sort out. Somehow it always helped me to see things more clearly. I actually solved a murder once, just sitting on a stone wall down by one of the water inlets.'

'I can believe that. There are no distractions. Is that why you chose this spot for today?'

'Gran chose it, I think because so few people come here.'

'Their loss.' Michael shook his head. 'How many different kinds of beauty are to be found in this world!'

'That's very true. In my old line of work I saw a lot of ugliness, hate and dirt, and sometimes pure evil. This place, and a lot of others, provided an antidote to the poison.'

'Nicely put, Stella. And it sums up what we are going to do over the next days, weeks, maybe even months. We are going to look for an antidote for what happened to you. We are going to find beauty of a different kind.'

'It sounds like an adventure.'

'It is, my dear. The greatest adventure you'll ever have.'

Stella looked at Michael. His eyes sparkled in the cold winter sunshine. 'Then I'm glad you are with me,' she said.

He linked his arm through hers and gave it a friendly squeeze. 'There's nowhere else I'd rather be — but before we freeze to the spot, let's go find that far horizon, shall we?'

They began to walk along the long, straight path. 'I spoke to your neurosurgeon this morning. He told me you'd already rung him, and he's very happy to have me on board. He's sending me your medical history and we are going to liaise closely.' Michael tightened his grip on her arm. 'I have already made one recommendation, and fortunately he fully agrees with it. We are going to change your medication. The drugs you are taking are very effective at what they do, but I've found that in some cases they can exacerbate depression. And that's the last thing you want. Field-Latimer says he will be contacting your GP about them today, so I suggest you call into your surgery tomorrow and collect the new prescription.'

They walked for little more than twenty minutes. It was only later that Stella realised just how much Michael discovered about her in that short time. His questions were casual and discreet, but obviously carefully thought out.

Stella pushed her hands deeper into her pockets. The breeze was growing stronger. The tide must be turning, she thought. 'Another ten minutes and we'll be able to see the river curving away towards the Wash and the North Sea.'

'And we've met no one at all.' Michael looked at her. 'Now, have you done your homework?'

'Yes, sir.' Stella gave him a cheeky salute. 'Although, considering all the extreme sports I used to do, it wasn't easy.'

'A life spent on the edge, huh?'

'Often quite literally. But I did dredge up something.' Actually she had recalled two occasions that had made her heart soar, but the second one was certainly not for sharing with Michael Lindenfeld!

A small group of sandpipers flew low over the water and their sharp calls echoed around them. 'Tell me,' Michael said.

'Has Gran ever mentioned that I was into photography before I joined the force?'

'I saw some lovely pictures in Beth's house. Were they yours?'

'Yes, but what I really loved was architecture, old buildings, especially derelict and abandoned places.'

'I've heard of this! Don't they call it decay photography?'

Stella smiled. 'Spot on. Decay makes the most amazing pictures.'

'I may be wrong, but aren't there people who seek out these old structures and get inside to photograph them?'

At last! Someone who didn't pull a face and look at her as if she were mad! 'That's right. They are called urban explorers, or urbexers. I had a group of trusted friends. I called them my crew, we had an amazing time infiltrating hundreds of wonderful and scary old places and photographing and cataloguing them. Before I became a copper they were the best days of my life.' She shook her head. 'Do you know, until you asked me to think about something that truly lifted my spirits, I hadn't thought about urban exploring for years.'

'I heard about it on the radio one morning. Is it a particularly British thing?'

'Not at all,' said Stella, and turned up her collar against the strengthening wind. 'Germany has always been popular with explorers, especially those with a penchant for Second World War or Cold War structures. Unfortunately the German urbexers won't share their info. They don't want foreigners finding their secret sites.'

'I can believe that. But it's the same idea? You do no damage, and you record and photograph your findings?'

'Right. The idea is to preserve something for others to see, before they are destroyed.'

'And it's damned exciting, I imagine. Dodging the authorities and discovering hidden treasure.'

Stella laughed. 'Oh yes! It was such a buzz! But when I decided to join the police force, I soon realised that my passion and my career were not exactly compatible!'

'Something of a conflict of interests, eh? So the urban explorer had to go.'

'And my career became everything to me.'

'So tell me, Stella, what was the particular occasion that moved you so much?'

'We'd been on a really dangerous excursion abroad.' She raised her eyebrows at him. 'Pripyat in the Ukraine was an incredibly difficult trip to make.'

'You went to Chernobyl?' Michael's eyes widened.

'Pripyat is the urban explorers' Holy Grail. There's not just one deserted building, but a whole town. I've never felt so overwhelmed by a place in my entire life.' She shivered. 'Although it wasn't the place itself that I was thinking about, but the moment when I downloaded the photographs I had taken. I was in my study at home. When I saw those images, I was blown away. I had managed to convey the very essence of the desolation of that place. I would be able to share it with people who would never have the opportunity — or the wish — to go there themselves.'

'Do you still have your photographs?' asked Michael.

'Sure. Most of the collection is packed away in a cupboard in my house. I haven't looked at them for donkey's years. The digital stuff will still be on computer file.'

'Can I see them?'

'Of course. They're not exactly fluffy kittens or picture postcard views. They are pretty gritty in fact. Some of them are quite hard to look at. Most people think they are an acquired taste.' Stella looked at the darkening sky. 'We'd better get back. I think the turn of the tide is going to bring in some squally weather.'

He nodded, and with a last glance across the marshy wetland to the silver strip of the sea, they turned back.

'Was that the kind of thing you meant, Michael?' It was easier to talk with the wind behind them.

'Very much so. I didn't expect it to be such a powerful memory, but it's perfect. Our next step is to see those pictures.'

'Okay. Gran said lunch is at one thirty, then after that we can all go round to my house and dig them out.' Stella whistled to Frisbee and quickened her pace. 'I'm afraid we need to step it out. We might just make it back to the car before the heavens open.'

* * *

On a different part of the fen, Beth was running steadily, checking her watch and noting how her body was reacting to the unaccustomed stress. She thought she had around ten minutes before the rain came, but it didn't matter. It would help to disguise the tears that were running down her face. When they had talked the night before, she had told Stella that she had no regrets. It wasn't true. Seeing Michael again so late in her life was more of a shock than she would have believed.

She still loved him.

Beth stared down the long narrow lane ahead of her. If Michael could turn Stella's life around, it might just make this agony worthwhile.

As the raindrops began to fall they joined the tears spattering her running jacket. Beth ran on through the driving rain. She would finish her course. *Nothing* would break her until Stella finished hers.

CHAPTER SEVEN

Lexi sat in the big cheerful waiting room and watched the families trying to keep their offspring amused until it was their turn to see the doctor. Some of the children, unaware that anything was wrong, happily played with the toys on offer. Others were fretful or silent. Thankfully Ethan was one of the former, and was trying to work out the mechanics of a toy spaceship.

Every time she heard footsteps coming down the corridor, Lexi looked up. Maybe Edward had managed to get away from work after all.

The door opened and two nurses walked through, heads together in deep discussion. Lexi sighed. All the other mums had someone with them. Only she was alone.

Edward always came with her, but when she'd reminded him this morning he'd practically bitten her head off.

'You *know* I've got a meeting with the Scandinavians this afternoon. No way can I be late for that, and there are figures to prepare!'

'Sorry, Ed, but you told me that they were here for the whole week. You said that a morning appointment would be fine.' She hoped she didn't sound whiny.

'Hell, it's only a check-up about his sleep disturbances. Get your mother to go with you if you can't go alone. '

'Mum isn't free today, and I'm perfectly capable of going alone. It's you who always insists that we go together. You said you need to, in case the doctor says something I don't understand.'

'I just can't make it today.' Lines of worry crossed Edward's brow.

Lexi softened. 'What's wrong, sweetheart? You look totally strung out.'

'Work,' he mumbled. 'Just work. Sorry.'

She kissed his neck, rubbed his shoulders and told him not to worry about the paediatric clinic. She didn't believe him, not for a moment. This was nothing to do with work.

'Ethan Byrne, please!' A nurse stood beside an open door and beckoned. 'Doctor Acharya will see you now.'

Separating a reluctant Ethan from the Starship Enterprise, Lexi realised that even after all he had said, she had still expected Edward to decide that his son was more important than the Scandinavians.

* * *

As his wife sat in the clinic, trying to make sense of what the consultant was saying, Edward was in his car in his company's staff parking area. The Scandinavians were being ferried off to visit one of their other facilities, under the watchful eye of his very able workshop manager. Edward had no qualms about not going with them. He had never intended to. What he needed right now was some time alone. He turned the key in the ignition and drove out of the gates.

Fifteen minutes later he pulled into the entrance to Westgate Woods, just outside Boston. He liked this spot. It was a newly planted woodland area with winding paths and a large wildflower meadow. It was the ideal place to lose yourself for a while to the sound of birdsong and the wind through the branches.

There were benches scattered beneath the trees. Edward locked the car and made for his favourite one. It was a little way off the path and hidden from passers-by. It had a small plaque screwed to the wooden back that read, "In memory of Andrew and Belle Weaver, who loved this place." He'd like a memorial like this. Nothing fancy, just a solid wooden seat where others could sit and share your appreciation for a special place.

Edward slumped forward and put his chin in his hands. He couldn't remember ever feeling so down and so alone. He wanted to go and talk to Stella, but how could he? After all she'd been through in the last six months it would be callous and unfeeling. He would just have to shoulder this by himself.

Edward stayed on in the cold and windy wood for about half an hour, impervious to the weather. Eventually he got to his feet, and with a last look at the little brass plaque, slowly walked back to the car.

* * *

Stella's house was nothing like Beth's barn conversion. It was a three-bed, Victorian-style new build in a small development on the edge of the village, but it was not without character.

Michael hung up their wet jackets in the porch. 'This is lovely! I wish my home was as tidy. My mind is orderly, but I attract clutter like a magnet.'

Stella gave him a brief tour, explaining how the previous owners had moved up from London to retire and live the rural dream. Unfortunately, even though they lavished a great deal of money on it, they soon discovered that they hated the sleepy village of Sutterthorpe.

'My neighbours tell me they moaned constantly about missing the theatres, the restaurants and cinemas. I suppose they also missed the constant traffic noise and the rumble of planes coming into Heathrow! Even worse, they had believed that their family and friends would be queuing up to come and visit, and no one came.'

Beth sniffed. 'A classic example of "be careful what you wish for."'

'I gather they didn't last long,' said Michael.

'A year, which fortuitously coincided with my divorce. I had the cash, and they wanted out — and fast — so I bought it with all the extras thrown in. Bargain! Now, we need to find those photographs. Would you help me, Michael? The boxes are pretty heavy, and with this weakness in my arm I might well drop them.'

Ten minutes later, they were gathered around three metal document holders that a panting Michael had deposited in the middle of the lounge floor.

'This isn't all of them, but I seem to remember they're the best. They were all taken with a "traditional" camera, if you get what I mean. I'm a bit of a dinosaur, I'm afraid, and I've always been a fan of single lens reflex cameras which take film. I had to be dragged, kicking and screaming into the digital age. All the ways you can enhance and fine-tune your shots are very clever, but I never really took to it. It seems to take away the integrity of the images.'

Michael nodded. 'I can appreciate that. I'm something of a purist myself.'

Stella bent down over the first box, then stopped. Did she want to go back to the world she had once inhabited? The Stella of that world had been at the peak of her physical strength, confident enough to climb the Shard with no safety rope. But that woman was long gone, and the Stella of today wasn't totally convinced that this was a good idea.

Michael spoke softly. 'It's alright, you know. Yes, you'll be looking at the past, but those were wonderful times. Maybe they will be stepping stones leading to your future.'

'I'm scared.' Stella was surprised at herself.

'This part of the past won't hurt you. It was an achievement. So let's celebrate it.'

'Okay,' said Stella reluctantly. 'Though I'm not sure what you'll make of it.'

'Rubbish. They are quite brilliant,' said Beth. 'Michael, you are in for a surprise.'

Stella gave an apologetic smile. 'Listen to the adoring grandmother! Forgive her, she has this delusion that I'm actually David Bailey.'

'Then I can't wait!'

Stella began to sort through the piles of photographs.

'Oh my! I never expected that.'

'Memories?' asked Michael gently.

'I'll say! Now I know why I spent all those years sneaking through fences into locked buildings, burrowing down tunnels and going into places I wasn't supposed to!' She glanced at Beth and saw pride in her eyes. Michael had started something. Stella was becoming more animated than she had since the shooting.

'I think you'd better start handing those around,' said Beth. 'Michael is drooling here.'

With frequent exclamations of amazement, Michael examined photograph after photograph. Finally he laid them down and shook his head. 'As I said, I'd heard of decay photography but I'd never seen it before. These are so powerful! They have such a strange, eerie beauty. Beth is right, they *are* very special! And Stella, you cannot leave these to rot in a box! There are image libraries out there that would pay very good money to use these. Or make up a library of your own on a website. Use them! Sell them! But please, don't waste them.'

Stella was taken aback by his enthusiasm. 'They aren't *that* good. We all took pictures — urban explorers *always* take them. Type "urbex" into a search engine and you'll be inundated with images, amazing ones. There are dozens of sites to choose from and they all have brilliant picture galleries.'

'I'm sure they do, but I know a master when I see one. You have a natural ability to use light to its fullest advantage. You have a first-rate talent, Stella. You *have* to use it.'

Beth looked at Stella. 'See? I told you they were something else. Do you have any wine in that fridge of yours? I think we need a toast.'

'The fridge is off, but there is a half decent bottle of red on the kitchen unit. Open that.'

Stella stared down at the photographs scattered across the floor. They showed derelict country houses, abandoned theatres, factories, underground railway systems, bunkers, churches and even an obsolete power station. She picked up an enlarged shot of the deserted foyer of a once magnificent cinema, and smelled again the damp and decay.

'Did Edward go with you on these explorations?'

For a moment Stella was confused. 'Oh, yes, well, sometimes. It wasn't really his thing. He preferred climbing and caving, and fast sport like squash. I used to have three close friends that I went out with. I think I told you that I called them my clan.' She smiled. 'We were good, really good. We understood each other, our strengths and weaknesses. We all had a particular role to play and we had some really exciting times.'

She rummaged through the case, and then the next one, until she found what she was looking for. She stared at the photo, and then passed it to Michael.

It was a black-and-white picture, showing the silhouetted figures of three young men grouped together in the centre of a vast railway tunnel. Stella had set up lighting that glowed like a halo around them, and accentuated the size and extent of the deserted underground station.

'Cave Bunny, Storm Zero and Hex. We always used nicknames, mainly for the stuff we posted on the various urbex websites, but it was also part of our unwritten code. Sometimes it helped us if we fell afoul of the authorities, although that didn't often happen.'

'So what was your name?' asked Michael.

'Starburst.' Her smile broadened. 'It's a play on the name Stella. And when I joined the force, I discovered it's the term used for when a group of car thieves or joyriders burst out of their vehicle and scatter in different directions.'

Michael handed the picture back. Stella held it for a moment, staring at it fondly.

* * *

An hour later, Beth declared that she ought to get back home to walk Frisbee before preparing supper.

'You go on ahead. I need to tidy this lot up,' said Stella, looking down at the pictures strewn across the floor. 'They need cataloguing at some point, they're all just thrown in together.'

'Perhaps I can help you?' said Michael. 'It would be a pleasure just to get a really good look at them.'

'You're on.' Stella grinned at him. 'Maybe we could work on them during our sessions?'

'Good idea. But right now, I think I'll go back with Beth and help her with the meal.'

'Fine. I'll follow on in a while.'

The front door closed, and Stella began to put away the photographs. Each one brought back a vivid memory of a place, a time, and sometimes a smell, but always the thrill of discovery. She wondered how she could have forgotten all that. How could her time on the force have wiped out such an important part of her life? Until this moment she had been mourning the loss of her precious job, grieving for the fact that Detective Sergeant Stella

North no longer existed. But was that really the case? Maybe she was actually mourning a lost identity.

But had she lost it? Here, contained in three metal boxes and a digital photo file, was the old Stella. Surely she could be that person again? The damage to her brain wouldn't allow her to climb parapets, but she could still explore. She could still do it!

On their walk, Michael had said that she should not waste precious time and energy regretting what had been lost, but channel her energies into creating a new future for herself. Forging a future would be the greatest challenge yet! Lexi had said something similar at their lunch the previous day. Now, seeing her photographs and remembering those exciting times, she had suddenly found a reason to live. Her grandmother was restoring her physical abilities, now Michael was helping her to deal with her mind.

She stared at the black-and-white photograph of her clan. Could she? Could she go out again?

She turned the picture over. The ink had faded a bit, but the number was still legible. She breathed in deeply. Then, still carrying the photo, she walked over to the telephone.

It was a local number, a village to the north of the town. She didn't expect her old friend to still be there — it had to be over ten years since they'd last met, but you never knew. Village people, born and bred, tended to stick around their family home. Tom Chalk, aka Cave Bunny, came from a farming family, so maybe . . .

A woman answered, speaking with a Lincolnshire accent and Stella immediately recognised Tom's mother. She explained who she was and how she wanted to get back in touch with Tom. The most she hoped for was another number to call.

'Stella North! Well, I'll be jiggered! How are you, me duck? It's been years! Oh, but our Tom will be tickled pink to hear you again. Hold on, dear, I'll go get him.'

Stella grew nervous. Had she done the right thing? Her doctors had told her to be wary of acting on impulse. Her judgment was, so they told her, radically impaired.

'Starburst! As I live and breathe! Why the hell haven't you been in contact for so long?'

On hearing her old tag used so warmly, Stella's reservations melted away. 'Things have been, well, uh . . .' She faltered. 'Difficult would be one way of putting it, I guess.'

'Oh shit, look I'm sorry. We heard what happened, I mean about the . . .' Now Tom was stuck for words.

'It's okay. I won't have a hissy fit if you say "shooting." I don't remember any of it, or much else either around that time. Anyway, I'm on the mend now.'

'I should have looked you up. I meant to, but, oh fuck it, Stella, you know how it is.'

'I do. And it is a bit of a conversation stopper when someone rings up and says, "By the way, I was shot in the head."'

'Well, for a girl wearing a bullet, you sound pretty good to me.'

Stella wasn't sure quite how to respond, but her friend was speaking again.

'So, I guess now you're better, you want to get out and about again?'

'You still explore?' Stella crossed her fingers.

'Hell, yes! Although the old team has moved on. Hex has married a Kiwi girl and moved to New Zealand, and Storm Zero is working on an oil rig somewhere in the North Sea.'

'And you?'

'Oh, me and my brothers are still working the farm, Stel. I've taken on a lot more work here since my dad died, but I still spend my spare time infiltrating whatever and wherever I can. Mainly rural stuff now, but there are some fascinating places right on our doorstep. So? Are you coming out with us?'

'Us?'

'I've got a new crew. You'll love them! Two brilliant kids. Real eager beavers! They'd love to meet the famous Starburst! Your crazy pictures are still on the websites, even after all this time.' His enthusiasm fizzed down the phone line.

'I don't know, Tom. Thing is, the injury has left me with a lot of shitty problems. I can't do heights anymore, so cranes and high buildings are out. And, well, I wouldn't want to hold you up, or more importantly, put anyone in danger.' She paused. 'I'm not the same anymore, Tom, and I really don't know how I would react. I guess I just don't know if I can hack it.'

'One way to find out, isn't there? Have you still got your gear? Your cameras? Boots and all that?'

'Yes, I guess so.'

'Right then, Tuesday night, my place, 7.30 p.m. Razor and Butterwitch are coming over to plan an outing for next week. You are in, my friend, and forget about the health issues. We'll be there for you. It's in your blood, Stella. You were one of the best.'

But maybe I no longer am. 'Just don't expect too much.'

'Tell you what, you research a location. Choose somewhere you'd be happy with. We'll use your first bimble as a practice run.'

It was a long while since she'd heard the word "bimble," the explorers' term for an expedition. Her stomach tightened in anticipation. 'Okay.'

'If it makes you feel better, we took Darren Kemp out to an old deserted quarry last month. He had the time of his life.'

'Darren Kemp? Didn't he lose a leg in a motorcycle accident?'

'That's the one.'

Stella laughed. 'It's great to be back in touch, Tom.'

'Too right! This is the best thing that's happened since I don't know when. So we'll see you on Tuesday, Stel, and no excuses.'

She replaced the receiver and shook her head. What had she just done? Tom's excited voice still rang in her ears. She wondered if he'd changed over the years. Probably not. Tom was a country boy, born and raised on the farm. She stared at the photo and gently touched his face. Tom had always been oblivious of his good looks. He had been the first boy she ever slept with. My God! It was a lifetime ago!

Stella sat back on her haunches and remembered. On her thirteenth birthday, she had promised herself that her first time would be on *her* terms. And it had been. When her body was ready, she had set about selecting a candidate. No way was that auspicious moment going to happen because of too much cheap wine at some dodgy party.

Edward, her dearest friend, was not on her shortlist. They'd had an especially close relationship, but it was not sexual. Stella laughed. How could she have had such insight at thirteen, and then lost it when they grew older and embarked on that disastrous marriage?

In the end, Tom Chalk was way ahead of the field. When she turned sixteen, he'd been only too happy to oblige. She was his first too! It made it even more special. They were never boy and girlfriend, but their secret was a bond between them and a great friendship had grown from it.

Suddenly her memories evaporated and she found herself back in the present. What on earth would Michael and Beth say about her decision? She really should have run it past them first. That impromptu call could have been one huge mistake.

Stella quickly gathered up the photos from the lounge floor and stuffed them haphazardly back into the boxes.

Right now she needed to get back to her grandmother's house and admit to making an immense cock-up!

As she picked up the house key ready to go, she was surprised to hear the doorbell ring.

Edward stood leaning on the door frame.

'I called at Coggles Barn but Beth said you were here. Have you got a moment?'

She stepped back. 'Of course. But whatever's wrong? You look terrible.'

Edward went into the lounge and flopped onto the sofa. 'Oh, work has been a nightmare recently. And we have buyers in from abroad. It's all been totally manic.'

'Surely that's good for the business?' She stared at him. 'But you look worried sick.'

'Can I talk to you, Stella? I mean confidentially, just you and me, with nothing getting back to Lexi or anyone else?'

Stella began to worry. Lexi had seemed cagey about Edward recently, saying he was overtired and worked off his feet. Was there something else going on? Stella wasn't sure she wanted to know. 'That sounds a bit heavy, Ed. Are things alright with Lexi and Ethan?'

He paused, clearly uncertain where to start. Then she saw his gaze land on the boxes of old photographs and he suddenly stiffened. He spoke in a clipped tone. 'I hope you're not planning on going back to that.'

Stella frowned. Now what? 'Well, sort of. I . . . I was thinking about a local trip out with the camera, that's all. Nothing dangerous. And Tom says he has a new crew that I could tag along with.'

'You can't! You just can't!' Edward's pale face was a mask of disbelief and anger.

Stella stared at him in amazement. Edward had just ripped the rug from under her feet. She felt as if he had slapped her.

Wasn't this her best friend? The man who knew her better than anyone? What on earth had she said to deserve

79

this outburst? 'I thought you'd be pleased . . .' Her voice shook.

'Pleased? You are joking!' Edward stood up and began pacing the room. 'Have you really thought it through? You're not ready for this. And what does Beth say about it?'

Stella shook her head. 'She doesn't know yet. I've only just talked to Tom. I was going to ask her and Michael what they thought tonight at supper.'

'Great! You haven't considered anyone else, have you? We'd be worried sick about you. Or don't you care about that?'

She had never seen him so angry. Even when they were struggling through their divorce and all its accompanying garbage, he had never once raised his voice to her. Now a vein at his temple pulsed dangerously, and Stella felt a stab of fear. 'Edward! This is no big thing. Just calm down and let's talk about it.'

'Calm down! Ah!' He continued to pace the floor. After a few moments he said, 'You really have no idea, have you, Stella? What we all went through when . . . when it happened.'

Now Stella was angry. 'Okay, I probably wasn't fully aware of everyone else's emotions. Maybe because I'd had two bullets fired into me at close range and I was fighting for my life at the time.' She frowned. 'But I can assure you that from the moment I regained consciousness, I've been grateful for everything you have all done for me.'

Edward's voice became tremulous. 'We suffered, you know. Beth put her whole life on hold for you. And now she's even brought Michael Lindenfeld over from Germany. Months and months of care and love. And then you say, "Thanks, folks, I'm good now. You can all stand down. Sod you, I'm off on an adventure."'

Stella exploded. 'It's not like that at all! In fact I'm pretty sure that Gran and Michael were pointing me towards this all afternoon! That's why the pictures are here. They are part of my therapy. If you can bear to remain in my company for ten more minutes, you can come with me to Coggles Barn and we'll ask them, shall we?'

Edward crossed his arms. 'It's too dangerous and too soon.'

'Jesus! I'm not planning on driving to London and doing an abseil off the Gherkin! It will be just a gentle trip around an abandoned country house or something. *And* it's with three others who will all be aware of my . . . my problems.' She tried a smile. '*You* know Cave Bunny. Tom Chalk was a good mate of ours for years. We all had some great times together.' Her smile widened. 'Remember that old theatre you discovered? The one that had been sealed up with all that 1930s stuff still intact! It was awesome, wasn't it? And Tom is as solid as a rock. He'll watch my back, I know he will.'

'More likely he'll watch your back*side*. He always fancied you, didn't he? I saw the way he looked at you when we all went out together.'

Stella drew in a long breath. 'Eddie, I've lost my career. I need to get out and do something with my life before I go crazy.'

Edward stared at his hands, clasped tightly in his lap. 'Your idea of rehabilitation is foolish in the extreme, not to mention childish. Sorry, but I've grown up, Stella. I've got responsibilities, and so have you.'

Stella was not certain which of these new Edwards was worse, the hopping mad one or the patronising one who was just bloody rude. Was Lexi the "responsibility" he put such heavy emphasis on? Was something wrong at home? Surely not! Unlike her, Lexi was perfect for him.

Stella didn't understand it at all. Edward was a mild mannered, gentle man, competitive in a healthy, sporty way, practical and conscientious at work and home. His reaction to something she had considered a really positive move forward was utterly out of character. To say that he'd overreacted was a major understatement.

Maybe the root cause of Edward's upset wasn't anything to do with her? Had she just taken the flack for something else entirely? 'I want to get back into photography, Eddie. I need a hobby and I was good at that.'

'Then do it. No one's saying you weren't good, you were bloody amazing. Take pictures of the fen on a misty morning, photograph flowers, wild birds, or Beth's bloody dog. Just forget about going back to urbex.'

Stella looked at his drawn, pale face and held up her hands. 'I'm sorry I've upset you, Edward. I suggest we leave it there. I certainly never meant for this to happen.'

Edward abruptly stood up and snatched his car keys from the coffee table. 'I never thought of you as selfish, Stella, but this, well . . .' He shook his head vehemently and strode from the house.

Stella suddenly realised he hadn't told her the important thing he had come to say, that Lexi must not know about.

Stella walked back to her Gran's place, feeling as if her head would explode. Was it her? Or was it Edward? She had absolutely no idea.

CHAPTER EIGHT

Michael frowned. 'Well, I have no idea where that young man is coming from, but I think it's a wonderful idea for you to go out with this Tom and his friends. It couldn't be better!'

Stella sniffed. 'Well, I thought so too.' She looked at her grandmother. 'He was so angry. You know Edward, Gran, he's just not like that.'

'Why did he react like that, then?' Beth shook her head. 'He did look dreadful when he called in earlier. Before he went off like a rocket, did he say there was anything worrying him?'

Stella decided not to mention the fact that he'd wanted to tell her something that no one must know about. 'He didn't tell me anything.'

'Maybe we should speak to Lexi?' said Beth. 'Or would you like me to try to talk to Edward?'

Michael shook his head. 'I think it would be best to leave him for a while to calm down. Stella doesn't have to answer to him for what she does with her life.' He smiled at her. 'Try to forget what he said and go ahead and plan your outing. Hopefully you'll be driving again by the day after tomorrow, and by next Tuesday you'll be free to go urbexing, or whatever you call it. Just don't tell Edward.'

'You're right. What he doesn't know won't hurt him. Don't let his outburst spoil things for you, Stella. Michael and I are delighted.' Her gran touched her arm. 'It was very brave of you to ring Tom after all these years. I'm proud of you.'

But Edward's words still echoed in Stella's head.

Michael went into the kitchen to check the food. 'Any idea where you'll go?' he called back.

'I haven't had time to think yet, although there is an old house out at Friskney that's always fascinated me. I need to get on the Internet and do some research.'

'Then start tomorrow. Strike while the iron is hot.' Michael stirred one of the pots, while stealing a glance at Beth.

'I'm sous chef tonight,' Beth said. 'Michael always was a better cook than me.' Stella heard the wistfulness in her grandmother's voice.

'Supper in ten minutes.' Michael announced. 'And I hope you're hungry.'

* * *

Robbie hated the gym. He had only joined because Stella had encouraged him to, and now he kept coming in case he bumped into her there. That, and the need to work off all the junk food he consumed. He wasn't alone in his crap diet, few coppers ate healthily. Their shifts and odd work patterns didn't allow them to be choosy.

Not trusting the timer on the cross trainer, Robbie glanced up at the big wall clock. There were ten more gruelling minutes to do.

This was hell. But there was nothing for him at home, so at least it passed the time. The best thing about this place was that although it heaved with people, no one wanted to talk to him. The big studio was filled with dedicated fitness freaks, all with headphones clamped to their ears, or totally absorbed in the loud music that pounded through the room. How could Stella and Beth enjoy this? Right now he was hard put to imagine anything worse.

His thoughts of Stella brought him to the CCTV footage. Somehow he had to smuggle her into the station to see the damn thing — *without* the super hearing about it. Croxforth had been adamant that he should have nothing to do with Stella. He had set it up okay, but how would he get Stella North in and out of the station without half the force turning out to greet her? Maybe he could talk her out if it. But if she really needed to see it, he didn't want to be the one to stop her.

He upped his pace on the trainer. There was another way, but it would put him in serious trouble if he got caught. Sod it! It looked as though his days in the police force were numbered anyway.

'How long are you going to be hogging that piece of equipment, mate?'

Robbie saw a bald, tattooed man wearing a sweaty vest top and tight shorts. He was standing too close.

'Four minutes and it's all yours.'

'How about *one* minute?'

A bully. Robbie had met plenty of them at school. Despite appearances, Robbie was no soft target. He smiled coldly. 'Better still, how about you sod off and let me finish? Oh, and I'm not your mate.'

For a moment the bald guy looked taken aback. Then his face contorted with anger. 'Don't upset me, *mate*, you could regret it.'

On another day, Robbie would probably have backed off for the sake of keeping the peace. Today he didn't feel so generous. 'You started this, so cool it, chum, or it will be you doing the regretting.'

Baldy took a swing at Robbie.

Robbie slipped the punch and watched the man fall heavily to the floor. He knelt on the small of his back and pulled an arm sharply up. 'Like I said . . .' He hauled the man to his feet. 'You can have the bloody machine. From the size of your gut, you obviously need it more than me.'

Robbie turned away and saw one of the instructors hurrying towards them.

He grinned broadly. 'It's okay. My *mate* here took a bit of a tumble. He's alright now. Aren't you?'

The man grunted. 'Yeah.'

'You really should log this in the accident book you know.' The young instructor looked worried. 'Health and Safety.'

Robbie smiled sweetly. 'I'm sure he won't want to make a fuss. He's not the kind of bloke to make trouble for anyone.' He turned to the man. 'Are you, *mate?*'

'I'm alright. Now leave me alone, will you?'

'See. Everything's fine.'

Robbie left the gym. He would have to pick a different time of day for his workout. He thought back to his problem: what to do about Stella's CCTV.

There was no other way. He would "borrow" the tape and copy it, and Stella could view it unofficially in the comfort of her own home. Damn the consequences. He really didn't care that much anyway.

* * *

Lexi sat alone in the lounge and read through the notes she had made after seeing the paediatrician. It seemed that they would just have to wait for Ethan's sleep disturbances to settle, although he had not ruled out several possibilities. The scariest was some kind of mental problem, such as attention deficit disorder. Lexi tried to push this worrying thought aside and clung to the words, 'But most likely he'll grow out of it.'

She exhaled slowly. She had been so worked up about Edward's absence that she might have been mistaken, but she thought that the consultant had been holding something back. In the past, the doctor had been reassuring, but today he had seemed reluctant to commit to anything concrete. When she had mentioned that there had been a couple of incidences of night terrors, he had seemed even more distracted. She had seen him write the word, "parasomnia" in Ethan's notes, and underline it. And now he had brought forward Ethan's next review, which to Lexi's mind was not a good sign.

She really needed to talk this through with Edward, but he was in his study with the door firmly shut. He had come in earlier looking thunderous, and Lexi had decided to keep out of the path of the impending storm. That had been two hours ago. Supper was still on the stove, probably dried out by now. Lexi had never seen Edward like this. She waited for the inevitable showdown.

CHAPTER NINE

On the way to police headquarters, Stella had trembled with anxiety. Her conversation with Tom had made her realise how important it was for her to get back on the road. She had to pass this medical exam.

Michael and Beth had dropped her off and gone for a coffee. An hour later Stella was on the phone, excited to share her good news. 'So who's driving home, Gran, you or me? I passed!'

Now she was mobile again, free to think about planning an expedition with Tom and his new crew. But first there was Robbie and the CCTV tape of the shooting.

She had spent a long time talking it over with Michael. To her surprise he had said that if she really believed it was impeding her progress, then she should see it, and move on. But he wanted to be with her when she viewed it. She had readily agreed, and somehow Robbie had managed to get the tape signed out for today. He had just phoned to say he was on his way.

Stella hoped that she was doing the right thing.

Michael was in the lounge with his new best friend lying contentedly across his lap. He grinned. 'I thought these guys were supposed to be working dogs?'

'Oh yes, they are, but Frisbee's not trained to the gun, he's trained to the sofa.'

'So I see.' He looked up. 'What time is your friend due?'

'Any minute.'

'I don't want you to worry about this, Stella. I've known several cases where it would have been a massive help to the people concerned if we could have shown them what really happened, but such footage is rarely available. If it helps, I'm certain that knowing your temperament, you are absolutely right to do this.'

She heard a car pull into the drive. 'So I can blame you if I have a wobble?'

'Of course you can, but you won't need to. I think I've got you sussed by now, and you'll be fine.'

Stella believed him. Gran, however, was unconvinced and had gone out running rather than have to watch her only granddaughter being gunned down.

Stella opened the door. 'How goes it, Robbie-boy?'

Robbie looked pale and unusually weary. 'Can't complain, I suppose. I won't use the 'Q' word again, but it's still pretty dead.'

'Won't last. It never does.' She took his arm. 'Come and meet Michael.'

The two men shook hands. Stella put the kettle on. 'We may need strong coffee after this.'

'More like a large whisky,' muttered Robbie. 'I've copied the footage to a memory stick, so we need to see this on a computer. Is that okay?'

'Sure. We can use Beth's in her study. It'll be cosy!'

Stella didn't feel nearly as relaxed as she sounded. Privately she wondered who had given Robbie permission to copy a tape that was part of an ongoing investigation. She hoped it was all above board, but decided not to mention that now.

'Well, shall we get this over with?'

The three of them trooped into the office and Stella inserted the device. 'Here goes nothing!'

'It's not the best quality footage, I'm afraid,' said Robbie. 'The village store didn't have up-to-date equipment.'

'At least what they did have was working, *and* had a tape in it.' She smiled at him. 'That's more than a lot of the scenes we've visited in the past, right?'

'True.'

Stella drew in a breath and clicked play.

Robbie had been right. It was grainy and the indistinct figures stopped and started as in an old film. But it was clear enough. Stella watched impassively as two men tried to kill her.

When it ended, she ran it again. She felt detached, as if it was happening to someone else. Maybe that commendation wasn't without merit after all, she mused. The figure that she knew to be herself had certainly tried hard to get the men to lay down their weapon. She had put herself between them and the people in the shop. She was doing her duty — what she'd been trained to do. Then they shot her, jumped onto a motorbike and roared off.

She turned to look at Michael. He seemed more shocked than she was.

'Tell me what you're thinking,' he said.

'Nothing, really. It was like it wasn't me. I've been so fixated on the effect it would have on me, and now . . .' She shrugged. 'It was like watching an episode from *Emmerdale,* except *Emmerdale* seems more real.' She frowned. 'I didn't much like seeing that "me" lying in a pool of blood, but I wouldn't relish seeing one of the Dingles like that either.'

Robbie heaved a relieved sigh. 'And to think I've been agonising over how you might react.'

'Thanks for organising that, Robbie. I really do owe you one.'

'No problem.' He smiled at her, but he still looked drawn. 'Is that coffee still on offer? I need to get back to base pretty soon.'

'Of course. Same for you, Michael?'

Michael nodded. 'And that's really all you felt?'

'I'm not hiding any anguish, honest.' Absently, she touched the scar on the side of her head. 'Maybe I'll feel differently if I recover real memories of what happened, but seeing it like that hasn't freaked me out at all.'

'That's good. And you were right when you said it was like watching someone else. It's the fact that you have no personal recall that makes it feel so unreal. Now it's time to draw a line, and move on.'

'In which case, I'll make those drinks.' She squeezed his arm as she walked past. 'Perhaps you should ring Gran and tell her she can come home now, and that I'm not a quivering heap of jelly on her lounge carpet!'

After Robbie had gone, Stella sat with Michael and the dog. 'Should I have felt something more?' she asked. 'I'm not going to have some kind of delayed reaction, am I?'

He shook his head. 'Don't talk yourself into feeling something that isn't there. It is what it is, that's all. There's a very good chance that if you were going to react to that tape, it would have happened at once. You'd either have been hysterical or gone into shock. And I didn't see any evidence of that, did you?'

Stella gave a short laugh. 'Not at all, and that's what's worrying me. I had expected *something*.'

'Try not to analyse your reaction too much. Before this happened, you were a very well-balanced woman, just believe that you still are. I'll be watching you closely, never fear. Let me worry about your reactions. You can move on now, go adventuring and enjoy yourself.'

She nodded. 'Yes. And now that I can drive again, I'm ready to check out that old house I was telling you about.'

'Perfect. It ties in nicely with my lecture tour next week. That's only two days, so it won't interfere with our sessions. As soon as I'm back, we begin in earnest. Are you up for it?'

'Try to stop me.'

'Good.'

'Michael? Don't think I don't want you here, but shouldn't you be going home after your lectures? Won't your family be missing you?'

'I'm a rolling stone, my dear. Always have been. My family is quite used to me coming and going. I'll go home when the time is right, never fear.'

Stella felt an enormous rush of relief. She knew that she must not use him as a crutch, but she also knew that he was vital to her present state of well-being. Right now, she needed Michael Lindenfeld to see her through, and knowing that he would brought tears to her eyes.

* * *

That afternoon Stella walked across the village and let herself into her house. She had no plans to move back immediately. In fact, she was thinking of staying on at Coggles Barn until her sessions with Michael were well underway. She certainly felt much better, but she was smart enough to know that she was still very vulnerable. Since her gran wasn't kicking her out, she'd stay a while longer.

Inside, she cranked up the heating, made tea, and went up to her office. Today she would get started on finding somewhere to take Tom and his friends and get some new photographs. She had already bought some 35mm film online, so all she needed now were her cameras, her boots, and a plan.

She pushed the office door open and looked around. Her study was, as always, impeccably tidy. Beth had said it was clean enough to conduct minor surgical operations in, but Stella wanted a place of work, not a showroom. It didn't take long to cover the empty surfaces with piles of reference books, camera equipment and chargers, and a sizeable collection of local maps. Having done that, Stella set herself the task of finding an interesting place to visit.

She sat down at her desk and switched on the computer. How many times she had sat here looking for new places to explore! Some she had come across easily or by chance, while others took months of careful planning to get into.

Stella recalled her most difficult, and certainly her most memorable, find. She bit on her lip. Was she ready to go there? Maybe. If she could survive the CCTV footage, a trip down memory lane ought to be a piece of cake.

She leaned closer to the monitor. The file she wanted was called *Chateau Sapin Noir, Belgium*. And there it was. The images of the abandoned chateau, with its haunting interiors, overgrown gardens, and the dark surrounding forest, all came back to her with almost shocking clarity.

For years she had believed the chateau to be just an urbexer myth. Then, while checking an online local paper for the area, she had come across a paragraph about a proposed railway line. Apparently there was a dispute over the ownership of the land, which contained some very old buildings. After another few days of research, she put two and two together and headed for the airport. None of her clan was free to come along, so she went alone. It was her first solitary bimble abroad.

It had taken days of scouting the area on a hired moped to locate the place. And then, when she finally found the hidden driveway, someone had beaten her to it. The car was well concealed, in exactly the spot she would have chosen — invisible from the road, but ready if a swift getaway was needed. It had a British license plate, and when she saw the personalised number beginning with JH, she knew who had stolen her glory.

If he was upset by her arrival, Jack Hammond didn't show it. After all, he had found the treasure first. And what a site! Stella had been to Belgium several times before, and seen the infamous Chateau Miranda and a host of other ruined castles, but this was a real find.

The sound of her boots resonated on the tiled floor. She didn't want to frighten the other urbexer by creeping up on him.

She had never met him before, but she recognised Jack Hammond the moment she saw him. She had followed his web site for long enough to be familiar with his tall, athletic form and long chestnut hair. He was silhouetted in candlelight, in the process of setting up some atmospheric shots.

'Well, well. If it isn't Starburst.'

His voice was soft, as if he didn't want to disturb the spirit of the place. Stella blushed, glad of the dim lighting. The legendary Jackhammer knew who she was!

'Jackhammer. I'm very pleased to meet you.'

He laughed. 'I'd have thought you would hate me for getting here first.'

Far from it, thought Stella. This was a blinding piece of luck. Jack was a legend, and always worked alone. And now, here they were, in a miraculously undisturbed piece of history. It was unheard of.

She knew he would not object to her presence, even if he was a loner. Urbexers respected each other, as well as the places they discovered. He would have admired the fact that she was there at all. The place had been hard to find, and for decades had evaded the adventurers.

Jack looked at her. 'This place is . . . I don't know. "Unique" seems inadequate. It is simply the most breathtaking find I've ever made.'

Stella added, 'It's almost been eaten up by the forest. It's as if nature is taking it back.'

Jack nodded.

'Have you explored the whole place?'

'Almost.' He looked around. 'But you mustn't miss an inch. The atmosphere here is . . . It's like somewhere sacred.'

'It is sacred.'

Jack took his shots, and then they explored the ruined chateau. Unlike many deserted old buildings, this one was in remarkably good condition. The wooden panelling still retained a warm patina beneath the dust. The intricate tiling on the floors was cracked and worn in places, but the pattern could still be discerned. Even some of the thick, heavily decorated wallpapers were intact. There were huge arched windows, some still stubbornly holding on to unbroken panes of glass. The ceilings had carved panels, inset with intricate painted bosses and tablets.

Jack opened a studded door and gasped. The room had been a library, but the window and some of the surrounding stonework had fallen in and the whole place was a mess. Books cascaded from the shelves and were scattered everywhere, their leather covers now a mosaic of mildew and mould. Along with long tendrils of ivy and other climbers, animals and birds had found their way in and added to the destruction. Somehow the damage these animals had caused was different to the desecration wrought by humans. Stella had seen what vandals could do, and it broke her heart. This more natural scarring just seemed like evolution, nature taking back what was hers.

They sat on the staircase. 'I have to come back tomorrow in full daylight and get more pictures.' Stella had taken a whole series of low-light photos using a tripod and one of her favourite old SLR cameras, but she needed daylight for some interesting digital stuff.

'I'm leaving first thing.' Jack traced a finger along the ornate wrought iron of the staircase panels. He gave her a searching look. 'Can you feel it, Starburst? Can you feel the mystery here?'

Stella had felt it the moment she set eyes on the chateau. 'Yes. It's as if we've stopped, stepped out of our lives. As if we've let go of the clamour and all the torrents of information we are flooded with. What really matters is here, in the silence.'

'This is pure, unpolluted history, and we are part of it for a brief while.'

They lit a couple of the tea-light candles that urbexers always carry, and placed them on the stone steps above them. In the flicker of the tiny flames, Stella saw hunger in Jack's eyes. And when he leaned forward and kissed her, the same desire ran through her like a flame.

'Where are you staying?' he demanded breathlessly.

'A small inn, a couple of villages away. I hired a moped to get here.'

'Will they miss you if you don't go back tonight?'

'I paid up front. I don't think they'd care what I do.'

'Good.'

He pulled her up and kissed her again. He gathered his equipment and said, 'Come with me.'

In the dim twilight, Stella followed Jack out of the gates and down the track to where his car was hidden. Jack unlocked it and pulled a large bundle from the boot.

The two-man pop-up tent went up in seconds. He threw Stella a handful of pegs and a small hammer. 'Peg it down. I'll get the bed roll.'

There was no need to say more.

Stella's whole body was alive with desire for this man who had, until a few hours ago, been just a name on a website.

When they were both naked, they knelt and stared at each other. It was almost dark but Stella could see his lightly tanned, muscular body, and his glinting, hungry eyes. She wanted him more than she'd ever wanted anything in her whole life. Then his hands were touching her, caressing, softly but urgently. She lay on her back, moaned softly and tried to pull him closer.

'No, wait,' he whispered. 'Let me . . .' His hands ran along the inside of her thighs, up and down, parting her legs with a smooth stroking motion. Stella's body began to arch towards him.

She heard herself begging him to take her.

And then he was inside her, and the rhythm as they moved together matched the pounding of her heart. He cried out as he came, and Stella felt as if she had exploded like a true starburst.

She began to explore his body, and soon he was erect again. Stella hadn't ever taken control before. She felt like a completely different woman. Was it because they were strangers to each other? There were no expectations, and no set pattern. Stella felt free, free to throw all her usual reserve to the wind and behave like — what? She didn't care. Tonight she need keep nothing back.

Much later, they lit a storm lantern and shared the food they had brought with them. Jack produced half a bottle of red wine from his rucksack, and they drank it from a plastic cup.

'I don't do this,' said Stella. 'I mean it. I never do this.'

'Then maybe you should. I think you're the most exciting woman I've ever met.'

Stella felt like a goddess.

Jack looked at her steadily. 'I don't do relationships.'

'It's okay, I'm not a bunny boiler.' She took another sip of wine, and for the first time thought about Edward. 'I am engaged to be married.'

'It's irrelevant. This doesn't concern anyone else. It is all just part of the magic of this place.'

He smiled at her. 'I'm glad we are sharing it, but it has nothing to do with the real world.' He drew in a breath. 'You know, I'm not sure that I want to post this place on the web. Maybe it should remain as it is, until the railway builders arrive.' His gaze had sadness in it, and pleasure too. 'For the first time since I started exploring, I'm not sure that I want to share this with anyone — except you, Starburst.' He took the cup from her and drank some of the wine. 'But right now, I think we have some unfinished business, don't you?'

He touched her face gently. She lifted her hand and covered his, then moved it slowly down her neck to her breast. 'Now I understand where your tag came from.' Her other hand strayed downwards and lingered over the growing bulge in his pants. 'Most fitting.'

'I'm glad you approve. So how would you like me to apply myself this time . . . ?'

Stella sat and stared at the photograph on the screen. What had happened that night? All she could think was that they had absorbed something powerful from the deserted chateau. She had never experienced anything like it again.

Jack Hammond left at dawn, and she never saw him again.

He didn't post his images of the chateau on his blog, or in any of the usual urbex sites, and a few months later he disappeared.

Stella sighed. She often wondered what had happened to him. He was such a vital man, so full of energy. How could he be there one minute and gone the next? Word was that he had died, and Stella was inclined to agree. In a way it was a little like what had happened to her. One minute she was on top of the world, and the next she was lying in a pool of blood.

She closed the file and stood up. She needed a break before she got back to the job in hand. She was still wandering through the majestic skeleton of a long dead chateau with an amazing man who might not even be still alive.

CHAPTER TEN

As they walked back to Coggles Barn, Michael noticed something different about Beth. She seemed quieter, reserved. He wanted to talk to her about things that concerned the two of them, but maybe the time was not right. He had come to England willingly — happily — but maybe too eagerly. He had been desperate to see her again, and from the moment she opened the door to him, he knew he still loved her. He wanted to leave Germany and his life there. His wife, his children, his grandchildren, his patients and his colleagues. If he could, he would walk away from it all for Beth. But Michael wasn't a heartless bastard, so it wasn't going to happen.

When they reached Coggles Barn, she said, 'Oh, damn! Would you hold the fort here for ten minutes to save me locking up again? I need to run to the village store. I forgot to get crème fraiche.'

'Your tiny village store sells crème fraiche? I'm impressed.'

'We aren't in the outback, Michael. It sells lots of nice stuff.'

'Shall I go for you?'

'No, it's all right. I'm bound to see something else I need. My mind has not been on domestic duties for the last few days.'

A few minutes after she left, the doorbell rang. Frisbee barked excitedly, his tail rotating furiously. 'Someone for you, I guess?'

Michael opened the door to a young woman standing with a howling child strapped into a purple buggy.

'Lexi?' It had to be.

'Michael?'

He smiled at her. 'Please come in. Beth will be back soon, and Stella is around at her own house right now.' He looked at the child's contorted face and said above the screams, 'Oh dear, someone's not happy.'

Lexi seemed to dissolve in front of him. Her eyes filled with tears and she began to sob. 'I'm so sorry. I'm at my wit's end. He's been like this all day.'

Michael resurrected the grandfather in him. 'Right, let's start with you, young man.' He deftly released the clasps and lifted Ethan up. 'Ever heard of Nana? Now most people think she was a St Bernard, but actually she was a Newfoundland, and she was the nursemaid to the Darling children.'

'*Peter Pan*!'

'Hey, you know the story! That's great, because . . .' Still talking, he carried the boy away from his mother and into the kitchen. 'I don't have Nana here, but I do have the amazing Frisbee!' He plonked the unsuspecting child into the dog's bed and called for the spaniel. 'You're in charge, Fris. It's worth double treats if you do a good job. Okay?'

Frisbee duly snuggled into the soft padded bed and gazed adoringly at the red-faced boy. Soon, the only sounds coming from Ethan were giggles and a toddler version of Spaniel-speak.

'Now it's your turn, young lady. Sit and dry your eyes while I put the kettle on. I've enough English in me to swear by the restorative powers of a nice cup of tea.'

She dabbed her eyes with damp tissues. 'Oh dear! Our first meeting and I make a fool of myself! You must think I'm some kind of nutter.' She blushed, remembering what he was, and looked at him apologetically.

He smiled at her. 'Don't worry. You're not psychotic, just a very tired and emotional young mother.' He went to make the tea, and found Ethan sleeping, curled up against the long-suffering Frisbee.

'Nice work, boy. I meant what I said about the treats,' he whispered.

Lexi appeared at the kitchen door. 'That's the first time today he's been quiet and actually slept.'

'Maybe you could get a dog?'

'Edward is allergic, or I'd have had one ages ago. Ethan loves animals and it seems sad that he can't have a pet.' She shrugged. 'Although I'm not sure I'd have the time to look after one. Ethan is a full-time job these days.'

And Edward? thought Michael. Is *he* a full-time job? 'Little ones are. Comes with the territory.'

They carried their tea through to the lounge and then Beth arrived, carrying a bag full of groceries. 'Lexi! Oh good, you've finally met Michael, and I see he's being the perfect host.'

'Shh.' Lexi held her forefinger to her lips. 'Look in the dog bed.'

Beth went into the kitchen to unpack her shopping. 'I see. Dr Dog is taking his job very seriously.' She looked at Michael. 'He won't budge from the child's side until we tell him to. He just seems to know.'

'Dogs are greatly underestimated. In my book, dogs and horses should rule the world.' Michael spoke brightly, but kept a careful eye on Lexi. She seemed more cheerful now.

'What about cats?' asked Lexi.

'Sorry, but I think there's a frightening similarity between cats and politicians, and I don't trust either.'

They all laughed. To Michael's trained ear, the laughter sounded forced. 'Lexi is very tired, Beth, and very upset.' He knew it was time to draw out what was behind Lexi's visit. 'Maybe you'd like some time to talk without me butting in. As the youngster is asleep, maybe I could walk Frisbee for a while?'

'No, please stay.' Lexi's voice trembled. 'I . . . I just needed to let off steam, and I didn't know who to turn to.'

Beth looked concerned. 'What about your mum? Have to talked to her?'

'Mum is great,' said Lexi, 'but she doesn't live in the real world. When things don't run according to her concept of the "perfect family," she falls apart. And you've been so good to me. You've never made me feel like an outsider.'

'Heavens, child! Why would I? You are the best thing that ever happened to my ex grandson-in-law!' Beth sat down next to Lexi on the sofa. 'Now, tell us what's wrong. Maybe we can help.'

Lexi drew in a shaky breath. 'I think Edward is having second thoughts about having divorced Stella.' Her voice was heavy with sadness and disappointment. 'Another reason not to talk to Mum. She utterly adores her wonderful son-in-law.'

'But Edward loves you to bits!' Beth exploded. 'He and Stella were terrible together as a married couple! What on earth has given you that idea?'

Lexi told them. He was distant, bad tempered, volatile, working all hours and just not himself. 'He even left me to take Ethan to the hospital on my own. He's never done that before. Now the doctors are talking about ADHD! And something called parasomnia.'

It's no wonder the girl is at breaking point, thought Michael. 'Ethan has sleep disturbances?'

She nodded.

'Are they getting worse?'

'Yes, much worse.'

Michael bit on the inside of his cheek. He guessed Ethan was picking up on the tension between his parents. 'Try not to worry too much, Lexi. I'm not a paediatrician, but I do have some disturbed children among my patients, and from what I've seen I'd be very surprised if he has attention deficit disorder. I think Ethan is simply very sensitive and he's showing signs of stress.'

'But how can I prevent Ethan picking up on Edward's moods? Especially since they're getting worse.'

'Overdose him on love. I know that's not easy when you are exhausted, but he needs to know he's safe and loved.' He looked at her. 'And find out what's bothering Edward. You can't fight something when you don't know what it is.'

'Know thine enemy,' added Beth. She took Lexi's hand in hers. 'Keep this to yourself, but Edward had a go at Stella too. So we know that what you are saying is true.'

'Forgive me for asking, but are there any financial worries? Business worries maybe?' Michael had seen this kind of behaviour with men that had been made redundant or had secret addiction problems.

'Edward says that the business is thriving, it's almost too much to keep up with. And there's always money in the bank.' Lexi frowned. 'Although I don't really know about that side of things. Edward takes care of business, and I take care of home and family. I rely on what he tells me.' She looked at Beth. 'And you say he lost his temper with Stella? Why?'

Beth shrugged. 'No idea. As far as we know, she was telling him that now she feels so much better, she was planning on going back to photography, you know, her old pastime of taking pictures of abandoned buildings. Edward went ape.'

'But that doesn't make sense! I think it's a great idea, as long as she doesn't go alone, of course.'

'Oh no, she has some old friends lined up to look after her.' Beth sniffed. 'It was a completely uncharacteristic and extreme reaction.'

'So maybe I'm right.' Lexi's voice dropped. 'He's jealous of her going out with someone else. He's certainly not been right since she got shot.'

Michael wondered. Could Edward be in love with two women? After all, wasn't that the case with him? Was Edward tearing his life apart because he was torn between Stella and Lexi? He wanted to catch Beth's eye, but didn't dare.

Beth cuddled Lexi and said, 'You mustn't doubt that Edward loves you. It has to be something else.' She looked across at Michael. 'I suppose it wouldn't help if you talked to him? Man to man? He might be more inclined to open up to you since you're an outsider.'

'I'll help if I can, but I really don't think it would be appropriate for me to wade in. He might think I'm interfering where I had no right. If I meet him and he wants to talk to me, that's different, but I can't intrude.'

'I suppose you're right.' Beth sighed. 'But we need to get to the bottom of this before he does something really stupid.'

CHAPTER ELEVEN

Stella wandered round her apology for a garden. Her next-door neighbour was taking out her rubbish, and she assured the old lady that she would be returning home soon. Nan Rowland smiled at her, saying she was pleased, she always felt so safe knowing that a brave police officer lived right beside her. *Not anymore*, thought Stella.

She went back up to the office, flopped into her chair and picked up her favourite SLR camera from the desk. It was almost an antique, but they had travelled many miles together. She smiled at it fondly and wondered if she had left any ancient film inside. Then her mind went blank. She didn't even know how to open it.

Slowly she replaced it on the desk and stared at it, frightened.

Remember what the doctors said and put it to one side, she told herself. *It's only temporary. You'll be fine again soon, just don't try too hard.* She took a deep breath, put her beloved camera in one of the desk drawers and turned to her computer. She needed a distraction. It was a good opportunity to look for a new venue to explore with Cave Bunny.

After half an hour she had whittled it down to two possible locations. Both were places she'd noticed some time ago when she was still working, and both were worth a look. Her first choice was an empty old country house, set way back off the road and surrounded by trees. Then there was a deserted military hospital about ten miles outside town that had fascinated her for years. Tom probably knew it well.

Before she made her decision she thought she should check out a few urbex sites, just to see if either the house or the hospital were already featured. It might be sensible to see the pictures that other curious urbexers had taken before walking into a situation that could upset her. For a while she fought through her mixed-up memory for the site names, then one came back to her and she typed it in. In moments she was scrolling down lists of buildings and places of interest that would never appear in the guidebooks. Most were new to her — after all it had been ten years — but she was pleased to see that some familiar places were still accessible.

Then her mobile rang.

'Starburst? It's me — Cave Bunny. Listen, Stel, have you sorted out a location yet?'

'I'm working on it now and there's a shortlist of two. Why?'

'Slight change of plan. If you've got your gear ready, we'll go out tomorrow afternoon, no prior briefing. We'll discuss it en route.'

Stella's heart sank. She didn't do spontaneous anymore. She needed to plan, get her head in order. 'That could be a problem, Tom.'

'Listen, I talked to the others and they can't wait to meet you. You are one of their all-time urbex heroes! I gave them your history, the potted version, and Butterwitch reckons that if we give you too much time to think, you'll chicken out. So, let's just jump right in, shall we?'

'So this Butterwitch is a psychologist specialising in neurological trauma, is she?' Stella hated her waspish tone.

'Actually, yes. Well, almost. She's studying neuroscience at Nottingham University.'

Stella's heart sank. That was all she needed. The last thing she wanted was to be a lab rat for some student. For a moment she felt panic, then a feeling of being let down. She had really believed she could do this, and now it was all slipping away from her.

'You've gone rather quiet.'

'I think this is a bad idea, Tom. I'm sorry but I'm going to back out.'

'No way! Look, maybe I should have kept shtum about the kid's career choice, but you'll love her, Stel, honest. And what she doesn't know about the Cold War isn't worth knowing.'

Tom had obviously remembered Stella's penchant for 1960s nuclear bunkers and subterranean complexes. 'Nice try, but sorry, Tom. I guess this is all a bit too soon. Hell, I'm still in therapy!'

'Please, Stella. Just one little venture and I swear you'll be hooked again. If you're not after that, then I'll back off, I promise.' He paused. 'The two kids are really dedicated. They have all the right ethics. They want to document these lovely old sites before they are torn down. They respect the past and want to catalogue all they can before there's nothing left.'

Stella hesitated. Tom could have been describing their old crew. Their credo had been, *Take nothing, damage nothing, and take your crap home with you.* 'And is the other guy a student too? Will he be studying my every move?'

'He's an architectural historian, specialising in the 1930s. He'll watch your back, just like you will his, and so will Butterwitch. She's awesome on a bimble! Totally focused. I'm telling you, Stella, I'm lucky to have met them, and you, old girl, couldn't have better company on your first trip out.'

'I can't promise.'

Tom was silent for a while. Then he said, 'What were your two choices?'

'The military hospital at Snaresdyke, or there's an old house out Friskney way, at Seas Meet. It was bought by developers, but hasn't been touched for years. I get the feeling it's slipped into no man's land. I only know about it because we used to get calls at the police station from the original owner, who was worried about vandals.'

'What's the name of the place?'

'Hall Place Manor, up an unmade track called Tin Lane.'

'Security?'

'Probably minimal, if anything. I would think they've given up after so long. Long-term security is costly, and if the deal's fallen through, well . . .'

'That one really is new to me. What's special about it?'

'It's pretty old, maybe dating from the mid eighteen hundreds. I saw it years ago when it was still a residential property. Lovely fireplaces, if they haven't been ripped out, and some good stained glass. I do know it has a pretty impressive Victorian orangerie.'

'I can't believe I've not heard about it. Have you checked it out online?'

'Briefly, but there's no mention of it. I was just about to look more closely when you rang.'

'Look, Stel, I really want to see this place, and the others will too. Hey, that reminds me, did you get your medical sorted? Can you drive now?'

'Thankfully, yes. I've got my freedom back.'

'Then if you have time later today or tomorrow morning, why not drive out to Seas Meet and do a recce, then we'll all meet there in the afternoon or early evening.'

Stella sighed. 'I'll do the recce. And even if I can't make it, I'll ring you with a suitable rendezvous point for your kids, and anything else that I think is relevant about gaining access. Okay? It's the best I can offer.'

'Good girl.' Tom gave her a mobile number and rang off.

Had there been a smile on Tom's face as he hung up?

She continued to trace the history of Hall Place Manor, but found precious little, and there was nothing at all on the urbex sites. So it was either a little gem or a total wash-out. Stella glanced at the clock. It would take around twenty to twenty-five minutes to get to Friskney from the village, and there was plenty of time before it got dark. Why not? She was gripped by the old urge to walk into somewhere she shouldn't. Well, nothing was engraved on stone tablets, so if she didn't want to go through with it, she'd be able to pass the directions on so Tom and his crew could check it out.

Stella closed down her computer and pulled her camera from the drawer. Without thinking she opened it and checked that it was empty. *See? Just a glitch.*

She locked the door and walked quickly back to Beth's place. *Okay, kid, all you have to do is have a pleasant drive out there, enjoy yourself, and that's your first baby step taken!*

* * *

After Lexi had gone, Beth and Michael took the dog for an extra walk around the village to reward him for his babysitting duties.

Beth looked over towards the green and saw her granddaughter hurrying towards them.

'I'm just going back to collect my car and take a drive out to Seas Meet.' She grinned. 'I'm going to check out that old house.'

'Alone?' Beth tried to keep the anxiety out of her voice.

'It's okay, Gran. I'm just making sure that the developers haven't demolished it yet. I'm not going inside, I promise.'

Beth watched Stella hurry away. 'Is this the dawn of a new era?'

Michael sounded thoughtful. 'I hope so. You know, having seen those amazing pictures, and now knowing the kind of dangerous structures that those young people infiltrate, if it were anyone else other than Stella, I'd say this was,' he made air quotes, 'a seriously bad idea.'

'And I'd agree,' said Beth. 'But we *are* talking about Stella. And I haven't seen her look so bright in ages. She needs stimulation, always has done, and this really could be her way back. I just didn't think you'd be able to light the blue touch paper so easily.'

Michael did a little bow. 'We aim to please.' He kicked a pebble, and Frisbee darted after it as it rolled ahead of them. 'Did you worry about her when she used to go off on these expeditions?'

'Oddly enough, I never had any qualms about her exploits, even when I got a phone call saying that she was just about to enter some defunct underground military facility, or a sewer system beneath the Paris streets. Other than the time when she said she was going to Chernobyl, it never worried me. She always had a sensible head on her shoulders. She was careful, fit and very capable.' Beth pushed her hands deeper into her pockets. 'Stella was born curious and she never lost that attribute. I'm certain that was what made her such a damned good detective.'

'She misses that job more than she says.' Michael spoke more seriously. 'I understand how she feels. That's why I want to see her find a new direction, a new path to follow.'

'Well, she certainly seems to be embracing this one wholeheartedly.'

'As long as another depression doesn't hit her. It can happen. So let's just cross our fingers, shall we?'

'And our toes. She's going to be okay. Isn't she?'

'If I have anything to do with it, she will.'

* * *

Stella returned from her trip buzzing with excitement. She'd had some trouble finding the entrance to Hall Place Manor, and it looked lonely, derelict and very inviting. It had taken considerable strength of will not to go inside. Now she was actually looking forward to tomorrow's adventure.

She parked the car in her gran's driveway, and her phone rang.

'Stella? It's Connor Dixon from the nick.'

She would have recognised the officer's soft Irish accent anywhere. 'Connor! How goes it?'

'Pretty good, thanks, but more to the point, how are you?'

Although she hadn't been on his team, Stella had always found the young detective constable friendly and fun to be around. 'I'm getting there. Too slowly for me, but at least I'm moving forward.'

'Good to hear. So, are you planning on coming back to us at some point?'

Stella frowned. 'Has Robbie put you up to this by any chance? He's been nagging me stupid about applying for a desk job.'

'Hey, no! Not at all, although frankly I can't see you in that role, Stella. But my call *is* to do with Robbie. He's off sick today and he'd asked me to arrange a time for you to come in and look at that CCTV footage. As I've no idea when he'll be back, I thought I'd better check with you and get it sorted.'

Stella frowned in confusion. But she'd already seen the footage, so what on earth was Connor on about? She stalled for time by dropping the phone into the foot-well of the car.

A picture of Robbie handing her the memory stick flashed into her head. Oh, the silly fool! What had he done? Surely he hadn't made a copy? 'Sorry, Connor, I'm in the car and I dropped the phone.'

'I was asking about the CCTV? We can do it tomorrow morning, if that suits?'

'Look, I'm really sorry to be a pain. I haven't spoken to Robbie yet, but I've decided against it. No one thinks it's a good idea for me to see it — except me, that is.' She hoped she sounded convincing.

'Excellent! To be honest, Stel, I thought it was a rubbish idea. I'll be delighted to cancel the whole thing, to be sure.'

They talked for a few moments more, and when the call ended Stella rang Robbie. It went to voicemail, but she decided not to leave a message.

She stared at her phone and wondered why Robbie would have done such a stupid and dangerous thing. Taking something away from the station while an investigation was in progress could cost him his job. New CCTV cameras use digital storage, but the old style, like the one at the village post office, were on video. The originals were seized and used as evidence, but a working copy was sometimes made for the investigating officers to use. One thing was for sure, they were not readily available to download to a memory stick or a DVD. Robbie had said he had obtained permission, but now she knew that was crap. Robbie owned a piece of kit that converted VHS tapes to DVD. She was pretty certain that he had taken the working copy of her shooting home, then converted and downloaded it to the device he had given her. But why, when she could have gone to the station and seen it there? It was true that she hadn't really wanted to face everyone just yet, but she'd never told Robbie that.

Stella got out and locked the car.

She was furious at Robbie. He was so damned lucky to still be in the police, but he seemed to not care a hoot about the precious vocation that they had both loved so much. He was carelessly wasting something that she would give her eye teeth for. And that was so out of character. Her anger abated. Connor had said that Robbie was off sick. He was *never* sick. In their time together he'd valiantly worked through coughs, colds, gut-rot, hangovers, the lot. Something had to be wrong. She needed to talk to Robbie Melton, and fast, before the silly sod did something else that could get him the boot.

Stella returned to the car and reversed off Beth's driveway. It was only fifteen minutes' drive to Robbie's place. The sooner they talked the better.

Robbie lived in a two-bed Boston riverside apartment. It was in a three storey block in well-kept private grounds and had a view across the river to the Marina. It was neat, tidy, and perfect for professionals who needed a place to crash in the working week but went away for the weekends. It reminded Stella of an upmarket Premier Inn. Robbie, however, loved it, even though he had no idea how to make it look like a home instead of a motel suite.

Stella stood outside and rang the intercom. After several attempts, the door swung open and a young man in a sharp suit and shiny shoes swept through. Stella smiled and entered, then took the stairs up to the top floor.

Robbie's door was closed and after three long rings on the bell, Stella stooped down and peered through the letterbox. There was nothing to see, and from the silence inside the flat it seemed to be empty.

Stella straightened up. She took out her phone and rang his home number. Seconds later she heard ringing coming from his lounge, but no one answered. She sighed and shut off the phone. He was supposed to be ill. She wondered if she should ring his mother, but hesitated. Victoria Melton was not an easy woman to like and they had crossed swords several times in the past. And Stella might drop Robbie straight in the shit with his over-protective mother.

Stella walked back down the stairs. Was she worrying over nothing? Maybe he just needed some space. She knew he wasn't coping too well at work, so that was most likely the answer. Despite his scruffy appearance, Robbie had money. If he chose to bog off for a few days, it would be no problem financially. It was just odd that he hadn't told her before he went.

Before she drove off, Stella left a message on his mobile asking him to ring her. Her earlier anger became concern. Where was he?

CHAPTER TWELVE

Razor stared at Stella with undisguised awe. 'Ray Zachara. It's an honour to meet you, let alone get to explore with you.' He offered a long-fingered, artist's hand.

'I'll second that,' said Butterwitch, giving Stella a warm smile. 'I'm Emily Butters, and I can't believe I'm actually meeting the woman who took those awesome shots in the linen mill in Northern Ireland. *Weaver of the Past?*'

Stella experienced a powerful wave of nostalgia. The great Victorian mill rose up in her mind's eye and she recalled the particularly unusual light on the day she got inside. 'Has Cave Bunny paid you guys to be nice to me?'

Tom grinned. 'No need, Stel. Starburst is legend in the Urbex world.'

Stella's reservations about meeting the two other crew members were already evaporating. She had begun to grow accustomed to being a nothing — an *ex*-copper, an *ex*-wife. An *ex*-human being. It was nice to hear words of appreciation, even if those pictures were taken a long time ago.

Her new acquaintances were nothing like she'd imagined.

Razor clearly came from money — unless she was very wrong, they both did. There was something in their manner that shouted "expensive education," and it had nothing to do with the way Razor dressed. There was no room here for designer labels, it was impossible to dress to impress. Flooded tunnels, filthy basements and tight crawl spaces demanded dispensable clothes. They all wore jackets, trousers and vests covered in pockets. These were vital for holding the multitude of equipment that UE required, from cameras and torches to first aid kits, antihistamines and even inhalers or EpiPens. A country house didn't call for ropes or survival gear, but every decaying place had its dangers. It paid to think it through before you even left home.

Stella thought that Tom had probably been right about Emily. If she could just get over the fact that she was a neurology student, Stella would really warm to her. She was tall and lithe, with dark blonde hair pulled back into a casual chignon. Her features were sharp, and her skin was clear and lightly tanned.

She exhaled. In the company of kindred spirits, she could let down her guard. They would understand.

They were in a small car park that backed on to a wildfowl reserve about a mile away from Tin Lane. They sat together on a low wall that skirted the reserve, and Stella briefed them on everything she had noted on her visit the previous day.

'No neighbours, and the house has extensive grounds as well as outbuildings surrounding it. There is some crappy old wire fencing across the gates and also across a back entrance, but the boundary wall is low enough to scale with no problem.' Stella realised that she hadn't once stuttered or mixed up her words. She felt comfortable and in control of herself. It was like finding a favourite pair of old trainers and slipping your feet back into them.

'There are warning boards all over, saying it's protected by a security company called the Galleon

Guarding Group, but they're the kind of firm you use only when you are running out of funds.' She knew this from her days on the force. 'They don't man the place, they just send out a bloke with a van to do an occasional walk round.'

'The kind of place we love,' said Razor with enthusiasm.

'It hasn't been lived in for donkey's years, and I know for a fact that the alarm system doesn't work.'

Tom rubbed his hands together. 'So, guys, we have around two hours of daylight left. Shall we go investigate this Hall Place Manor?'

They began to walk.

Razor said, 'Strange it's on none of the Urbex web sites. It's certainly the first we've heard of it.'

'I think you'll see why when we get there,' said Stella. 'I was actually called to the place way back, otherwise it would mean nothing to me either.'

They walked for around ten minutes, talking amicably about cameras and photo-editing software.

'Tin Lane is over there.' Stella pointed to an unremarkable-looking track.

The others looked around blankly.

'Where?' asked Emily, staring at an overgrown field and a track that seemed only to lead to an open barn.

Stella smiled. 'I remember driving past this bloody place in my squad car three times until I spotted it. I bet even some of the locals don't know it's here.'

She led them a short way up a farm track past a high tangle of wild rambling roses and elder bushes. Completely concealed from the road was the entrance to an unmade lane. 'Welcome to Tin Lane.'

It was easier than they had expected to gain access, as the last security man had left the wire gates unfastened. They switched their mobile phones to silent and walked along the grass that edged the gravel drive. In minutes they were standing in front of the old building.

Razor waved an arm. 'Oh this is fantastic! High Victorian! Look at those pointed gables!'

'It looks Gothic to me,' murmured Emily, staring at a leaded stained glass window.

'It is,' said Razor. 'This place dates to around 1860 to 1870. High Victorian was also called Neo-Gothic or Gothic Revival.'

'Just don't get your hopes up about the interior,' warned Tom. 'I can see signs of people who aren't urbexers.' He nudged at a lager can with his boot, and scowled at a scattering of screwed-up food containers.

'Let's find an access point.' Stella was eager to get inside. She suddenly realised that she hadn't once thought about any of her limitations. And Emily hadn't given the slightest indication that she was interested in her neurological anomalies. She was totally absorbed in Hall Place Manor.

They circled the building, until Razor whispered loudly, 'Over here! We have access! There's a small sash window that we can lever up without causing any damage.'

Okay, it wasn't virgin territory. They were not the first to walk the echoing halls, but it was good! Most of the furniture and belongings had gone, but at least the period features hadn't been bastardised, and Stella was pleased that the owners hadn't been tempted to "modernise." There were a few indications of half-hearted attempts at vandalism — little kids probably — but nothing substantial, and in the main it was undamaged.

They walked from room to room, taking photographs as they went. Razor gave them a running commentary on the features, such as the decorative encaustic tiles around the fireplaces and the plaster vaulting on the ceilings. He was enraptured by what he was seeing, and Stella felt proud that she had been able to provide something new and interesting on their very first trip out.

In the kitchen, Emily pointed out an old carved wooden key box on the wall. 'All the keys are labelled!

Listen. *Orangerie. Wine cellar.* And, oh look! This one says, *Ice House.*'

Razor looked like all his Christmases had come at once. 'I just love ice houses! Although I shouldn't be surprised. They were really popular on large estates in the nineteenth century. Most manor houses had one, even small ones like this. I saw a small lake from one of the bedrooms, which would be a perfect source of ice in winter.' His eyes sparkled. 'We have to find it!'

'You really are in your element,' laughed Stella. 'It's nice to see someone so passionate about their work.' As soon as the words left her mouth sadness washed through her. That was how she'd felt about policing. For the first time she noticed Emily looking at her thoughtfully. *She's astute, that one!* Stella gave her a smile, and Emily's grin said, "You haven't fooled me."

It took them a while to locate the entrance to the ice house, and longer to photograph it. Razor took several close-up shots of the weathered doors and the eroded brick surround. 'Classic!'

Tom turned the key in the undamaged lock and opened the door wide. 'Okay, Mister History Channel, give us the gen.'

Razor stepped inside and let out a low whistle. 'Brilliant! This is a great example of a nineteenth century ice house. The brickwork is first class.' He ran his delicate finger over the surface. 'It seems to have been insulated with charcoal. As I said before, they used to cut ice from the local lake or pond, and pack it in the central cellar, sometimes with straw in between blocks to make it easier to separate. It was used in the manor house kitchen for all sorts of things like preserving, cooling drinks and making desserts. This one really is classic — it's circular. Come inside and look. It's in remarkable condition.'

The stairs led down some eight feet into a large circular chamber.

'I don't think this is the original flooring, because I can't see any drainage for the melting ice. It may have been added later, and I wouldn't be surprised if that bricked-up area over there was a passageway to the main house at one time. Some of the gentry preferred the servants to use tunnels and passageways, rather than be seen about the grounds.'

Stella shone her torch around. 'Someone's used it as a garden store, by the look of it.' She saw some ancient dismantled bunk beds in the piles of junk. 'And prior to that, as an air-raid shelter.'

Razor's voice echoed in the cold, domed room. 'Isn't it incredible that it's still so cold, but it isn't damp? That shows the quality of the design and the skill of the builders who insulated it.' He sighed. 'This place is really awesome. Thank you, Stella. What a brilliant find!'

Despite the bitter cold in the ice house, Stella felt warm. For the past hour she had not once thought about her problems, or Edward's. 'I'm relieved. I'd have felt a right numpty if it had turned out to be a crock.'

Tom looked at his watch. 'Sorry to break up the party, but daylight's fading. We need to make a move.'

As they climbed back up the steps, Butterwitch gave an exclamation of surprise. 'Well, well! Look at this, guys.'

The beam of her torch had lit upon a small intricate symbol etched on the wall near the steps.

'So we aren't the first UEs to find this place.' Tom grinned. 'Jackhammer beat us to it.'

Hearing Jack Hammond's tag spoken so casually made Stella freeze. She examined the mark. It was his mark all right — a triskelion, a Celtic symbol with three swirling branches representing motion, which was the logo on his website.

'Did you know Jackhammer, Stella?'

It was difficult to hear the voice through her racing thoughts.

'I met him once.'

'Respect,' whispered Razor. 'He was the King of Urbex, along with Jeff Chapman and of course, our Starburst.'

'He came here?' said Stella, puzzled. 'How very odd.' She hadn't known that Jack had ever ventured into her neck of the woods. And why had he checked out this humble site when he spent most of his time and money infiltrating the spectacular and the inaccessible? And why leave a tag? Urbexers never marked their discoveries.

'Maybe there's more to this place than meets the eye,' Tom said thoughtfully. 'I think we should schedule a return visit, don't you?'

They made their way back to the car park. Stella was in turmoil. Everything had been going so well, and then Jack Hammond had forced his way back into her thoughts for the second time in as many days.

'I think Jackhammer must have been here many years ago,' Emily said. 'Rumour has it that he was killed on a trip abroad.'

'I heard he went out to some place in Europe, met someone and decided to stay,' Razor added.

'I know different,' said Tom, looking smug.

Stella's eyes widened. 'You know what happened to him?'

'Not exactly. But I know a man who does.'

'Is Jack alive?' Stella's mouth was dry.

'My mate wouldn't actually confirm it, like it was some deep secret, but I'm certain he is.' He grinned at Stella. 'I bet he'd tell *you* though. Walt was always a sucker for a good-looking woman.'

Stella cuffed Tom around the back of the head. 'You can pack that in for a start, Bunny-boy. Hey, is this a wind-up?'

Tom shook his head vehemently. 'Absolutely not. I'll give you this bloke's number, and you can ask him yourself.'

Stella drove off, glad that no one could see her expression in the twilight. Knowing that Jack had been here had really shaken her. And then to learn that someone actually knew what had happened to him was a further bombshell.

She saw again the chateau in the forest, and felt Jack's body close to hers. Stella gave a moan and wondered whether this trip would turn out to be the good thing she had first believed. Or was it a very dangerous one?

* * *

That evening, after Stella had gone to bed, Beth and Michael sat in front of a crackling log fire and enjoyed a snifter of brandy.

'So much for the training regime.' Beth looked reproachfully into the glass, as if it were to blame for her lack of willpower.

Michael laughed. 'Beth, the three-quarters of an inch of Remy that you have there isn't even medicinal. And I think you deserve it. I know how edgy you've been, waiting for Stella to get home.'

'I worried over nothing, didn't I? She coped brilliantly.'

'Oh, ye of little faith.'

'Excuse me, but I believe I saw you give a few anxious glances at your watch?'

'Nonsense. I never doubted her for one minute.'

'If you say so.' Beth pulled a face at him and he stuck his tongue out.

For both of them, seeing Stella return home full of enthusiasm for her outing and her new friends, was worth more than a haul of jewels.

Beth gazed into the glowing ashy logs. She could not recall a time in the last few years when she had felt so relaxed. Maybe it was the brandy.

'I need to get back to my room and pack a few things.' Michael sounded reluctant to move. 'And I really ought to go over my talk. I know it backwards, but everything that has happened here recently has rather dulled my enthusiasm for giving a lecture on cognitive neuropsychology to a group of new generation shrinks.' He finished his drink.

'I'm sorry, Michael. We've taken over your life in the last couple of days, haven't we?' Beth wondered silently how much of his preoccupation was with her, rather than Stella's problems.

'I'd have it no other way. In fact—.' He stopped abruptly.

Beth decided not to pursue it. Maybe it was something for another time. Maybe she wouldn't even want to hear it. 'Can I get you a coffee before you go?'

He shook his head, persuaded a sleepy Frisbee to return to the floor, stood up and stretched. 'The longer I stay the harder it will be to leave at all.'

Beth smiled too brightly and said, 'Yes, it's bitterly cold outside tonight.'

Michael's look told her that his reluctance to leave had nothing at all to do with the Lincolnshire climate. 'I'll be gone for two days, but you have my mobile number. Not that I expect any particularly bad episodes with Stella.' He touched her arm lightly. 'But if you feel like ringing me in the evening, it will be good to keep abreast of what is going on.' His hand lingered. 'Even if you just wanted to talk?'

'Of course.' Beth spoke lightly, but she was in turmoil. What would she do when he had to leave for ever?

* * *

Tom Chalk looked around at his half-built home. It was a barn conversion, but nothing like Beth Cartwright's. Past thirty, living at home had proved too much for him and in desperation he had commandeered one of the defunct farm buildings and begun to work on it. Since Tom was the eldest son, the main farmhouse had been left to him when his father had died, but it still housed his three brothers and his mother, and was far from being a personal haven. Tom flopped down on the old futon that he was using until the planned mezzanine bedroom area was finished, and let out a sigh. At least he had privacy here.

The barn had the potential to be something really special. The high interior shell was constructed in warm red brick, and sandy coloured arched wooden beams made it light and airy.

He had designed it himself, and was pleasantly surprised to discover a hidden talent. He kept the basic shape of the old place, and added windows and a mezzanine bedroom area where he thought these seemed right. It was beginning to look pretty good. He had had to get a professional to sort out the plans and get them approved, but it was *his* baby. And although it was far from complete, he was getting there.

He just prayed that he'd find the time and the money to finish it because right now, it had all the homeliness of a building site. Farming was tough, with long hours, and he allowed himself one trip out every fortnight with his new clan. He didn't go to the pub much and he didn't smoke. His only indulgence was urban exploring, his one release from twenty-four seven farm work.

He rested his feet on the lid of a five-litre paint can, opened a Dutch beer and downed a good quarter of the foaming liquid.

It had been quite surreal going out with Starburst, as if time had gone into reverse and they were hungry and excited kids again, hunting for treasures in some deserted and unloved building.

Stella looked amazing. He had been mega-anxious about seeing her again. What did you say to someone who had been shot twice at close range and lived? Normal conversation seemed banal and inconsequential in the light of what she'd suffered, and he didn't actually know the extent of her disabilities. But as it turned out, she was simply Stella. From the moment she had stepped through the gates of Hall Place Manor, she was back on home territory, and he was right beside her, where he'd always been.

He took another swig of beer, leaned back and closed his eyes. Times past. They had been good, probably the best times of his life. Back then, his dad had been there to shoulder the day-to-day running of the farm. Not that Tom was ever afraid of hard work. Unlike his brothers, he never moaned or slacked off, in fact he broke his balls every day to keep on top of the weather, the changing seasons and the crops and harvests that went with them. Now Dad was gone and it was his yoke to carry. But he didn't regret a moment of it. He loved the countryside, working the land, and he wanted his dad to be proud of him and what he was making of the farm.

His thoughts returned to Stella. He had known about the shooting almost before the gun had cooled. Gossip travelled fast in the country. He hadn't told Stella because he didn't want her to know why he hadn't visited her in hospital.

It had been bad enough when she joined the police force and gave up urban exploring. He had been devastated, and it had taken a while for him to go back out without her. Then she'd been shot, and Cave Bunny had buckled under the sheer weight of his emotions. He hadn't gone to see her because he couldn't face what he might find. So he had shut her out. Then she rang, and he realised how stupid he had been.

He shook his head. 'All that time. What a bloody waste.'

He finished the can, thought about opening another, but as usual he had to start at the crack of dawn. He needed a clear head. Tom threw the can into a sack of builders' rubble and decided on a shower and then bed. His conversion project had started with the installation of an upmarket shower room and a separate toilet. The rest would follow as time and money allowed.

He was still amazed by Stella North's return to his life — and to urbexing. She'd been like a fish going back into water. Even the kids had been impressed with her. Razor had looked dazed and Butterwitch . . . Butterwitch was obviously head over heels in love! Tom laughed.

Life was definitely looking up.

CHAPTER THIRTEEN

The morning had started badly and was getting worse. Lexi struggled to get breakfast out of the way, and finished up shouting at Ethan. Edward turned on her.

'You are not helping by behaving like that! Don't shout at the boy!'

This made Lexi's blood boil. '*You* get him to bloody eat then! Look, half of it is on the floor and most of the rest is up the wall.'

Frustration was getting the better of her. She wished Michael Lindenfeld had been able to talk to Edward, but she understood his position. Lexi was no fighter. She had spent most of her life in the role of peacemaker and she didn't relish the coming battle.

'I'm sorry, Ed,' she murmured. 'I know it's not Ethan's fault. I'm just tired and so worried.'

'*You're* worried.'

Ethan began to howl, the volume increasing with each breath.

'I can't handle this.' Edward jumped up and pushed his chair back. The front door slammed and his car roared away.

Lexi let out a moan. Then she looked at her child's scarlet face. They couldn't go on like this. Their family life had become intolerable, and Ethan would suffer the most. She might not want to have that battle, but she was going to have to force Edward's hand.

She stood up and gathered the boy into her arms, whispering soothing sounds that had no echo in her head. She would take Ethan to her mother's house and then she would go and see Edward at work. She knew how important his father's business was to him, but he had a family of his own now and they had to come first.

Lexi suddenly felt much better.

* * *

Beth and Stella drove across the fen towards the gym. The landscape gleamed in the harsh, glaring light from a low winter sun. The fen looked dark and rich, the muddy furrows etched into deep brown relief.

'At least the weather has improved for Michael's trip to East Anglia,' Stella said, squinting in the sunlight. 'I just hope he has a pair of sunglasses. This glare is wicked.'

Beth nodded.

'It's weird, not having him around. He's only been here five minutes but I feel that I've known him forever.'

Beth gave a dry laugh. 'He has that effect on people. I just wish he would talk to Edward. I'm sure he could help.'

Stella looked out of the window. 'I rang Lexi this morning after breakfast, but there was no answer. I left a message, but she hasn't returned my call.'

'I feel for her, but I suppose it really is *their* problem, isn't it?'

Stella patted her grandmother's leg. 'I think so. And I suspect even Michael's wise words would fall on deaf ears. Edward is behaving like a complete prat and refusing to listen to anyone. I'm sure that eventually, when he's had time to think, he'll realise what an idiot he's being and tell us what's wrong.'

Beth looked at her. 'You're very upbeat about something that had you crying your eyes out not so long ago.'

'Look, you know I love Edward to bits, I always have. I thought he'd be thrilled that I'd decided to get out and do something to help myself for once. Edward was always so courageous, so practical and so in command of everything. To hear him talk to me like that, like I was some rebellious child, it really hurt, Gran. But now I've decided that Michael was right. Edward had no right to try to put me down like that. It wasn't easy finding the courage to go out and meet new people yesterday. After that awful outburst, I could have easily abandoned the whole thing. In fact, if I hadn't had Michael's support, I don't think I would have gone.' She smiled. 'And then I'd have missed out on a real turning point in my recovery.'

Beth grinned at her. 'You loved it, didn't you? Just like years ago.'

'Did I ever! And those two youngsters were just like Tom and I when we were their age. It was great to see that a new generation of explorers are out there, with exactly the same goals and principles as we had.'

'So you'll go out again?' Beth asked.

'Already booked. Next week. We're going back to Hall Place Manor, only much earlier to catch the light. We didn't have time to see it all, particularly the orangerie and the wine cellar, and I want a lot more photos.' She frowned. 'If I could only get hold of Robbie and stop worrying about him, things would be pretty well perfect.'

'It's a bit of a mystery, isn't it? The second man in your life to be acting out of character.' Beth indicated and pulled into the long drive up to the sports centre. 'By the way, have you thought any more about setting up an image library on the web?'

Stella nodded. 'It's actually a very good idea. I have far more material than I thought, and even I know some of it is pretty good. Plus it's all original, so I can copyright it or allow free use, whatever I choose. I even wondered about a studio, somewhere where I could produce proper pictures, big enlargements either framed or on canvas, but for sale as serious artworks.'

'That sounds absolutely brilliant.' Beth could have jumped for joy. Stella was getting herself out and enjoying something and most importantly, she was making plans for the future. Was it all too good to be true? Depression didn't just vanish overnight. There would be bad times, but maybe with new interests to pursue these would be fewer. Right now, the kid was on a high.

An hour later, with a gruelling circuit on rowing machine, treadmill and cross trainer behind her, Beth relaxed in the swimming pool. *This is bliss*, she thought, as she glided through the turquoise water. As Stella chatted to an old friend in the steam room, Beth's thoughts wandered back to the first time a very young Stella had gone exploring.

Every town and village has a haunted house. The one in Sutterthorpe was simply called The Laurels and no one, including Beth, had ever known it to be inhabited.

Nine-year-old Stella came running into her kitchen, her clothes dusty and her eyes wide. 'Gran! You have to come and see this!'

Beth indicated the mixing bowl and asked, 'Is it more important than chocolate brownies?'

'Oh yes!'

'Then I'd better wash my hands.' Chocolate brownies were Stella's favourite.

Beth followed her into Love Lane, where Stella suddenly slipped through a gap in a rickety fence and into an overgrown garden. 'Did your father ever explain about something called trespassing?' she asked, picking her way past a bed of six-foot-high nettles.

Stella had clearly thought it through. 'Oh yes, but it's a bit of a grey area. I think if anyone stops us we should just act dumb.'

Beth wasn't too sure about the law herself. When did an abandoned building — and this one had been abandoned for many years — cease to be private property? If her dog ran into the garden was she entitled to go after it?

Stella was beckoning to her impatiently. 'This is an old downstairs toilet,' she whispered. 'And the window catch has fallen off. Look.' She pushed the small sash window. It juddered and stuck a bit, then slid up.

'And I'm going to climb through that, am I?' Beth was beginning to have serious doubts about her suitability to be a surrogate parent.

'You will be gobsmacked, Gran! Honest!' Stella swung easily through the window. 'Come on, hurry up!'

The house was intact, as if the owners had gone out for a moment and never come back. It was like wandering into one of those Second World War museums where they enacted scenes from nineteen-forties life.

She followed Stella from room to room, wondering why no one had ever been inside. There was no graffiti, no rubbish and strangely, very little dust.

Stella pulled at her hand and pointed out some of her finds: a red-and-white metal Oxo tin filled with yellowing cigarette cards, a bottle of something called Brilliantine, and a piece of apparatus that was like a strange swirled cane tennis racket. 'It was used for cleaning rugs, Stella. You threw the rug over your washing line and gave it a damn good thumping with the beater.'

'Cool!'

But the things Stella most liked were the carved wooden staircase, tiled fireplaces and the stained glass panels set into the tops of the doors. Beth watched her. She disturbed nothing.

'I have to come back with my camera,' she whispered urgently. 'We got in so someone else might, and they could wreck it. That would be terrible, Gran, really terrible.'

Beth dived under the water and resurfaced halfway down the pool. After all these years she could still recall the smell inside the Laurels. She had never been able to adequately describe it, except that it smelled of 1944, when the Paisley family went to visit an old friend in Boston and never returned. A local historian later told her that he believed they had been caught in an air raid. Their car was rumoured to have taken a direct hit from a doodlebug. The Laurels had been the start of a lifelong passion for Stella.

Stella called from the poolside shower. 'Gran! I'm through. How about you?'

Beth waved. 'Last lap coming up.'

CHAPTER FOURTEEN

Lexi was motoring along the main road towards the small industrial estate where Edward's factory was situated. She had no idea what she was going to say to him, but one thing was for sure. She was not leaving until she found out exactly what was wrong with him.

She was pulling into the slip lane for the entrance to the estate when Edward's silver Range Rover crossed the junction ahead of her onto the main road. Lexi glanced in her rear-view mirror, spun round and followed her husband's car.

She had never tailed anyone before and found it difficult to keep sight of the powerful car ahead. She had no idea where he was heading, until he turned into the Pilgrim Hospital. Was he hurt? Had someone at the factory had an accident and he was racing to A&E?

Concern for his well-being replaced her cool resolution. Something had to be wrong.

The car park was heaving. She saw Edward take a single space at the end of a bay, leaving her searching for a free spot. By the time she found somewhere, Edward was already disappearing through the main doors.

Lexi grabbed her bag, locked the car and dodged between the parked cars. Inside, she looked around. But this was the main hospital, not the emergency department. She frowned. As far as she could remember, no one they knew had been admitted for anything recently. So that left outpatients and the various clinical departments. Of course! He was coming to see Ethan's consultant! He must have realised that he should have been with her on that last trip, and although he hadn't admitted it, he must have felt guilty and asked to speak to Dr Acharya.

Lexi hurried towards the paediatric clinic. This might turn out to be a good thing. It would be the perfect time for them to talk. She turned the corner into the waiting area. It was empty.

'Can I help?' asked a nurse.

'Is Dr Acharya here, please? I think my husband has an appointment to see him about our little boy.' Even as she asked, Lexi knew what the answer was going to be.

'There is no paediatric clinic today, and I'm sorry but Dr Acharya is away until next week.'

'My mistake,' she said hurriedly. 'Must have got the date wrong. Sorry.' She turned and rounded the corner into another waiting room. This one contained five or six people sitting stiffly in uncomfortable plastic chairs.

Edward sat in a corner, elbows on his knees, staring blankly at the floor.

'Mr Byrne, please!' Someone called from an open doorway.

'Wait!' Lexi ran to her husband. 'Edward? What's going on? Why are you here?'

Edward looked at her in surprise, then gathered himself, stood up and took her in his arms. 'Oh, Lexi, I'm so glad you're here!' He looked at the nurse. 'Please, could you give us a few minutes, maybe see the next patient?'

The woman nodded, disappeared back into the consultant's room, and called another name.

With their arms around each other they walked to the deserted children's area and sat down.

'Darling? Is this what it's all been about?' Lexi asked. 'You are ill?'

Edward ran his fingers through his hair. 'I don't know where to start. I just know I'm out of my depth.'

'What sort of clinic is this?'

'General medical.'

'What is the matter with you?'

'I'm here for the results of some tests for renal cell cancer.'

Lexi took it in slowly. Cancer? Then the word seared itself into her brain. Her Edward? She closed her eyes and struggled to keep calm. So this was what lay behind all the moods and tempers. 'Why on earth—?'

Edward was shaking. 'Don't! Just don't! I have no idea why I couldn't tell you. Probably because I'm supposed to be the strong one. I should be protecting *you*.' Tears began to run down his face. 'The thing is, when they told Dad he had cancer, he was so brave. He just took it on the chin. So why am I like this?'

Lexi squeezed his hand and felt her strength returning. 'You said you were here for results? So nothing is confirmed yet?

'No, but—'

'Come on, darling. Let's take this one step at a time, shall we? No use being terrified of something that might never happen, is there? We'll go and see your consultant together.' She stood up. 'And Edward? For God's sake, no more secrets. Okay?'

'No more secrets.' He straightened up slowly, and for the first time in many weeks looked into her eyes. He smiled.

'Right. Let's do this.'

* * *

Stella had just returned from walking Frisbee and was towelling him down in the yard when she heard her mobile ringing.

'Hi, Stel! Just wanted to tell you that we all had a great time with you last evening. I for one can't wait to go out again,' Tom said.

'Oh hello, Tom. Me too. It felt just like it used to.'

'No ill effects?'

Stella walked into the kitchen and sat down at the table. 'The opposite. I feel energised.'

'Well, the kids were well impressed with the famous Starburst. Butterwitch has already posted a glowing blog about you.' He chuckled. 'Forgot to mention that she's gay, and I think you've made quite an impression.'

Stella laughed. 'I'm honoured. Gay girls have great taste in women, you know.'

'Anyway,' continued Tom, 'that's not why I rang. Er, tell me to bog off if I'm being nosey, but did I imagine that you almost fell down when you saw Jackhammer's Celtic sign in that icehouse?'

Stella stopped laughing. 'Well, no. I was shocked. I honestly thought he was dead.'

'Thing is, you told the kids that you'd been on a bimble with him once. I don't remember that, and our crew went everywhere together.'

Stella had never mentioned the chateau to anyone.

'Not quite. I just bumped into him when I was abroad. None of the rest of you could make it, so I went alone.'

'Ah, I see. But you seemed really gobsmacked when I said he was still around.'

'I was. As I said, it was a shock.' Stella felt rather at sea. She had nothing to hide, but nevertheless she felt that Tom was too probing.

'Well, if you want it, I've got the telephone number of the guy who supposedly knows where Jack is. I rang him earlier and he says he'll talk to you. One thing he did say though, Jack is still living in this country and apparently not too far away. That's all he'd tell me. You might have better luck.' Tom was joking again. 'Use your detective skills, Officer, interrogate him and find the missing urbex. You'd not just be a Starburst, you'd be a Superstar if you could track down the celebrated Jackhammer.'

Stella wrote down the number. 'I might ring, I'm not sure, Tom. Maybe he really doesn't want anyone to find him. He's been down for a long while now.'

'I'll leave it with you then.' Tom sighed. 'Better go. I've two ditches to dredge out before evening, and I very much doubt that my lovely brothers will have got round to it. See you next week?'

'Dead right you will. And by then I should have sorted out all my cameras for some better shots.'

'Take care, Stel. See you then.'

Stella stared at the telephone number. So much was happening right now. Maybe getting involved in finding Jack was too much, too soon.

She entered the number into her contacts. Right now there was another missing man to hunt down — Robbie. Her messages had gone unanswered and she was beginning to get really worried. Edward was another worry, but he had Lexi. Robbie had no one.

She went inside and put the kettle on. Gran was in her office checking out the dates of forthcoming marathons on the computer. When she was through, they would make a plan for the search for her missing friend. She was just trying to list some priorities when her mobile rang again.

'Stella North?'

Stella automatically straightened her back at the sound of the superintendent's voice. 'Superintendent Croxforth! This is a surprise.'

'Stella, I'm sorry to bother you, only we have something of a dilemma and we are hoping you can help us.'

It sounded more like an order than a request for assistance.

'It's DC Robbie Melton. Do you know where he is?'

'I have no idea, ma'am. I understood he was on sick leave. What's the problem?'

'Something has occurred regarding an investigation that he is assigned to and we need to contact him with some urgency. He is not answering his home or mobile phone, or our repeated messages.' The superintendent added, 'That young man is going to get himself into serious trouble if he's not careful.'

Stella had never warmed to Andrea Croxforth. She was a soulless, driven, company woman. Suddenly Stella realised that she was no longer beholden to gold braid. She didn't answer.

The super was speaking again. 'For some reason we have no record of his parents' telephone number. The one we have is defunct. Even that is against the regulations.'

'They moved very recently. Maybe the files haven't been updated yet.'

'Do you have the new one?'

She did. Should she give it to this woman? Stella thought quickly. If something was wrong with Robbie, she didn't want to prevent his getting help. And another thing. Why shouldn't Andrea Croxforth have the pleasure of talking to the prickly Victoria Melton instead of her? 'I'll get it for you, ma'am. I'll put you on hold for a moment while I access my contacts.'

Amazing that the superintendent had phoned just as she was thinking about Robbie. She only hoped she was helping her friend and not dropping him in the brown and sticky stuff.

Stella relayed the family's home number, and said, 'I'm worried about him, to be honest.'

'Thank you for your help, Stella, but it's DC Melton that should be worried. His conduct is far from the shining example that it used to be. He's on thin ice. If you should hear from him, you can tell him so, and get him to ring me immediately.'

Stella ended the call and stared hard at her phone. 'How about a bit of, "How are you, Stella? How are you coping? Can we offer any assistance? It would be good to see you back, Stella, *do* think about it, won't you? There's always a place for you here." Bollocks!'

Beth stood in the doorway, the corners of her lips twitching.

'Sorry, Gran, but that woman! I could swing for her. She's got the heart of a hunk of granite and all the charisma of stale beer!'

'That could only be your very own favourite superintendent.'

'Got it in one. She's really out for Robbie's hide.'

'No news about the boy?'

Stella puffed out her cheeks. 'Off the radar. He is supposed to always keep the station informed of his whereabouts. He's done a bunk and the fur is flying.'

'So where do you come in?'

'I'm to be the deliverer of exceedingly bad tidings should he contact me. And I handed over Mummy Melton's home number. Those two women deserve each other.'

'I spoke to Michael early this morning,' Beth said quietly. 'He asked if anything was worrying you, other than Edward, that is. I mentioned that Robbie seemed to have taken off without warning, and he asked if the lad had had any counselling after the shooting.'

Stella pulled a face. 'I was rather out of it at the time, but I doubt it. I think he would have told me.'

'That's what I thought. Michael said that the powers that be should take his behaviour seriously, rather than threatening to punish him. He thinks Robbie's going through a grieving process. After all, it was a terrible shock and as he'd been your partner for such a long time, he could well be feeling guilty.'

'But why? He wasn't even there. There was nothing he could have done.'

'Exactly. He wasn't there. Plus he's lost his partner, which is where the grief comes in.' Beth spoke gravely. 'Michael said it's serious. Is there any way we can help find him?'

Stella puffed out her cheeks and exhaled. 'I was just trying to work that one out when Granite-face rang. I just don't know where to start.'

Beth's eyes narrowed. 'Maybe I can help. I still remember a few of the criteria we used when I worked for the government. People are creatures of habit, so I'm betting that if we put our heads together we can find him before your lovely superintendent does.'

'That would be a real pleasure. And probably a godsend for Robbie.'

They sat down together in the lounge, and Beth began.

'As a rule, when people are upset and can't cope, they run to a special place, a bolt hole, somewhere they feel safe. Or they might bury themselves in a pastime, something to take their minds off the pain they are going through.'

'A bit like when I took off on a walking holiday or went scaling rocks after a particularly gruelling case had come to an end?'

'You were just recharging and preparing yourself for the next assignment. Robbie really isn't coping with anything right now, so I suggest he's gone down the "run away and hide" route.' Beth looked at her. 'You know him well, probably better than anyone. Has he got a safe place that you know of?'

Stella thought hard. Robbie was such a career copper that there seemed to be nothing in his life except the job. Even when they had days off, and she went off and did something energetic, Robbie just sat in his apartment, ordered a takeaway and downloaded some movies. She gave a hopeless shrug. 'Nowhere that I can think of.'

'Okay. Well, you used to talk a lot. Was there something that he really loved doing as a kid? Something that he spoke fondly of?'

'I don't think his childhood was a happy one, Gran. I got the feeling that his parents were disappointed in him. Robbie always believed that he hadn't lived up to their expectations, so he rarely spoke about his childhood.'

'What about holidays? Where did he go, and who with?'

Again Stella was stuck. 'In all the time I've known him he's never been abroad. He reckoned his parents used to drag him around the south of France and the Med during his school holidays, drinking and socialising with what he called their arse-licking friends. He hated it.'

'After he grew up, where did he go? Every young man takes a break at some point, especially someone in such a demanding job.'

Stella felt a memory glimmer in the back of her mind, tantalisingly close, but she couldn't retrieve it. 'Damn! There *is* something, Gran, I know there is, but it won't materialise.'

Her grandmother smiled at her. 'Relax. It'll surface in its own time. It happens to everyone, it's not just you and your glitches.' She reached down and fondled Frisbee's ear. 'How about someone he cared for? You say he was not a happy child but there must have been someone close to him when he was younger? Someone he trusted.'

'That's it!' Stella sat up. 'Cornish mines! He had a carved wooden engine house in his lounge, and a collection of quartz and amethyst crystals. He said he had an aunt, his father's sister, who lived close to the sea, and as a boy he loved roaming over the cliffs hunting for rocks and minerals.'

'Is she still alive?'

'I think so. In fact I'm sure she is. She's an artist. She sent him a special hand-painted Christmas card last year.'

'Do you know where in Cornwall she lives?' Beth's eyes sparkled.

'Ah, now . . .' Stella puffed out her cheeks. 'This is where it gets difficult. He told me that there was this old tin mine, not long closed down, and the paths up on the cliff edge ran along the slag heap. He said it was full of interesting rocks and crystals.'

'We can look that up on the Internet.' Beth stood up. 'Any more clues?'

'The mist used to come in suddenly. Robbie said how eerie it was with the sound of the lighthouse booming out around them. He said the foghorn went off every twenty seconds.' Her smile broadened. 'I've got it! It was called the Pendeen Watch!'

Beth nodded. 'Then I know exactly where you mean, and unless I'm mistaken the mine is the old Geevor Tin Mine. My father came from Cornwall and it was one of my old haunts. It's a heritage museum now. And you say the aunt lives close by?'

'In an old converted miner's cottage in a village that begins with Tre . . . something.'

Beth strode to her office. They soon found the village of Trewellard, then a link to local artists and on to a woman named Hazel Melton. 'Bingo! Oh, I love it when it all comes together!' Beth grinned. 'Who needs police computers when you have Google, huh, kiddo? I do believe we've found your friend.'

'*If* he's there.' It had been far too easy. 'Gran, Robbie could be anywhere.'

'So find out.' Beth picked up her phone and held it out to Stella. 'Hazel is a well-known landscape artist. Her number is on her site. Ring and ask.'

Stella took the phone and stared at it. A dark confusion swirled through her mind and all at once she had no idea what to say to this woman.

'Gran?' She passed the telephone back to her grandmother. 'I can't.'

Beth smiled at her. 'No matter. Shall I?'

Stella nodded, sick to her stomach. It was a simple task, something she would normally have done without thinking about it. But a frightening void had opened up and she was floating.

She listened to her gran talking easily to this stranger, with no alarm or consternation in her tone. She would have made a bloody good police officer, thought Stella.

'Well, if you hear from him, Hazel, do get him to ring his friend Stella, and put her out of her misery.' There was a break. Beth laughed and added, 'I'd love to. And I'm delighted to hear that the Meadery is still there. Next time I head southwest I promise I'll call in, and maybe we could meet and have a glass of something?'

There was more laughter and then she hung up. Her smile faded. 'Nice woman.'

'But no Robbie?'

'She hasn't heard from him in months. She promised to ring us if he materialises.' Beth sighed. 'Hell, I was so sure we were on the right track.'

'Things rarely go that smoothly when you're tracing someone.'

'I just had a good feeling about it, my version of what you call your policeman's nose.'

Stella knew the feeling well.

'Maybe a cup of tea would help.' Beth stood up and walked to the kitchen. Stella had no idea where to try next. Her heart was heavy.

CHAPTER FIFTEEN

'So it isn't cancer,' Edward said tentatively.

Lexi grasped Edward's hand and squeezed it harder. 'Thank God for that!'

The consultant looked thoughtful. 'Not cancer, but nevertheless, polycystic kidney disease is a very serious condition. We will need to keep a very close eye on you.'

'Is there a cure?'

'Unfortunately no, not at present.'

'But it's manageable?'

'It is, and now that we know what we are dealing with, any complications that occur can be dealt with promptly.'

'How did I get this?' Edward asked, his voice cracking with emotion.

'It's an inherited condition, Mr Byrne, a faulty gene. It generally doesn't show itself until between thirty and sixty years of age.' He sat back. 'You have multiple small fluid-filled sacs, called cysts, in your kidneys. Now we need to draw up a suitable treatment plan and spend some time with you so that you understand what is going on in your body, and what to watch out for. Diet, and so on.'

Lexi took in a deep breath. 'What's the prognosis, Doctor?'

'It is highly variable, Mrs Byrne. You are both sensible adults so I'll be frank with you. Some patients go into kidney failure, requiring either dialysis or transplant, and others live the rest of their lives with their kidneys functioning pretty well.' He held out his hands. 'It's a bit of a lottery, but the cysts are very small and with a good diet and a healthy lifestyle, I have high hopes that Edward won't suffer any serious problems until he's well into his sixties.'

Edward shook his head. 'I thought I had just months to live, maybe a year at best, and now we are talking decades.' He smiled wanly, then suddenly looked worried. 'Just a minute! You did say it's hereditary, didn't you? Does this mean our son could have it too?'

'It's possible, so he will need to be screened regularly.'

Lexi's face tightened. 'And the chances of Ethan actually having this faulty gene?'

'Fifty per cent, I'd say. But that doesn't mean the condition will develop. Other factors influence that.'

Lexi nodded slowly. 'Thank you for your honesty. We appreciate it.'

'The most important thing is that we have diagnosed it before it has become a serious problem.' He paused. 'And hopefully your son will not have inherited it. Considering what we feared, it is positive news.'

The consultant promised to get an urgent referral letter to a kidney specialist at Nottingham Hospital. Edward and Lexi stood up to leave.

'Not cancer,' Lexi whispered as they walked hand in hand along the corridor.

'Not cancer,' Edward echoed.

'We'll get through this.'

Edward stooped and kissed the top of his wife's head. 'I now know that, sweetheart, and thank you so much for coming and finding me. You're my rock.'

'Right, and don't you forget that, Edward Byrne. I'm a damn sight tougher than you seem to think!'

* * *

Robbie had spent his whole life being criticised. He should have been used to it by now. Parents, teachers, tutors and superior officers alike were all constantly pointing out his shortcomings to him. Everyone except Stella. She might call him a "plonker," or a "wally," but it was merely in fun, to a mate.

Yet Robbie had been totally unable to cope with Superintendent Andrea Croxforth's particular brand of vitriol.

Robbie sat on a slippery outcrop of rocks and stared at the crashing waves. There was something very special about being alone on a day like this, when nature was playing out a drama just for you. Usually this calmed him. Today the remote spot and the wild weather only amplified his loneliness.

Salty spray drenched him, and although he tried to concentrate on the crash and hiss of the water rushing up the beach, he could still hear his superintendent's harsh words playing on a loop inside his head.

He should have either walked away or fronted it out, but had done neither. He stayed silent behind the half-opened office door and took it all in.

'Get him on side, Detective Inspector, and quickly. I don't carry makeweights in my teams.'

'Forgive me, ma'am, but DC Melton is a good copper. He's obviously having trouble adjusting to what happened, but all he needs is a strong partner, then he'll come into his own again.'

'Good grief, man! You make him sound like some hothouse flower. He's a policeman, a detective, and he's not producing the goods.' A long pause had followed this. 'If you say he needs a prop, find him one. Why not? Find him another hero to dance attendance on. Sorry, but he either shapes up or ships out. End of.'

Robbie shivered.

No one seemed to understand that he could be a hard-nosed bastard if he wanted to. Lord knows, he had enough role models! He simply refused to be like that. He considered the long list of exemplars, headed by his mother. He gave a short laugh. Her undisputed role as Queen Bitch was now being contested — by Superintendent Andrea Croxforth.

A massive wave hit the rocky cliff and spewed a plume of white froth some twenty feet into the sky. Was she right? He knew he wasn't firing on all cylinders, so if he really was a burden to the team, he had no right to be there. Then what did he do next?

He stood up and clambered over the wet rocks, closer to the sea. He knew he was letting people down, and by staying out of contact he was probably in deeper shit than ever at work. His phone was still in the glove compartment of his car, missed calls piling up. Not that he cared. The only person he regretted avoiding was Stella.

He wiped a hand across his face and tried to see through the fine, soaking spray. He had been too afraid to call her. He knew exactly what she would say, and he didn't want to hear it. He was rejecting the one thing she would give her right arm to have. She wouldn't forgive him for that. Stella North, his guide star, would finally join the long list of people who took pleasure in condemning him.

Robbie stood and stared into the North Sea, wondering just how cold it really was.

CHAPTER SIXTEEN

Michael arrived early and Beth could not believe how pleased she was to see him. It had only been two days! How could she have missed him so much when they had been apart for decades? Suddenly she saw Michael as he really was. No longer the handsome young student she had loved so deeply, or even the older, learned doctor that had hurried to her side from Germany. He was a perfect amalgam of the two. In his youth he had been vibrant and headstrong, ready to leap into whatever life threw at him. Now age had calmed the flood of impatience and he was gentler. Beth liked what she saw.

Michael looked cheerful, clearly invigorated by the young people he had been teaching. He pulled off his coat and beamed at her. 'They were a great group. We got on well, and there were one or two that will be top doctors one day.'

'That's reassuring.' Beth gave him a wry smile. 'Although maybe a little late for you and me.'

Michael hung up his coat. 'So, how have things been here? How's Stella?'

'Come into the kitchen, coffee's brewing.'

He followed her through and sat down at the table. 'Any disasters?'

Beth took coffee cups from the cupboard. 'Remarkably, no. She did wake up yesterday with those black dogs snapping at her heels, but she seemed to get on top of it by lunchtime. This morning she's been a bit edgy and showing the vagueness and mild irritation that sometimes heralds a bout of depression. She said she'd had bad dreams last night.'

'Any obvious reason?'

'Robbie Melton is still missing and she's worried sick about him.' Beth placed the sugar bowl in front of Michael. 'But other than that, she has been good. She even went over to see Tom Chalk, to get ready for their next outing. They have done some more research on their house at Seas Meet and they think there may be all sorts of exciting finds there.' She smiled. 'Anyway, it's doing her good, and that's fine by me.'

'And Edward? Have you heard from him?'

'Ah! This is where the good news starts. I suspect you might have worked out that he was ill?'

Michael nodded. 'I guessed as much. That's why I couldn't interfere. But it's not serious?'

Beth smiled. 'They went to the hospital the other day, and he told us everything. It's such a relief that the old Edward is back. He apologised profusely to Stella, but I get the feeling that she's still hurt.'

'That could take a while. I'm sure she'll come around with time. And at least he's not living under the imminent death sentence that he must have feared.' He paused. 'And how about you?'

'Oh, I'm fine. I've been trying to help Stella track down young Robbie, but so far my deductive skills have deserted me. He's vanished.'

'Not hard to do.'

'Sounds like the voice of experience?'

'I did take some time out once, after my hand was injured. It was a pretty dire time, and I needed to get away from everyone and everywhere that I knew.'

Beth felt sad that he had been suffering and she hadn't known about it. 'Where did you go?'

'Not too far from where I lived. A remote village in the mountains that I'd visited at some point. I thought I needed to be away from people and close to nature, God knows why. I guess I'd forgotten that wherever you run, you take all your baggage with you. I avoided everyone for a wasted month, then went home and got myself some proper professional help.'

'I thought that was what Robbie would do — run away — but he's not staying at his favourite haunt, and no one knows enough about him to think of other places he would go.'

'I'm really angry that his employers seem not to understand that he is ill and needs help.'

'Even I never realised just how badly he reacted to Stella leaving the force.' Beth sat down opposite Michael.

Michael frowned. 'He is having to cope with multiple traumas, and they will have made him question everything. If he'd had the right counselling immediately after the shooting, he would most likely be back on track by now. As it is, he's floundering. And he's doing it alone.'

Beth sipped her coffee. 'Would you talk to him when we finally find him? I don't mean full-on counselling, just a few encouraging words?'

'Of course I will. But the lad needs something more regular to get him back on track. If nothing else, I could certainly suggest the most suitable therapy for him and possibly recommend a good practitioner.'

'Michael! You're back!' Stella ran into the kitchen, hesitated, and then threw her arms around him. 'I'm so glad you're here.'

She sat down and nodded at the coffee pot. 'Any left?'

'Of course.' Beth got another cup. 'So what have you got planned for today?'

Stella looked at Michael and raised her eyebrows. 'If you're not too exhausted after your lectures, I'd really appreciate a talk with you. Actually, I've been feeling a bit shaky.'

'Well, luckily I'm on top of the world, young lady, and completely at your disposal. In fact I've been wondering how you would feel about a session in your house. There are some issues that I'd like to explore, and I feel they would be better approached on home ground — if you're okay with that?'

Stella nodded. 'Bring it on. I need something to take my mind off Robbie Melton, that's for sure.'

'And this evening, I'd like to take the two of you out for a meal. Do you know any really good restaurants round here?'

'That would be lovely,' said Stella, 'although there are not too many Michelin stars in this neck of the woods.'

'There's the old coaching inn out near Swineshead. I've been told the food is something special,' Beth added. 'But I'd like to treat *you*. You've given up all your precious time to help us, and we're grateful.'

Michael brushed her offer away. 'Another time maybe. This is my treat. Should we book a table?'

'Probably. I'll do it as soon as I've walked Frisbee. Oh, there's the phone.' Beth lifted the phone then put her hand over the mouthpiece and whispered, 'It's Robbie's aunt from Cornwall.'

"I've been thinking about it ever since you rang," said the woman, "and last night I had an idea. He did this once before, when he was much younger. His father, my brother, was never exactly supportive of poor Rob. He had set his heart on the boy going to Sandhurst, but Robbie was having none of it. He told me once that he'd rather run away and beg on the streets than join the army."

Beth laughed. 'I can believe that. He doesn't strike me as being cut out for that kind of career.'

"I agree with you. Anyway, my brother and his lovely wife made life hell for Robbie. And one day, just as he was about to finish senior school, he simply took off."

'Where did he go?'

"That's what I've been trying to remember, and last night it came to me. It was a place like Cornwall, but much closer to you, *your* stretch of the Jurassic Coast, in North Yorkshire."

'Do you recall where exactly?' Beth tried to keep the excitement out of her voice.

"Around Ravenscar, I think. He liked to go fossil hunting along that stretch of the coast. It's really wild and he always said if he didn't have the time to get down to Cornwall, that's where he'd head for."

'That's only three, maybe three and a half hours from here.' Beth's mind was racing.

"Well, it's not guaranteed, Beth, but I'll bet ten-to-one that my nephew is hiding out up there somewhere."

Beth thanked her and promised to let her know if they had any news. Then she told the others.

'It's tempting to just jump in the car and go. But he could be anywhere along that rugged chunk of coastline. It would be like looking for a needle in a haystack.' Stella bit her lip.

'Not necessarily,' said Beth. 'It's winter, and that east coast only gets serious walkers and hardened fossil hunters at this time. The fossil beaches that Hazel was talking about stretch from Robin Hood's Bay, through Whitby, right down to Scarborough, but the area at Ravenscar is different. There's nothing there except for one big brooding hotel stuck way up on the cliff top.'

'I've been there!' Michael exclaimed. 'The Victorians planned to make it a luxury holiday destination, but it all went wrong, and the project was never realised. Nothing was ever built. It is one of the most intriguing places I've ever been to. I think that's exactly the kind of place that Robbie would run to.'

'But if he needs time alone, should we seek him out?' Beth wondered.

'I think *I* should,' Stella said softly. 'This is my fault, even if it was unintentional. I think I owe it to him to go and find him, even if it's just to know that he's safe and not thinking too many dark thoughts.' She shrugged. 'And it's not as though I don't have the freedom or the time.'

'Maybe we should ring that hotel and ask if he's staying there. It is very remote up there. At this time of year he'd be hard pushed to find anywhere else. Just knowing that he was booked in there could help put your mind at rest.' Michael looked at her.

Beth agreed. 'I'll look up the number on the Internet. And if he's there, well, you know how much the dog loves long walks on the beach. Why don't you and Michael take Frisbee and be beachcombers for the day? Who knows what you might discover.'

* * *

Stella sat in her room and tried to clear her muddled thoughts. It seemed that their search for Robbie was doomed. Gran's call to the hotel had produced a big fat zero, and dashing off to trudge miles of freezing beach on the off-chance of spotting him seemed a bit crazy, even for her.

She decided that she might have to admit defeat and wait for Robbie to call her. Surely he had to check his messages at some point? She was his closest friend, and she was hardly Superintendent Andrea Croxforth, was she? Stella was certain that the super was behind Robbie's unexplained disappearance. She had to have put too much pressure on him too soon.

Stella lay back on her bed and sighed. With a more understanding boss, things might have been very different for both of them. She thought about other officers that she had worked with, and one in particular came to mind. She had once been seconded to help out in the nearby market town of Saltern-le-Fen, where she had worked with a team headed up by an Inspector Jackman and a detective sergeant called Marie Evans. She had become friendly with Marie, and was still in touch with her. Marie had sent her a card when she had come out of hospital, and a message promising help if she ever needed it.

A smile crept across Stella's face. Marie! I wonder . . .

She jumped from the bed and grabbed her address book. It was a long shot, but worth a try. She glanced at her watch. Ten o'clock. Perfect. The early morning meeting would be over and Marie should be free to talk. As she searched for the number she recalled Marie's tall, athletic figure and long, dark hair swept off her face. And the motorcycle leathers she usually wore. Marie was a brilliant, intuitive detective sergeant with a gentle manner, and a demon on her high-powered motorbike. Her Amazonian looks were a great help to her, but she had earned the respect of her colleagues through her loyalty, commitment and efficiency.

Stella grinned smugly to herself. Marie Evans was the perfect teammate for Robbie Melton.

Marie answered almost immediately and sounded pleased to hear from her. They chatted for a few minutes, then Stella told her that she needed her help.

'Fire away. We are pretty slow today, so whatever you need.'

Stella told her about Robbie.

'That's a damned shame. You and Robbie were two of the best. Bit Batman and Robin maybe, but definitely Defenders of the Realm!'

'I need to find him. And when I do I need to convince him to move away from Croxforth.'

'Well, on the first point, I have a mate who works out of Scarborough. He's a really good bloke, and I'm sure he'd be happy to make a few discreet enquiries. I'm sure

that if your Robbie is there, my Jimbo will flush him out.'
She paused. 'If he is up there we'll locate him, but we
won't interfere. You'll need to go and pick him up. Okay?'

'That's a deal.'

'And on the second point, we might be able to help
there too. There are a couple of vacancies coming up in a
month's time. They are not yet common knowledge —
one is a maternity leave that I happen to know will most
likely extend into a permanent post, and the other is a bit
more complicated. I can speak to DI Jackman for you and,
knowing him, he'll be sympathetic.' She gave a chuckle.
'He *really* dislikes Croxforth. She's not his kind of police
officer at all.'

'He'd be an asset to you, Marie. He's a great guy and a
brilliant second-in-command.'

'He won't be chasing after my job, I hope!' Marie
laughed.

'That's not what he wants at all. He needs a good
leader, and if he respects you, he'll follow you to hell and
back. And he's brilliant undercover. He has the knack of
becoming a non-person. He can blend in and disappear —
until he's needed, then watch him go.'

'If what the grapevine says is true, his record speaks
for itself. If he applies, I'm sure he'll get the job. And there
should be no bad feeling about the position going to an
outsider because as I said, there are two jobs up for grabs
and the second one could stay in-house.'

Stella heard a phone ring in the background.

'Sorry, Stella, I've got to go. Leave it with me, okay?'

'Thank you, Marie. I really owe you.'

Stella hung up and sank back on the bed. If Marie and
her Jimbo were successful, she would have to talk Robbie
into salvaging his precious career. That wasn't going to be
easy.

As she tried to decide on a strategy, her phone rang. It
was Tom.

'I don't mean to push you on this, but Walt is going off the radar for a month or so. He's doing some back of beyond foreign jaunt and will be out of reach. If you did want to talk to him, you'll need to do it sooner rather than later. No pressure, Stel, even though I'm practically wetting myself waiting to find out where the Jackhammer is.'

'Message received and understood, though I'm still in two minds about it.'

Stella closed her phone and pulled a face. Was this a wake-up call or a warning to let sleeping dogs lie? And which should she choose? Maybe today's session with Michael would give her some insight, and if it didn't, she could always resort to flipping a coin!

She sucked in air. It wouldn't hurt to just talk to this Walt, would it? It didn't mean she *had* to contact Jack, but she would at least have his details if she decided to do so.

'Oh, sod it!' she muttered. She found the number in her contact list and pressed call.

The voice on the other end had an almost familiar Cockney accent.

'So you're the infamous Starburst? Ol' Tom Chalk's mate?'

Stella said she was, and added that she was also an old friend of Jack Hammond, and that his disappearance had been worrying her for some time.

'But he never got in touch with you, did he?'

Stella stammered, 'We were very close, many years back.'

There was an audible sigh. 'Sorry, but you must have realised that he's been silent because something happened to him, and he hasn't wanted to share it with anyone.'

'Except you.'

'Yeah, except me, and he didn't have any choice about that. I was there when it happened.'

'When what happened?'

'Bugger! Look, I really don't wanna say.'

'Walt, I don't want to make a big issue out of this. If Jack doesn't want to talk to me, well, fine. How about you take my number? Give it to Jack. Tell him Starburst sends her love. End of. If he says, "Get stuffed," then fair enough. Okay?'

Stella was desperate to know what had happened to turn Jack the daredevil into Jack the Recluse, but she couldn't ask. 'Shall I ring off?'

'He had an accident. And since then he has never got his bleedin' act together.'

Welcome to my world, thought Stella.

He sighed. 'I'd been having trouble with transport. Eh, no car. And I badly wanted to see an old decommissioned power plant in Germany.'

To Stella that sounded like he'd been banned from driving.

'Jack said he'd take me, just as a one-off. You know he always travelled alone. Well, it was raining.' Walt sounded thoroughly miserable. 'Not just raining, it was blasting down. We were sideswiped by a bloody great artic that was speeding on the Autobahn and skidded.' Walt sniffed. 'I dunno how two people in the same vehicle could have such different injuries. I got away with a whiplash and a shedload of bruises. Jack shattered his femur and broke both his hip and his wrist in three places.'

Stella breathed in sharply. She'd seen enough RTCs in her time to know that femur breaks were very nasty. People with broken femurs sometimes bled out before the paramedics could even move them. 'I'm so sorry. I had no idea.'

Walt gave a mirthless laugh. 'Then it's worked. Jack didn't want anyone to know what had happened. He was airlifted to some big *Krankenhaus* in Cologne where they put him back together. Then later he was transported home for further surgery.'

'And now?'

'Devastated. It's ruined him.'

And do you feel you're to blame? she wanted to ask. Do you feel like Robbie does about me, even though there was nothing you could do and it really wasn't your fault? After all, Jack didn't have to go. It was his decision. 'I'm so sorry. But I'd still like to see him if he feels up to it. Will you talk to him for me?'

'Yeah, but no promises. He's . . .' There was a long pause. 'He's volatile. He hasn't seen anyone from the urbex world since. It's like he hates the fact that they are free to go where and when they want, and he's a prisoner in a wheelchair. So, like I say, it's not likely he'll talk to you.'

'If it means anything, you can tell him that I've suffered too.' Stella wasn't used to telling people what had happened to her. 'Bottom line, I was shot. I'm a . . . I *was* a copper. I loved my job with a passion, and now I'm out of it, with health problems of my own, so I can empathise with him. I'm not in a wheelchair, but I do have limitations that have put me in a sort of prison for a while. Tell him that, please, Walt?'

'Sure. I'll be talking to him later today.'

'Thank you. And I'll understand if he says no, and I won't bother you again.'

'Maybe . . .' Walt paused. 'Just maybe you'll be different. I'd like that. I hate to see the silly bugger all alone with no one to swap stories with. They were good times, weren't they, Starburst?'

'The best. What was your tag, Walt?'

'Riptide. As a kid I always had a hankering to go surfing down under.'

Stella vaguely recalled the nickname. 'Do you still go out exploring?'

'Not much anymore. I kind of look out for Jack most of the time. He has a lot of stuff like food delivered, but you need a mate to help you with some things.'

Yes, you *are* feeling guilty, thought Stella. 'But you are off on a long trip soon, according to Tom?'

'I need to. My life is going like Jack's, straight down the pan. I have to have a break.'

'I think you're very sensible,' said Stella honestly. 'Where are you going?'

'Canada. Way up north. I've got a cousin there.'

'Good luck, and thanks again for talking to me. You take care, Riptide.'

Stella stared at her phone. Jack Hammond, disabled?

It seemed impossible. Jack was their leader and their role model. He had superhero status, and people spoke of him with awe and admiration. Stella had had a number of lovers over the years, but Jack Hammond was the only one to leave a mark on her. It had never gone away, even though she'd tried hard to erase it.

She exhaled loudly. 'Well, life sure has a weird way of sticking decent people up to their necks in the shit,' she murmured to herself. 'And it sounds as if right now, Jack can't dig himself free.'

Stella stood up. It was time for her session with Michael. She thanked God that she had a small army of friends with shovels!

CHAPTER SEVENTEEN

Stella and Michael walked slowly back towards Coggles Barn after a scary but uplifting session at her house.

Stella felt safe when Michael was around. She never felt judged by him. Most people were critical, even if they didn't intend to be. Coppers were the worst of all, because they were trained to be that way. Michael was different. He just seemed to understand the reasons behind people's words and actions and didn't question them. But he wouldn't be staying forever and when he left, her anchor would be raised and she'd be cast adrift on the stormy seas.

'I guess they'll be missing you back in Germany?'

Michael shrugged. 'Probably not, although one or two of my patients might be feeling rather abandoned. Luckily I have a very good support team.'

'I was rather thinking about your family, your wife and children.'

He laughed. 'My children have children of their own. The only time they need me is when they want something — school books, holidays, riding lessons, computers, it's a bottomless pit.'

'Ah, I see. But your wife must miss you?'

Michael stopped and turned to face her. 'Frida and I . . . How can I put it? We are the dearest of friends, but we don't live in each other's pockets. She is in the mountains being nanny to our newest grandchild, and sometimes I go off for months to different universities and hospitals.' Suddenly Michael looked his age. 'We love each other, but I was only ever *in* love with one woman, and it wasn't Frida. We have made a good and fruitful life, but it was not the one I had hoped for.'

Stella stared back at him. 'Beth?'

He nodded. 'Beth.'

Stella didn't know what to say.

'Don't tell her this, Stella. I think it's better if she believes that my marriage was a great success. Otherwise it will all seem a terrible waste of both our lives.'

Stella slipped her arm through his and they walked on. 'She told me what happened. Neither of you had the heart to let Frida and Archie down, did you? You were both too honourable.'

'But was it right to live a lie?'

'You did what you believed to be the right thing, and you stuck by it. That took courage.'

'But was it *right?*'

'I can't answer that, Michael. I don't know what I would have done in the same situation.'

'You had the courage and the honesty to admit that your marriage to Edward was wrong, and you walked away from it. It was a very similar thing.'

'Not really. There was no one else involved, no one else to get hurt. We just did what was right for us at the time.'

'Speaking of angels.' Michael pointed to a silver car parked outside Coggles Barn. 'Edward's, I think.' He squeezed her hand. 'No telling Beth. Promise?'

'It won't come from me, but she's no fool. I'm sure she guesses.'

'Maybe, but guessing is very different to knowing.'

In the house, Beth was entertaining Edward, Lexi and Ethan.

Edward beamed at Stella. 'I've taken the day off!'

'Good Lord! That's a first!'

'We are taking Ethan to Cleethorpes for the afternoon.'

'Bit young for the white-knuckle rides, isn't he?'

'Pleasure Island is closed, dummy! We are just going to pig out on fish and chips and candyfloss, and maybe see the sea.'

'I thought you were on a strict diet?'

'I'm having a day off from that too, though I promise to be careful.'

Stella looked at Lexi. For the first time in months she looked truly happy. Her husband might have serious health issues, but she knew what the trouble was now, and she was clearly able to deal with that. And Edward looked completely different — relaxed and almost carefree. Maybe she should cut him some slack now. What he had said to her had hurt, a lot, and she was still smarting. Still, she of all people should understand what illness, or the fear of it, can do to your mind.

Ethan was tearing round the lounge in hot pursuit of Frisbee, yelling something unintelligible about donkeys.

'We've told him that the donkey rides on the beach are only in the summer, so I think he reckons Frisbee will have to do instead.' Lexi shook her head. 'Come on, young man, time to get you into the car.' She gathered up her excited son and hugged him. 'I'll ring and let you know how today goes, Stella. It could be bracing!'

Lexi carried Ethan out to their car.

Edward waited until they had gone. 'I know I've been a total arsehole, Stel. I'm really sorry for how I behaved. You must do whatever you want to get yourself back up there again, even if it does mean a spot of breaking and entering.' He looked her in the eyes. 'Forgive me?'

She hugged him. 'Forgive you for what?'

'Love you, Stel. Always will.'

'Save your love for that beautiful wife of yours.'

'Oh there's plenty left for her, no fear. And that little tyrant of a son of mine.'

'Good, I'm glad to hear it. Now go frighten the seagulls.'

Ethan waved his well-hugged rabbit and called out, "Bye-bye, Auntie!" Stella smiled at him, feeling an unexpected tug at her heartstrings. She had never drooled over new-born babies. Her lifestyle and career had left no room for motherhood. But she sometimes wondered what it would be like to have a child of her own. Would she be even capable of that much commitment and responsibility? She was positively neurotic about Frisbee, and he was not even *her* dog! What would she be like with a tiny person? The car disappeared but Stella remained, staring into the distance.

She turned back towards the barn. She needed to get her own life in order first . . . Hang on! What on earth had got into her? Stella North would be a crap mother! How suddenly the hormonal switch could be tripped!

Stella switched it off again.

'Penny for them.' Her grandmother was looking at her with an eagle eye.

'Not worth half that.' Stella smiled, and then it faded.

Behind Beth, Michael was sitting on the sofa, a cup of coffee next to him and Frisbee draped across his feet.

This is exactly as it should be, thought Stella. But it wasn't.

Stella had believed that at Gran's age, emotions would be tempered, and time would have cooled all passion, but she was obviously wrong. For both Beth and Michael, the fire burned as brightly as it had ever done. The problem was, they each sought to hide it from the other.

It was all her fault. She had been the catalyst that had brought them back together, stirring up all the old feelings, and all the pain.

She ran up the stairs and into the bathroom. It was the only room in the house with a door that locked.

* * *

Michael noticed Beth's look of consternation and said quietly, 'We did cover some pretty emotive stuff this morning. She's bound to be a bit shaky.'

Beth stared at the empty staircase. 'What on earth did you talk about?'

'Her feelings about seeing the CCTV footage of the shooting for one thing. And her future.'

Michael knew that Stella had coped remarkably well with their session. He suspected that her sudden flood of emotion was due to his revelation about Beth. Should he have kept silent? Maybe not. Sometimes the occasional sharing of a secret was beneficial. It introduced a more human aspect to the therapy and put relations on a more equal footing. Stella would be fine.

'Should I go to her?'

'Leave her for a while, then maybe take up a cup of tea. She's confronting a lot of confusing issues right now, but she is getting there. Though I think we'd better cancel tonight's dinner, don't you? We'll do it another day.'

'I agree.' Beth sighed. 'Robbie Melton doing a bloody Lord Lucan isn't helping her.'

'It's not his fault, poor lad. He needs support right now, not condemnation.'

'I know. But it's not easy when Stella is so upset.'

'I've got a suspicion that he will be back soon, with some different views on life.'

'I do hope so. I like Robbie a lot. They really were a crack team.'

'Robbie's young, and if he was as good as you say, he will find another partner.'

Just don't leave it too long until you show your face, young man, thought Michael. *Because it will be harder to come back.*

* * *

In a darkened room not far away, another casualty sat looking at a computer screen.

The picture on the monitor showed an old abandoned theatre. Skeletal chandeliers hung on rusted chains from the heavily embossed ceilings of the auditorium. The seats were heavy with dust and their smell of mould and damp was almost tangible. The faded curtains on the stage strewn with debris were heavy with dirt and cobwebs.

The emptiness and decay in the old building mirrored Jack Hammond's state of mind. He sighed.

The telephone number on the memo pad in front of him had just four words below it. *Starburst sends her love.*

So she had finally found him.

Jack shook his head, picked up the mouse and scrolled through another file of photographs, one he had not looked at for years. The images transported him back to their fabulous Belgian chateau. He started the slide show and lived again the magic they had found. He had never posted the Chateau Sapin Noir on his website. It was his one truly secret venue. Which did he want to keep for himself — the place? Or was it Starburst?

The chateau was long gone, razed to the ground to make way for a railway line. He thought of the commuters dozing or studying their smartphones, unaware of the magnificent building that lay beneath the iron wheels. This was what urban exploration was all about — keeping a record. Keeping the beauty alive.

Stella had been very good at that. Her photographs were stunning. He'd thought her first pictures owed their beauty to beginner's luck, or a bloody expensive camera. Those amazing shots had to be a fluke. But he was wrong. Shifting in his chair in an attempt to ease his pain, Jack thought about Stella North.

He had admired her long before they met. He enjoyed being thought of as a romantic loner, and he was a damned good photographer, but Stella was his personal urbex hero. She was beautiful, brave, artistic, and the most exciting lover he'd ever had. Starburst was the only person he would ever have considered exploring with. Now it was too late.

The thought that he would never go out again hit him like that runaway juggernaut. He ran his fingers over the name on the memo pad. According to Walt, something terrible had happened to her too. He stared at the scrap of paper for a long time. Then he crushed it into a ball and threw it in the bin.

CHAPTER EIGHTEEN

DS Marie Evans had asked her boss, DI Rowan Jackman, about Robbie Melton and had received a pretty favourable reply. Now she wanted to know more about this man before she committed herself to his transfer.

She scrolled through old copies of the force e-zine. After half an hour she had decided it would be no bad thing to have Robbie at Saltern-le-Fen, if he wanted to come. His record was spotless, and he was clearly not someone who hogged the limelight. Everything she read told her that he was a team player, which could not be said of many of her present colleagues. Stella North's old sidekick would fit in perfectly. Jackman was a fair boss and a good man, and Marie herself really wasn't *that* scary.

She yawned and sat back in her chair. If the kid wanted to apply, she'd do her best to make it work for him.

Her desk phone rang.

'Is that the Welsh Witch?'

She recognised Jimbo's voice immediately. 'Maybe, and is that the Yorkie Carrot-cruncher?'

'Your mobile is switched off and I tried your home. You're at work early. Couldn't you sleep?'

'Well, I wasn't out on my broomstick. My phone goes on when I start work.' She pictured the craggy-faced Yorkshireman and grinned. 'Do you have news, or have you just called to throw a few insults at me?'

'I've found him.'

Marie nodded, then remembered he couldn't see her.

'Mind you, he doesn't look like the handsome young poster boy in the picture you sent me. Your missing Robbie Melton is more like a cross between Catweazle and some dosser who kips under the pier.'

'Was he in the Ravenscar area?'

'Close enough. I found him on the Flat Scars, a rocky bit of coastline between Robin Hood's Bay and Ravenscar.'

'Did you let him know you were looking for him?'

'Course not. You said find him, not arrest him.' Jimbo laughed. 'We just exchanged a few words, mainly about the weather, as we Englishmen do, and I jogged on, figuratively speaking of course.'

'So we don't know where he's staying?'

'You might not but I do.'

'Good thing you're not anywhere near me, Jimbo. You're safer that way,' growled Marie.

'YHA, Boggle Hole, Fylingthorpe.'

'Thank you.'

'No trouble. Any other missing souls I can find for you? Glen Miller? Or maybe Lord Lucan.'

'That would be good. Thanks for what you've done, Jimbo. It's much appreciated.'

'Are we going to see you and that hulk of a motorcycle around this way soon?'

'You might just do that. On my next few days off, I'll ride up and buy you a drink.'

'You're on. See you soon! Go well.'

* * *

Stella woke disoriented and with a cracking headache. The early morning winter sun lit her room with a pale silvery glow. She realised that her phone was ringing. She reached for it and mumbled her name.

'Stella? Oh damn it! I woke you, didn't I?' Marie was obviously wide awake. 'Thing is, I'm sure you'll want to know this. Jimbo located Robbie Melton, had a few casual words with him, and we have an address for him as of this morning. I'd move fast though. Jimbo doesn't know but maybe Robbie smelled a rat and has decided to up sticks.'

It took Stella a while to realise what Marie was saying. She'd found Robbie! 'Thank God! I was really beginning to worry!'

'Understandable. We see so much crap in our job that it's no wonder we often think the worst.'

Marie still referred to her as one of them. Stella liked that.

'So what have you planned? Are you going to go and gather up the lost lamb?'

Stella wasn't really sure. 'I guess so, though I keep wondering if I'm actually helping him. He's been so miserable at work.' She paused. 'Er, I suppose you haven't had a chance to talk to Jackman, have you?'

'I was coming to that. When you find him, tell him to apply directly to DI Rowan Jackman, and he will most certainly be considered.'

Stella felt a lump come to her throat. At least if she found him, she could offer some practical help and a free ticket out of Superintendent Andrea Croxforth's clutches. 'I can't thank you enough, Marie. It could be the saving of a bloody good detective.'

'And he could inject some new blood into this place. Jackman and me, we had a really tight team a while back, but it's not what it was. Your Robbie could be just the breath of fresh air we need.' Marie laughed. 'So I suggest you go grab the silly sod and tell him to get off his arse and do the right thing, okay?'

Stella promised to do just that, and hung up her phone, feeling one hundred percent better. The hurt she'd suffered had also damaged those she loved, but maybe she could put a small part of that right. She stretched and sat on the edge of the bed. Come to think of it, so was breakfast. Now that she didn't have Edward and Lexi to fret over, a drive up to the North York moors was a very pleasing prospect.

* * *

Michael and Beth were delighted that Robbie had been found, but not about Stella driving all that way alone. They both offered to go with her, but she would not be swayed.

Beth was about to protest again when there was a knock at the door. Tom Chalk walked into the kitchen and placed a tray of fresh eggs on the table. 'Thought you could use these. Mum's chickens have gone into overdrive this week.'

'Lovely!' said Beth. 'What do we owe you?'

'Heavens! Nothing. You'll be helping her out by using them up.' He grinned at Stella. 'I've decided it's time my brothers stepped up and pulled their weight, so I'm taking a couple of days off. I wondered if you might like to go on a little expedition. I wasn't planning on anything too strenuous, just the two of us and some old derelict building. That deserted Second World War airfield maybe?'

Stella told him about Robbie, and his smile broadened. 'That sounds brilliant! Mind if I tag along? I could share the driving. In fact we could take my 4x4. It spends half its life trundling round the fields and it could do with a decent run.'

Beth sighed with relief and Stella smiled back. 'Great, how soon can you be ready?'

'Give me time to change and grab a few things in case we can't find him today and need to stay over. I'll fill the vehicle and be straight back. An hour tops, okay?'

He drove away, and Stella ran up to her room to pack for the trip.

Michael said, 'I like that young man. He's uncomplicated. No airs and graces.'

Beth smiled. 'He's been that way since he was a little boy. I always thought I'd be proud to have him as a son.'

'Or a son-in-law?'

Beth shook her head. 'She likes him well enough, but not like that.' She laughed. 'If I remember correctly, he was her first proper boyfriend.'

'I could be wrong, but I think he still feels a lot for our Stella.'

'Whatever, she'll be in good hands on this rescue mission.' Beth began clearing away the breakfast dishes. 'Tom has had a tough life, having to take on that farm when his dad died, and trying to motivate three lazy brothers. Today will be a welcome break for him too.'

'So. What should we do with *our* day, Beth Cartwright?'

'It would be a shame to waste our free day, wouldn't it?'

Michael's eyes twinkled. 'My thoughts precisely. So how about a run out to Rutland Water for a long walk, then lunch in Uppingham. I know a delightful inn that is "dog-friendly," and the chef just happens to be an old school friend. Then we can browse the antique shops and art galleries in Oakham before heading home. What do you say?'

'I can't think of a better plan!'

'Perfect.'

It would be, thought Beth sadly, if only you didn't belong to someone else. They would be the very picture of a happily married retired couple out with their dog. The truth was breaking her heart.

Beth went to her room and looked for some warm clothes. For one whole day she would have Michael all to herself. She would put everything else aside and pretend that they were exactly what they appeared to be, a loving couple.

CHAPTER NINETEEN

Stella soon realised that for all her bravado, the solo journey might well have been too much for her. Signposts and landmarks loomed up and disappeared from sight, and the road she once knew well became a confusion of jumbled map references and blank spots.

'Shut your eyes and have a snooze. I promise to wake you up when we cross the Humber Bridge.' Tom's voice was soft.

'I'm fine,' she answered unconvincingly. 'Just a bit dizzy.'

'Shall I slow down?' Tom glanced at her. 'I'm tonking it a bit because I get the feeling you want this thing with Robbie sorted as soon as.'

'I do. And if he does suspect Marie's friend of being another copper, he could well do a second disappearing act.' Stella chewed her lip. 'He's good at that.'

'You're really worried about him, aren't you?'

'Of course I am. We were partners against crime for years. I can't sit back and watch him throw away a brilliant career.'

Tom slowed down for a sharp bend. 'And his commanding officers are no help?'

'His superintendent is an arsehole,' Stella growled. 'I have no idea why she's being so hard on him. He's a good detective, one of the best. He's shrewd, intelligent and great in the field, but for some reason Croxforth can't see that he's suffering.'

Tom shrugged. '*Won't* see, sounds more like it. And of course, she could be pissed off at losing you.'

'You're probably right. But luckily not everyone is that short-sighted. I've got good news for Robbie. If we can find him.'

'We'll find him. I can feel it in my waters,' laughed Tom.

'Yes, me too.' Stella nodded.

'I suppose you get pretty close, working together in stressful situations?'

'Your crewmate can be the difference between life and death. If you find the right one, it makes the job very rewarding.'

'And if you get lumbered with the wrong one?'

'You dread going on shift.' Stella grimaced. 'I worked with a guy once who was a nightmare. For a start, he got car-sick so he wanted to drive all the time, and his driving made whitewater rafting seem tame! *And* he couldn't last half an hour without sliding off for a crafty fag.'

Tom chuckled. 'A match made in heaven — not!'

'Then he transferred to another division, thank God, and I got paired up with Robbie.'

'Were you and Robbie ever, er . . . ? Like, did you . . . ? Oh, you know what I mean.'

'Haven't a clue,' teased Stella.

'Oh, all right then, were you ever an item?'

'No, although it certainly does happen. We were a good working combo. Anything more would have ruined both our friendship and our working relationship.'

'It never spoilt *our* friendship,' Tom said, and chuckled.

Stella nudged him. 'You concentrate on your driving, Cave Bunny! That was a very long time ago.'

Tom said nothing, but Stella sensed he was holding something back. She chose to ignore it.

The terrain began to change. Heather cloaked the moors rolling away into the distance. Stella grew nervous. What state would Robbie be in? Would he be angry? Would he even listen to her? Such a lot was at stake, for both of them.

'This place is like the Fens in a way,' said Tom. 'Many people think it's too bleak, and others see beauty in it.'

'What do you see?' asked Stella, already knowing the answer.

'I see peace, freedom, fresh air, and wonderful countryside, just like I do on my own land.'

'Why aren't you married yet?' she asked him suddenly.

'Blimey, Stel, that came out of left field!'

'Just wondered. You seem so at one with the world, but you're alone. Is that what you really want?'

Tom launched off into the usual, "Oh, no one would have me . . ." Then he added, 'I suppose it's like you with the police force — the farm comes first. Once a woman finds out that I'm on duty twenty-four/seven, up before the lark and in bed, exhausted, by eight thirty some nights, I no longer seem a very exciting prospect.' He pulled a face. 'Oh, and then there is the myth about farmers being rich. I put every penny I earn back into the farm, and if the weather decides to go against us, I crawl to the bank for help. It's not exactly a life most women hanker after.'

'I see your point. When your work is everything, it takes a very special kind of person to accommodate it.'

'And in my case, so far no one has applied for the post.'

'But they will, Tom, I'm certain.'

'Should I start handing out flyers? Contact the Job Centre, maybe?'

'Just be yourself, that's good enough.' She looked up. 'Ah, that's the first time I've seen Ravenscar signposted. We're only five miles away.'

'And then you can become a detective again, and go hunt down your man.'

* * *

Robbie stood on a rocky outcrop and watched two people walk along the windswept beach towards him. From this distance the woman looked a bit like Stella. Robbie moved quickly away, back towards the base of the cliffs. He couldn't face any more pleasantries about the bloody weather. It seemed the only thing that strangers could find to talk about. Unless they had a dog, of course, which was the usual reason for plodding along a cold beach in winter. Robbie narrowed his eyes and squinted in the sunlight reflecting off the water.

It couldn't be! Could it?

The woman waved, and Robbie swallowed hard.

How on earth had she found him in this godforsaken spot? And who was that with her? He certainly wasn't ready for a jolly chat with some unknown bloke. For a moment he was tempted to run away, to race up the cliff path and not stop.

He tensed. Fight or flight?

He saw the man lightly touch Stella's arm and move away from her. He stared for a moment at Robbie then lifted a hand and waved. Then he headed off along the beach in the opposite direction.

Robbie's hand went up automatically in response. Suddenly he felt very tired.

Stella approached him. 'Robbie! Bloody hell! You look like shit!'

For the first time in weeks, Robbie laughed. 'Lord, I've missed you,' was all he could say.

Stella walked up to him, threw her arms around him and held him tight. 'You bloody great idiot! I've been worried sick about you.'

'I've been a bit concerned about me too. I'm not at my best right now, Stella.'

Stella took his hand. 'Let's walk, shall we?'

'Who's the friend?' He pointed to the stranger, who was fishing a stone from a pool and examining it closely.

'Exactly that. He's an old friend who was kind enough to drive me here.'

'How did you know I was here in the first place?'

'Long story. We'll leave that for later. The main reason I'm here is because I've found the answer to all your problems.' She squeezed his hand and smiled at him.

'You're clever, Stella North, but not that clever.'

'Oh yes I am, so pin back your lugs.' She told him her news.

'DI Jackman and Marie Evans? But they are legendary!'

Stella stopped and faced him. 'Robbie, this is your chance to get away from Croxforth. She's the one who should be taking the blame for you wandering lonely as a sodding cloud and looking like a bleeding vagrant! Go to Saltern-le-Fen and see Jackman. Marie said they need new blood in her team, and she is an ace woman to work with. The job hasn't even been posted yet and I promise you, it's got your name all over it!'

Robbie sighed. 'I don't know. I'd just decided to chuck it all in and go abroad.'

'What rot! This is the chance of a lifetime. Take it. Don't waste your talents. Heavens, I'd give my right arm to work with Jackman. And what have you got to lose, other than carrying on with that old bag, Croxforth?'

Robbie thought of the casual way the superintendent had written Stella off. Stella, a brave and decorated officer, was history. Just like that. 'Well, working miles away from her is incentive enough, let alone anything else.'

'Will you do it?'

'But what if Marie and Jackman find out about this? They'll think I'm a flake! They won't want me on their crack team then.'

'Marie knows, you moron! *She* bloody found you for me! Marie Evans isn't Andrea Croxforth, okay? Take it at face value, Robbie Melton! Move to Saltern. It's no distance at all, and you'll have the scope and the support to prove your worth.'

Robbie looked out towards the horizon, then down to the glistening droplets on the tops of the waves as they rushed in to the shore. 'I'll come back tonight. Tomorrow, I'll ring DI Jackman and then see the superintendent. If she will okay a transfer and Saltern-le-Fen will have me, I'll do it.' He hugged Stella. 'Thank you.' He brushed some salty water from his eyes — sea spray, of course. 'And maybe you should tell your friend that he really ought to get out of that rock pool before he freezes to death.'

CHAPTER TWENTY

Beth's day had been perfect. She pretended that she and Michael really were just an older couple, still in love despite their years. By about seven that evening, she knew this was the truth. They had been apart for decades, but their love had never died.

Stella had phoned to say that her mission had been accomplished. Robbie was on his way home, and hopefully in a more positive frame of mind. She and Tom were going to stay over in a country house hotel near Whitby and would leave after breakfast. Tom had offered to drive her straight home, but Stella was tired. She decided to treat him to a meal and a luxury room for the night as a thank you for being the chauffeur. Beth was desperate to ask about the sleeping arrangements, but thought she'd better not pry.

So she and Michael — and Frisbee — were on their own for the evening.

Michael was putting more logs onto the open fire and staring thoughtfully into the flames. 'Can I ask you something?'

'You can ask.'

'Did Archie ever know about me?'

Beth let out a slow breath. 'He knew there was someone else. He just didn't know who it was.'

'Was that before you married him?'

Beth nodded. 'He said the girl that came back from Germany was changed in some way. But he decided that whatever had happened, I'd chosen him, and he loved me for that. So we got married. He never asked.'

'Never?'

'Not once.' Beth got up, went to the kitchen and poured them both a shot of brandy. 'And what about Frida?'

'Same thing I suppose, although she did ask me if there was someone else and if so, did I want to cancel the wedding.' He sipped the brandy. 'That was exactly what I wanted to do, more than anything, but I said no.'

'And if you had your time again?'

'I would follow my heart. People get over breakups and move on, even if they suffer at the time. Next time I would put the two of us first.' He sat staring into the amber liquid in his glass. 'And you?'

Beth hated hurting people.

'You hesitate,' said Michael rather sadly.

'Only because I know that we aren't heartless people. That's what makes us who we are. I think we'd do exactly what we did before. I don't believe that you could break Frida's heart any more than I could have destroyed Archie.'

Michael sighed and watched Frisbee edging closer to the fire. 'I suppose you're right.'

Beth raised her glass. 'To love. The most resilient of emotions.'

'And the most painful.'

Later they watched an old DVD of *The African Queen*. Beth could not remember a more peaceful evening.

Inevitably, the credits rolled. Michael would be going, and the perfect day would have to end. Beth went to the door to let Frisbee out for a few minutes.

Michael came and stood behind her. 'Can I stay? Please, Beth. I want nothing more than to be with you, to hold you. To remember.'

Beth turned and clung to him. 'Oh, my darling, it will only make things worse. I don't know how I'm going to cope as it is.' She looked into his eyes. 'I lost you once. I can't lose you again.'

'You never lost me, Beth. I've been yours since the day we met.' He gently cupped her face in his hands. 'And as for returning to Germany, well, there's a question mark over that.'

Beth's heart stopped for a moment. She was almost overcome by hope, but told herself to wait. After all, she didn't know what he meant.

'Please, Beth?'

Beth closed her eyes. What was there to lose? She'd survived before, and she was older and stronger now. After all, how could you break something that was already in pieces?

* * *

Stella and Tom sat in big leather armchairs in front of an open-fronted log burner in the hotel lounge. Sleepy from the warmth of the fire, they settled back and talked about their old expeditions.

'The owners told me that there is a footpath beside this property that leads to a waterfall. It's the highest in Yorkshire, and they said it's spectacular now, after all the recent rain.' Tom's eyes sparkled in the firelight. 'Fancy a stroll before breakfast?'

'I'm not sure. If it's that high we'd have to get down into the gorge and then back up again.'

A shadow passed across Tom's face. Then he grinned at her. 'We brought hiking boots, didn't we? Come on, Stel. I can't see us getting back here in the near future, and now you've sorted out your old buddy you can relax. We'll take it slowly. It'll be fun.'

Stella wanted to say yes. But her head ached and although she had managed to conceal it from Tom, the tremor in her left hand had returned. 'Can we see what the morning brings?'

'Sure.' Tom stretched his long legs out in front of him. 'I forgot to tell you that Razor and Butterwitch wondered if they could meet up with you some time and see some of your old photographs. I said I'd run it past you.'

'Of course they can. I've got boxes full of them, and a stack of them on the computer.'

'Maybe I could come too? I could bring pizza.'

'And wine. Then you've got a deal.'

'Butterwitch told me that she'd been looking on the Internet. She discovered that your record for a woman scaling the world's tallest freestanding climbing wall still stands. Did you know that?'

Stella did, but she shook her head. 'Oh, the Excalibur in Holland? A combination of being in great form, perfect weather conditions and a lot of luck. I can't believe that no one has bettered it. It was years ago.' Her smile disappeared, and she rubbed her temples to try and ease her worsening headache.

Tom got out of his chair and dropped onto his haunches in front of her. 'Are you okay?'

She hesitated. 'I'm fine. Nothing that some sleep won't cure.'

Tom frowned. 'This has been too much for you to take on.' He took her hand. 'All that stuff you told me about with your ex, Edward, and now this. You're pushing yourself too hard too soon. When I get you home, I want you to back off from everyone else's problems. They are *not* your fault.'

How perceptive he was! He was right. Guilt was obviously behind it all. Hell, she was so tired.

'And now, I suggest you go and get some sleep, and start enjoying that luxury suite you've paid for. I'll get up early and check out this Mallyan Spout waterfall. I've got my camera in my bag, so I'll take some pictures for you. Then you can tell everyone that we both went to see it at dawn, okay?'

Stella nodded. 'Sleep well, Tom, and thanks again for all you've done.'

Tom shook his room key. 'If you feel bad, I'm only next door. Just call me. Promise?'

'Promise.'

Soon Stella was resting her tired body in fresh, white sheets. She was 150 miles from home — from Michael Lindenfeld, and safety. The thought scared her. She heard him say, "Never believe that your therapist is the healer. Never think that you can't manage without them, because it's *you* that is doing the mending, not someone else." But if that was the case, why was she so scared? It was like being lost in a blizzard, knowing that your guide is on the other side of the mountain.

She was woken up at 3 a.m. by a dream about her father. It had been a long time since she had thought about him.

She didn't hate him anymore, although his suicide had affected her deeply. This extended to her job, and it had taken several years before she could deal with a sudden or suspicious death without judging the person involved.

When she was a child her father had been a thoughtful, intelligent, bookish kind of man, who loved to read her to sleep. She had once asked him why he had called her Stella. She wanted a softer name like her best friends, Millie and Chloe.

'Because the first time I saw you in your mother's arms, and saw that determined look in your eye, I knew that you deserved a strong name. You are my star. You see, ever since time began, the North Star has been used for navigation, and I get the feeling that you, my darling, will be a guiding light. You will keep others safe and lead them home.'

From that moment on, the young Stella had been proud to have a different sort of name. She was her father's North Star.

Stella smiled to herself in the darkness. Whenever she helped some drunk off the street, or put a down-and-out into a cell for the night, she remembered his words. She really was leading people into port, a safe haven with a hot meal and a bed. It was a pity that she had not been able to guide her father home.

Then she thought of Robbie, standing alone on a cold, rocky shoreline, with the icy waters drawing nearer. She had delivered her news, and he had walked away towards a new future. Had she done that? Had she been some kind of guide star, like her father had predicted? Perhaps. But all this life-saving certainly took its toll.

Robbie would be back home by now. Edward and Lexi would be sleeping with less fear in their hearts. And Beth and Michael? Maybe they would be her next mission. But for now, everyone who mattered was safe.

The headache had gone.

CHAPTER TWENTY-ONE

Stella did as Tom had suggested. She luxuriated under a hot shower, and then sat in her dressing gown with the morning paper.

She had heard Tom leave about two hours ago. He would be in his element, enjoying the walk to the waterfall. Today she could probably have managed the trek quite easily, but the horrible sick feeling of the previous night worried her. She hoped she had just been overtired.

She struggled with the crossword. Before the shooting she had found them easy. After a while she gave up. One more thing to contend with, courtesy of a thug's bullets.

She folded up the paper and began to get dressed, and then her mobile rang. Please don't let it be Tom, she thought, up to his neck in Yorkshire river water!

'Hello?'

The line was bad, but she made out the words, 'I'd know that voice anywhere.'

'And I'd know yours, Jack.' Stella's pulse raced.

'Walt gave me your number.'

She took a deep breath. He sounded odd, and it wasn't just the poor signal. She knew it would be a mistake to say, "How are you?"

'I'm really pleased you rang me, Jack. I heard what happened, and I wondered if we could meet up? For old times' sake.'

After a while, he said, 'Things have changed, Stella.' Another long pause. 'I've changed.'

'So have I. Perhaps I could come see you?'

There was a snort. 'Well, it won't happen any other way. I don't go out anymore.'

'Then that's fine. How about the day after tomorrow?'

'I suppose so. Make it the afternoon, sometime around two thirty.'

'I'll need to know where you are. Let me grab a pen.' His abrupt tone puzzled her. But he *had* phoned, and if she was the first person he had made contact with since his accident, then it was probably very hard for him. 'Okay, fire away.'

He rattled off his address. 'It's quite secluded, but I'll see you coming up the lane. The gates will open automatically, then just push on the front door. I have a security release on the lock, I'll let you in.' He paused, then mumbled, 'Look forward to seeing you.'

The call ended.

Stella stared at the address. He was barely twenty-five miles from where she lived.

She glanced at the clock radio beside her bed and stood up. She was late meeting Tom for breakfast. She pushed the address inside her wallet. She wouldn't tell Tom. Not yet.

* * *

'Stel, you *have* to see that waterfall! Not now, I realise that you're not a hundred per cent yet, but we must come back here when you feel better, and it will be on me next time. It's simply beautiful. You climb round this rock fall, and suddenly there it is! A torrent, cascading from way up high. Absolutely gorgeous!'

'I wish I'd got up and gone with you, but I still feel a bit shaky.' *Not to mention that phone call.* Stella was sure that if he'd received no answer, Jack would not have tried again.

'I'm sorry.' Tom looked at her. 'You seem a bit distant this morning. Will you be okay for the trip home?'

'Of course. I'm tons better after a good night's kip. Was your room okay?'

'Sheer luxury, and a view to die for. I mean it about coming back here. The people are friendly and the walks are breathtaking. I've been thinking. It's time my brothers stopped leaning on me. If they expect to get a living out of our farm, they are going to have to shoulder a bit more responsibility. Stel, while I was out this morning I decided that if they toe the line I'll be delighted, but if they'd prefer to opt out completely, I will give them that option. If they take it, I can get in some hired labour. One way or another I'm going to take that farm forward, for Mum's sake and for Dad's memory. But I need hard workers with me.'

'No one will work as hard as you do.' Stella smiled.

'Of course not, it's my baby. I don't expect anyone to kill themselves, just put in a good day's work for their money. And I also realise that if I'm to keep going, I need the occasional break to recharge my batteries, *and* I have my barn conversion to complete.'

'Well, this wasn't much of a rest, with you driving both ways.'

'No sweat. I love driving. And it's not that far, is it? I've had a great time with you, Stel, and staring into rock pools and standing under a waterfall has allowed me to get things into proper perspective. Oh, and by the way, I'm really glad it worked out well for your mate.'

'I just hope he follows it through.' Stella prayed that Robbie would not get cold feet. She made a mental note to ring Marie.

They finished their breakfast and Tom looked at her, tilting his head. 'You're sure you're okay for the drive?'

'Stop worrying.' She tousled his hair affectionately. 'I'm good to go.'

CHAPTER TWENTY-TWO

It was the day of her visit to Jack. Stella's headache had gone. She was feeling much better than she had in Yorkshire, apart from a severe attack of nerves. She had checked the route to Jack's address a dozen times, and the day before she had driven halfway there as a trial run. She knew that her anxiety was about more than the drive. It was what she might find behind Jack Hammond's security system.

She still didn't know what decision Robbie had made about his future, but she had decided not to push him. She agreed with Michael — she had done all she could. Now Robbie must take care of his own future. Marie had promised to ring or text with the outcome. Right now Stella was hoping that no news was good news.

Stella stared at her bed, littered with clothes. She had no idea what to wear, and suddenly it seemed terribly important to get it right.

After a while she pulled on her favourite pink sweatshirt bearing the logo, *Try and Fail, but Never Fail to Try*. She looked at herself in the mirror and shook her head. How could she wear something with an inspirational message emblazoned across the front when Jack had apparently given up hope? The last thing she needed was for him to think that she was taking the proverbial. She pulled it off and settled for a grey and white check shirt, a purple sweater and a pair of purple sports shoes.

She glanced at her watch. Three hours to kill before she left. She flopped down on the bed. Maybe she was being foolish. Perhaps she should have just forgotten him and moved on. What kind of hornets' nest was she about to stir up? Stella sighed.

She heard Beth calling her name and went downstairs.

'You look very nice,' said Beth. 'Is that what they call smart casual?'

'It's what they call indecision. I didn't want to overdo it, but I didn't want to dress in my usual old tat.'

Her grandmother beamed at her. 'You look perfect. Are you sure about this visit?'

'I need to see him, Gran,' she sighed, 'even though I'm scared to death.'

'Well, given the circumstances, I suppose you will have some common ground. That should help to make the conversation easier after such a long time has passed.'

'I guess. We are certainly going to be very different to who we were back then.'

'Try to enjoy yourself, darling, and remember, if it gets too challenging just come home, okay? At least you will have made the effort, which is more than he has.'

Stella nodded and watched Beth pull on her running shoes. 'What route are you taking today?'

'Here to Swineshead and back.'

'Around twelve miles?'

'Just under. It should be a doddle now the wind has dropped and there's no rain forecast.'

'Take care, Gran, won't you?'

'I always do, and don't worry. I'll be back long before you go. I'm getting stronger with every day that I train.'

Stella had seen a change in her gran since her trip to Yorkshire. She suddenly seemed more alive, more vital.

Maybe it was down to Michael's therapy sessions. It had to be a huge weight off her grandmother's shoulders to see her so much better.

'I thought I'd walk round to my house and get a few photos together for Jack to see.' She had thought of taking her pictures of Chateau Sapin Noir. She had never shown them to anyone.

'Good idea. Some shared memories are a good starting point.' There was a hint of amusement in Beth's expression, but she bent down to tighten a lace and Stella was not sure if she'd imagined it.

'Were you in love with Jack?' asked Beth.

Stella swallowed. She'd told Gran a bit about his legendary status, but little more than that. 'I . . .' She hesitated. 'I'm not sure, but I don't think so. He was just so powerful. I'd never encountered anything like it before. We just seemed to . . .'

Beth sighed. 'Oh dear. I know what you're telling me, really I do. So even more reason to be careful, Stella, and don't expect too much from this meeting.' Her grandmother looked anxious suddenly. 'Things are going so well at the moment, I'd hate to see you disappointed or knocked back.'

Stella shook her head. 'Don't worry, Gran. I'm not expecting anything, except maybe a very frustrated and bitter man. I'm going because he's hurting, and maybe because of what I've been through, I can offer him just a little of what Michael has given me.'

'You're a good girl, Stella, but don't do anything that depletes your own energies. Michael always says that healing others can drain you, and you don't have a surplus store of strength just yet. Look after yourself first.'

Stella hugged her grandmother tightly. 'I love you, Gran. Yes, I'll be very careful. After all everyone has done for me, especially you and Michael, I'm not going to risk slipping backwards for the sake of someone I hardly know.'

'Why not take Michael up on his offer? He is happy to wait in the car for you. He has a new lecture to plan, so it would be no trouble.'

'I really appreciate it, but I need to do this alone.'

Beth nodded. 'Okay, but phone when you're finished, just to put my mind at rest.'

* * *

Jack watched the clock on his computer edge towards two thirty. He should never have retrieved her number from the wastepaper bin. He'd existed alone, with only Walt as back up, for a very long time now, so why change things? What had he done? And why on earth hadn't he just got her email address if he wanted to talk? Even the Tesco delivery man never got across the doorstep. Talking to her on the phone had been purgatory so what would actually seeing her do to him?

The alarm system bleeped.

He tapped on his keyboard and a camera scanned the lane outside.

Jack watched the silver Peugeot approach the gates. His finger hovered above the keys. He could always switch the system off and leave her there. She'd soon give up and go away. Like an automaton he pressed the button. The gates swung back and the car moved forward.

Jack gripped the armrest of his wheelchair and squeezed until the pain in his damaged wrist made him gasp. Pain sometimes helped to focus his mind but it wasn't working now. He was confused and afraid.

* * *

Stella stared at the towering double gates and her heart sank. This was no secluded country retreat. It was a fortress of paranoia.

The gates moved slowly inwards, revealing what appeared to be a barracks. Instead of a garden, there was an expanse of hard paved area that resembled a municipal car park.

Stella parked and walked up to the front door. She pushed it. With a series of clicks and clunks the bolts were released. 'Welcome to Alcatraz,' she murmured to herself, and stepped inside.

Stella had seen some odd houses in her time on the force, but she'd never seen anything like this. The hall was very wide with wooden laminate flooring. The walls were painted an off-white colour, bare of pictures or photographs. There were few windows. The blinds seemed to be operated by remote control.

'Jack?'

With no carpet or curtains to absorb the sound, her voice echoed.

'In here!' The call came from the far end of the hall.

She walked towards him, glancing into the rooms she passed. They were all large, and almost empty. There was a feeling of transience about the place, as if the occupants were about to leave, or had yet to arrive. Stella shivered and increased her pace.

The room resembled a television studio. Jack was sitting in an electric wheelchair in front of a bank of computer screens, wearing a fisherman's jersey that sagged over his hollow chest. He had a full beard and long, lank hair. His skin was pasty, and jailbird grey.

Stella smiled brightly, hoping that her shock at his appearance hadn't shown. She bent down and kissed him lightly on the cheek, and smelled unwashed hair. Her resolve to keep their first meeting light and casual vanished, and so did the polite words that she had been rehearsing.

'Lord, Jack! What on earth has happened to you?'

'Nice to hear you say what you really mean.' Jack looked almost relieved. 'Good to see you too. Grab a chair.'

Stella noticed a couple of office chairs and dragged one around to sit beside him. 'Walt told me what happened. So, have they completed your treatment or are you due for more operations?'

'I'm pinned, plated, screwed and bolted together like Frankenstein. No, no more ops.'

'Physiotherapy?'

'I have home visits. I've gone private. After the haulage company finally paid out, I can afford it. There's not much else to spend it on. I did think of buying a jet ski for a bit of fun on the Med, or joining a Salsa class, but that's so boring.'

Stella grimaced. 'What do you really do with your time?'

He pointed to the computer. 'This. This is what I do. I watch the lane for the Tesco delivery lorry. I check that no one is trying to break in. I play games and sometimes watch films. That's what I do.'

Stella indicated the array of computer equipment. 'Pretty impressive.'

'State of the art, all new generation. Look.' He pressed a key and a slide show began to run on a huge wall screen above them. Urbex pictures. Images that caused the hairs on the back of her neck to stand up.

'Your work is superb,' said Stella.

'Praise indeed, coming from you.'

'You've seen my photographs?'

'Everything you ever posted. In fact I downloaded most of them. They are very good indeed.'

'People are saying that we shouldn't let all these images go to waste.'

'Who would want them?' He shrugged. 'I can't see decay photography ever making it big, can you? And there will be no more from me, not now.'

'Can you walk at all?' Stella had seen a pair of crutches propped against the wall.

'*Very* short distances. Getting to the front door and back almost kills me.'

'What about driving? Have you got a modified vehicle?'

'My *vehicle* was modified by a runaway twelve-wheeler, and it wasn't exactly saleable afterwards. I don't drive any more, Stella.'

Stella had a sudden thought. Hadn't Tom taken Darren Kemp, an amputee, urbexing in a disused quarry? Time of his life, Tom had said, and he'd been raring to go out again. But there was a world of difference between Darren and the Hollow Man sitting next to her.

'Shall I make us some tea?'

Jack nodded. 'I'll make it. I'm not totally useless.'

Stella followed him into a vast kitchen with low work benches, cupboards and drawer units, all custom made. 'Did you do all this?'

'No. The place actually belonged to my uncle. He was disabled by a spinal injury after a fall from a horse. He died just before I had my accident and I inherited it.' He shook his head. 'Sometimes I wonder if he put some demonic clause in his will that I needed to be unable to walk in order to qualify.'

He took two mugs from a cupboard and switched on the kettle.

'Was he the technical wizard? Everything here seems to be operated with remote control handsets and computers.'

'No, that's me. It's what I used to do for a living. I was an IT specialist.'

Stella realised that she knew very little about Jack Hammond. It also came to her that she had been practically interrogating him. It was nerves. Perhaps she should ease off.

Jack made the tea and asked her to carry it back to his office.

She placed the cups on the desk and sat down. 'I hate the thought of you shut away in here all alone. It's like a prison.'

Jack held up his hand. 'Stop. Don't say any more.' His face was hard. 'Alright, it's a prison, but I *chose* to be here. I feel safe here. No bright suggestions about a little drive into the countryside, okay?'

Stella said nothing. It was such a waste. He had been such a fit man, so strong and fearless. She'd seen some of the places he'd infiltrated in his urbex years — giant cooling towers, a lost underground mine, a defunct ballroom in a deserted castle. The list was endless. And he could do amazing things again, just different ones. Challenges took various forms, something Stella had discovered by chance. But Jack had sealed himself up in this sterile prison. He might as well be dead.

* * *

'So, what happened to *you*?' Whatever it was, it hadn't been that bad. She looked amazing.

'I was shot, twice. Once in the head, and once in the side. I even died at one point, or so they tell me.'

She lifted her hair away from her temple and he could see the scarring. Walt hadn't told him anything about this. Stella had been *shot*? But she seemed so normal. Jack stared at her, dumbfounded.

'And now I have problems. Weakness in one side, lack of balance, loss of concentration, memory glitches. Speech sometimes eludes me. Clinical depression, panic attacks . . . But I didn't come here to compare medical conditions.' She smiled. 'I just wanted to see the Jackhammer again.' She fished in her bag. 'I never posted these online, and I never showed anyone else, but I thought you might like to see them.'

She handed him a batch of A4 size photographs.

The Chateau Sapin Noir.

His hand shook as he took them from her.

'They aren't meant to hurt. I just wanted you to have them, because it was a very special time. I've never forgotten you, Jack.' She touched his hand. 'So alright, the present sucks, and the future has a question mark beside it, but I will always remember that time.'

The photographs were breathtaking.

The past came hurtling towards him. The beauty of that abandoned place, and of the woman he'd shared it with. He groaned aloud. 'I think you should go. Now.'

Stella stared at him, her eyes misty. Then she seemed to deflate. 'I hoped . . . I hoped that you'd let me help you.'

'I don't need your help, or anyone else's. Please leave.'

He watched her pick up her bag. At the door, she turned. 'I said that too, just a little while ago. But I was wrong.'

He pressed the security button and heard the door open. A few minutes later he watched the Peugeot pull slowly out into the deserted lane. The visit had gone exactly as he feared. A great big bloody mistake!

The gates closed behind her. 'Pull up the drawbridge, Jack,' he muttered. 'Time for lockdown.' Then he saw the two mugs of untouched tea, and burst into tears.

He slept all afternoon, and when he woke he was still shaken. He lay on his bed for a while, trying to make sense of his emotions. He had never expected that seeing her again would move him so. Then he thought about what she said had happened to her. Surely he would have seen it on the news? Was he so cut off from the world?

It took Jack almost five minutes to drag himself from the bed and back into his wheelchair. The effort left him gasping for breath and racked with pain. He sat for a while, breathing hard, and then went back to his office.

He tapped her name into a search engine and soon found the story.

According to the reports, she had managed to prevent a massacre in the village of Sutterthorpe. Two young men, high on drugs and armed with an automatic pistol, had been confronted by a ring of locals outside a post office that they had just tried to rob. There were children there, women, and older men, all under threat. Stella had managed to keep their attention, allowing the crowd to get to safety. She had taken a bullet in her side and another to her head. Her attackers made off on a motorcycle and had never been apprehended.

Jack shook his head. But she had looked so good.

Jack picked up Stella's pictures of the Chateau Sapin Noir and examined them more closely. The one that moved him most was the shot of the library. He clicked on his own picture file of the chateau and compared the shots. His conveyed the atmosphere of degeneration and sad decay. Stella's images showed nature bestowing new life on the ruined structure. It was quite bewildering. They were both brilliant photographers, but Stella had the edge.

She had said something about not wasting their images. Maybe she was right. Right now Jack couldn't see beyond the black hole that he had dug for himself, but she was obviously looking further. He wished her well.

He had been hard on her.

He had probably been quite cruel. But Stella could walk! Stella could drive. Stella could make love. Stella had come through. He had been defeated. He was no longer angry at the lorry driver, the terrible weather or Walt. He was simply angry at himself.

Each reacted to the card fate had dealt them just as their photographs reflected different viewpoints. Jack looked at the envelope that had contained Stella's photos. She had written her email address on it. He clicked on his message icon, typed in Stella's address and sent a one word message. *Sorry*.

CHAPTER TWENTY-THREE

Stella arrived at Coggles Barn to find Robbie, Beth and Michael in earnest conversation. In the kitchen sink sat a huge bouquet of flowers. No garage purchase this! She saw a mass of roses, gypsophila, orchids and various other exotic blossoms that she didn't recognise.

'They're for you.' Robbie beamed at her. He had a new haircut set off by cargo pants and a Ted Baker jumper. He enveloped her in a giant hug.

'I was this far, Stel,' he held up his thumb and forefinger, 'from booking a plane ticket to the back of beyond.' He shook his head. 'I really am a muppet, aren't I?'

'At the moment you look more like a Cheshire cat.'

'Well, thank God you found me. Heaven knows what your friend must think of me, the bloke at the rockpool!'

'Tom? Oh, he's just pleased we made contact.'

'Thank him for me, will you?'

'So what now?' asked Beth.

'I had a meeting with DI Jackman and DS Marie Evans yesterday, and I've already put in for a transfer.'

'Brilliant! What did Croxforth say?'

Robbie shrugged. 'She's making out that she couldn't give a damn, and is delighted that the weakest link is shipping out, but I don't think she's happy that Saltern CID has snapped me up so quickly.'

'I bet Jackman is pleased as punch to get one over on Croxforth. I'm told she's not his favourite police officer.'

'I got that impression. I can't wait to go now. In fact I'm taking the leave I'm owed in lieu of notice. I'd rather be out of her hair.'

'She'll regret the way she's acted, although she won't admit it. And you, sunshine, have made a damned good career move.'

'What about your trip, Stella?' asked Michael. 'Was it fruitful?'

Stella pulled a face. 'Let's just say I didn't exactly get the kind of welcome Robbie gave me.'

'Ah. You found him as bitter as you expected,' Beth said sadly.

'More than bitter, Gran. He was . . .' Stella couldn't find the right word.

'Resentful at what happened? Hopeless?' Michael suggested.

'All of that and more.' She shook her head. She didn't want to talk about Jack Hammond right now. She needed time to think about him.

'So when do you head out to Saltern, Robbie?'

'My post will be available in three weeks, so as long as everything goes through, I'll start then.'

'Are you going to commute?'

'Oh yes, it's only twenty minutes. Anyway, my friends are here.' He grinned at her. 'Aren't you?'

'Always.' It was her turn to hug him. 'Congratulations, Robbie. You're going to love working with that team. I have the greatest respect for both Jackman and Marie.'

'I just wish we were going together, that's all.'

Stella nodded. Then she recalled Jack in his peculiar prison house, his face etched with misery. 'At the risk of sounding like an inspirational speaker, I think we need to face up to change with hope in our hearts. We both have new beginnings ahead, and we shouldn't be afraid of moving on.'

Michael grinned broadly. 'Well said, Stella! Maybe you should try my job.'

'Forget it, Sigmund! Each to their own and right now, I'm looking forward to getting to grips with my old photo gallery.'

'Oh, that reminds me,' said Beth. 'Tom called by and asked if he and his crew could meet you at your house this evening for a picture show? He said you'd know what he means, and he'll bring the pizza and wine. Just ring him if it's not convenient.'

Stella was tired, and another headache was coming on. The drive and the tension of her meeting with Jack were beginning to tell on her. But spending time with two younger urbexers who clearly admired her work might be the perfect antidote. Why not? 'Wanna join us, Robbie?'

'Loads of pictures of rust, junk, and old ruins? Sounds riveting.'

'Oh, there are rivets too. They're usually pretty corroded.'

'I'll give it a miss, but thanks for asking.' Robbie picked up his car keys. 'I'm going to ring my aunt in Cornwall and go visit her for a couple of days before I start my new job.'

'Great idea. Now don't go getting all maudlin on those windswept cliffs, will you? I'm not up to another manhunt just yet.'

'No danger of that. Your work is done, Stella North. You can stand down now. Robbie Melton is back on track.'

* * *

After Robbie left, Stella sat with Michael, while Beth and Frisbee retired to the garage for a grooming session.

'I hope your thankless journey hasn't upset you too much?' Michael asked.

'At first I was gutted. I drove away from that godforsaken place in tears. Then I calmed down and started to appreciate what a big thing it was just for Jack to meet me.' She played with a loose thread on her sweater. 'I wonder what made him do it at all. There was so much I wanted to ask him, such a lot of questions — like when and why had he visited that old house at Seas Meet. Now I guess I'll never know.'

Michael looked thoughtful. 'Don't be so sure. I have a strong feeling he will make contact with you.'

'I don't think so.'

'Have patience.'

She smiled. 'Ah, the "P" word! I'm not very good with that one.'

'Watch your emails. He might not want to talk, but texts and email messages are a very good way of expressing what you can't say to someone's face.'

'And you can think before you send them,' added Stella.

'Exactly.' Michael lowered his voice. 'Stella, I wanted to talk to you about something, and as Beth is occupied with the dog, now seems a good moment.'

His expression was serious. 'I will be going back to Germany in a few days' time.'

Stella gasped. 'Oh. I see.'

He smiled at her. 'Actually you don't. I am only going to sort out some urgent business, and I'll be back in no time, a week at the most. Do you think you will be okay?'

'I think I can do that. Oh, you frightened me.' She exhaled. 'There's nothing wrong, is there?'

'No, not really. I am planning something a bit radical.'

Stella leaned forward, intrigued. 'Radical?'

'I have been offered a permanent position at the University of Essex, and I am going to accept it.'

'That's a long way to travel to work.' Stella was confused.

'I will be making my home in England.'

'Oh! But that's wonderful!' Then Stella thought of Michael's wife, his children and grandchildren. His home and practice in Bad Harzburg. Surely . . . ?

'I need to make a lot of arrangements, but there is nothing that cannot be sorted out, I'm sure.'

'Does Gran know?'

'Not yet. She knows that they approached me. I have also been asked if I might like to set up a local private clinic in conjunction with your Donald Field-Latimer at the hospital, which is rather appealing too. I just feel that I should put some rather important things in order before I tell Beth of my decision. I'd hate for something to go wrong.'

'And for Beth to get hurt?'

'Precisely. That is *paramount*. So please, please don't tell her.'

A loud bark followed by a fluffy, well-brushed dog brought a halt to the conversation.

Frisbee leapt onto her lap and she tickled his ears and told him what a handsome lad he was. It was an enormous relief that Michael was going to be around on a permanent basis. It was like the answer to a prayer. But she needed to curb her excitement, just in case things didn't work out.

'I'd better get back to my place and clean up before the crew arrive.'

'I wouldn't worry too much. I thought they liked decay and debris!' Michael's eyes twinkled.

Stella hadn't told the urbexers about her visit to Jack, and didn't want to. But she didn't like lying either, especially to Tom. She would just have to hope that the topic didn't arise.

By six o'clock everything was in its place. Stella guessed that her obsessive neatness derived partly from being an urbexer. When you planned an expedition you had to be meticulous about the equipment you took and where you put it. You needed to know the exact location of everything in your numerous pockets and bags, even in the dark. It could save your life.

She decided to load a couple of picture files onto the computer, ready for her visitors. Then she opened her inbox and found a whole heap of junk mail, plus one from a new sender: info@jackhammer.biz

With a gasp she opened it, and saw the single word, "*Sorry.*"

Without thinking, she replied. *"Me too. My fault, I was really thoughtless."*

The answer came back almost immediately. *"No, I'm entirely to blame. Let's start again, slowly."*

Her heart jumped in her chest. So he hadn't drawn a line after all. *"You lead, I'll follow."*

"Tomorrow, same time, I'll email you. And by the way, you have no right to look that good after what happened to you."

Stella smiled.

She put a bottle of white wine in the fridge. The boxes of photos were still in the lounge, and while she waited, she pulled out some of her favourites, and one or two that Michael had found particularly interesting. The only ones that would remain unseen were those of the Chateau Sapin Noir. She had only seen a small selection of Jack's photographs on his giant hi-tech screen, and they were quite awesome. Different to hers, but brilliant nevertheless.

She sat up sharply. What if they joined forces and started an online image library? Or produced a book? Between them they would be able to produce a stylish publication, something quite different from the usual pretty coffee-table books.

Stella had to stop herself from running back upstairs to the computer and putting the notion to Jack.

This could be the stimulus he needed to get him back into the world! Maybe she could help him after all. And what had he said? He'd been in IT and designed websites before his accident. His computers were state of the art, so surely getting an image library up and running would be easy for him. If she could only get him motivated!

The doorbell rang, and Stella realised that she was actually looking forward to seeing the new crew again.

She had been apprehensive about overdoing it, but as it was, the evening turned out to be great fun.

Stella watched Emily put away glass after glass of wine.

Ray looked sadly into his first and only glass of claret. 'Oh, I'm often the chauffeur,' he said.

The spicy smell of pizza reminded Stella of her time in the police force. Long, boring nights doing surveillance, made bearable by Rob, strong coffee and pepperoni pizza.

Tom was finishing another funny story about their former exploits. Stella realised that he had an almost photographic memory. He seemed to remember every single expedition, and could even date some of the photographs.

'I kept diaries,' he said.

Stella hadn't known. 'Do you still have them?'

'Yup. Every one.'

'So if I catalogued these, you could help me identify some of them?'

Tom smiled. 'I'd like to. Michael's quite right, they are far too good to moulder away in boxes.'

Tom had always been the most committed member of the clan. Storm Zero and Hex had been the daredevils. Edward, when he occasionally joined them, was reserved. She had been the photographer, and also the sleuth, even then. But Tom had been truly passionate. His enthusiasm was still infectious. So, given her often fuzzy memory, Tom and his journals could be of enormous help.

'Maybe we could help too?' said Ray. 'We both have computer skills.' He nodded at Emily. 'You have done several modules in it, haven't you, Em?'

She nodded. 'Before I decided on neuroscience, I was contemplating computational biology and medicine, so I kicked off with an undergrad course in computing.'

Stella was impressed. When she was Emily's age, the most important thing in her life had been outdoing the lads on the climbing wall. If her grand idea of using her project to "heal" Jack Hammond didn't come to fruition, then these two could be very useful indeed.

'Some of the books on urbexing are pretty awesome,' said Tom, 'but to my mind they try too hard to be sensational. For a start they enhance the shots.'

'Oh yes,' Emily said. 'I hate that! I've seen brilliant pictures ruined by putting in some robed figure lurking in the background.'

Ray added, 'Some even rearrange what they find, and that's sacrilege in my opinion. Your photography is honest, Stella. It respects the integrity of the place.'

'I hope so. Touch nothing, leave only footprints,' she murmured.

'Amen to that,' said Tom. 'Starburst, you are looking very tired. Have we worn you out?'

Stella gave him a grateful smile. She was done in, though it had more to do with Jack Hammond than Tom and his friends. 'I guess I'm not quite back to my old self yet.'

'Then we'll clear up this mess. Can I run you back to Coggles Barn?'

'No, I'm fine. This won't take two minutes. You guys get off. Tonight has been great, and as soon as I get my head around what I want to do with this lot,' she pointed to the overflowing boxes on the floor, 'we'll get together again and maybe make some plans. Okay?'

'Sure,' said Tom. 'Are you still up for a return trip to Hall Place Manor?'

'Can't wait.' *And I can't wait to find out when Jack went there and left his symbol scratched on those steps.*

After they had gone, Stella tidied up, locked the door and headed for Coggles Barn. What a day it had been! The heart-breaking visit to Jack, Michael's news, and finally an enjoyable evening with Tom and the others.

She wondered what tomorrow would bring.

CHAPTER TWENTY-FOUR

The worst part was seeing Michael drive away. It seemed as if something had ended, even though he had promised to return as soon as possible.

Gran, however, was on a high. Maybe she knew that he would take the job in Essex.

Stella felt unaccountably low. Jack had emailed her as promised, but their conversations were guarded. Stella looked forward to his messages, but found them hard going. There was so much she wanted to tell him, but she knew she had to play it cool or she would lose him for good.

She and the crew went on their second trip to Hall Place Manor. They had found nothing new other than a superb Victorian orangerie, still with its original wrought iron work and tiled flooring. Ray was carried away. He was going to get his filthy rich father to buy it for him. Stella had gone back to the ice house and looked more closely at Jack's triskelion. It looked rather crude, different from the one on his website. Maybe somebody had done it as a tribute or joke. Stella was determined to ask him about it.

That evening Jack said very little. Worried about his state of mind, Stella refrained from asking.

Now she had a phone call, and Stella stirred herself from her lethargy. 'Hi, Lexi! How's things?'

'Just thought you'd like to know that we have three bits of good news. Ethan is sleeping again, so Michael was right about him sensing the tension. He's a changed boy. And best of all, his scans show no sign that he's inherited the PKD!'

'Oh, that's great to hear! You must be so relieved. And the other good news?'

'We cheated and went private. Edward saw a specialist yesterday, and he's had a really positive prognosis. As long as he sticks to the diet, responds to his new medication and keeps his stress levels down as much as possible, they are sure they can keep it under control for now.'

'For now?'

'Things might change as he ages, in fact they probably will, but we'll cross that bridge when we come to it. At least it gives us some quality time with each other and our son.'

'I'm *so* pleased.' Stella felt tears welling up.

'And Edward is easing off from work for a while. He has a good team in place and there's no shortage of orders coming in, so he wants to spend more time with us.'

'So, he's finally seen sense!' Stella laughed, but felt a touch of envy too. It was that family thing again. She felt wistful when she hung up.

Beth was in her running gear. 'Would you hang around here and look after Fris for a couple of hours to save shutting him in? I'm doing circuits at the sports track today.'

'Sure, no problem. I've nothing planned.'

'There might be a call from Germany. He said he'd ring sometime today.'

'I'll be here, and I'll give him your love, don't worry.'

Beth paused at the door. 'I hate to nag, but you haven't been to the gym for two days. You lose your fitness very quickly when you aren't training.'

Stella hung her head. 'It's just this damned headache. It keeps coming back. I might go for a swim when you get back. Okay?'

Beth frowned. 'You must see the doctor, sweetheart. You can't afford to leave it.' She closed the door.

Stella looked at Frisbee. 'Okay, your lordship, it's you, me and the sofa. You can pick the film. How does that sound?'

The spaniel tore through to the lounge and leapt up on the couch.

'Well, that's settled then. But I refuse to watch *Marley and Me* again.'

* * *

Michael's head was about to explode. He had made lists, set a dozen reminders on his phone and planned numerous speeches. But first, he had to see Frida.

Now he was on his way to the mountains. He had booked a meal at their favourite restaurant, and then cancelled it. Much too formal. They needed privacy, somewhere they could talk without interruption. When he phoned she said that Helmut and his wife were out at a school function, so they would have the house to themselves for a few hours.

Michael looked up at the towering mountains. He had quickly come to appreciate the flat lands and marshes of Lincolnshire and now he found the height overpowering. Even the pine forest seemed menacing.

Frida met him at the door. She was as beautiful as ever, in chinos and a soft blue mohair sweater. Michael experienced a moment of doubt, and then it was gone.

Frida led them into the dining room, where she had set out a light meal. 'It's nothing fancy, but you didn't give me much notice.'

He replied in German. 'I know, and I apologise. Maybe I should have waited until tomorrow, but there are things I must talk to you about and they can't wait.'

There was a silence. Finally Frida said, 'Shall we eat first?'

'I'm really not hungry, but you go ahead and I'll talk.'

Frida poured two glasses of wine. 'I have a feeling we are going to need this.'

Michael forgot his notes and reminders, and blurted it all out. The job at the university, the private practice. How he wanted to accept one or both of them and make England his first home. 'The last thing I want to do is hurt you, my darling, though I'm sure that is what I'm doing. I'll make sure everything is sorted out and that money will never be a problem. I already do so much lecturing it won't be very different, really. You'll hardly miss me at all. And I'll visit. The house is mortgage free and is, of course, your home for life. I know this will be a shock, but I—'

'Stop! Michael, just stop and be honest with me. You are going to her, aren't you?'

He stared at her. She knew?

Frida sipped her wine and regarded him over the top of her glass. 'I'll make things easy for you, shall I? But in return, we do this my way.'

He waited for what she had to say.

'I don't want to live in the house. I want it sold. I will buy a small property here and be closer to the children. Helmut's job is uncertain, and in order to keep it, he has to take less money and work longer hours. They hate the thought of a childminder, so they will need my support. Kurt's work is taking him abroad next year, so I will be able to keep an eye on his home while he is away. It will save me travelling and will suit me much better.'

'If that's what you want,' Michael said softly. Who was this woman with her businesslike ideas? She seemed almost hard. It wasn't his Frida at all.

'Oh, darling, don't look so shocked.' Frida gave him a rueful smile. 'I've always known you would go. You said it will be a shock.' She gave a bitter laugh. 'Hardly. I've waited for this moment ever since our honeymoon.'

'But why did you stay with me if you knew?'

'Because I loved you, and every moment with you was a blessing. Because I still do love you, and I know that you love me and our children too.'

Michael nodded slowly. 'That won't change.'

'But some things must. I want a divorce, Michael, simple and fast. I think you owe me that much. I've lived the best years of my life with only part of you. Now I want my last years to belong to me. I want the independence to do whatever I wish, whenever I want. And if that should mean being with someone else, then I want the freedom to do it.'

Michael was dumbfounded. Whatever he had imagined, it was not this. He had expected tears, recriminations, not a well thought out plan of action. He drank a mouthful of wine. He was a psychologist, for God's sake. He was supposed to understand people. Well, he couldn't have got this more wrong.

'And I don't want to know anything about her. Not her name, or where she lives, or what she does. You never chose to share that part of your life with me in the past, and I don't want to know about it now or in the future. Is that understood?'

He nodded. She was right, of course. 'I'll do whatever you want.' He slowly swirled his wine in the glass. 'But know this. I always loved you, and I always tried to do my best for you and the boys. I cut her out of my life. I never saw her or contacted her, not once, until last month when she tracked me down because she desperately needed my help. And that's the truth. I swear that throughout our marriage I was never unfaithful, and I always loved you.'

She covered his hand with hers. 'I never thought otherwise. But love isn't always enough, Michael.'

* * *

What do you know about Hall Place Manor at Seas Meet? There, Stella had finally asked the question via instant messenger.

You've found it? When? Jack replied.

A couple of weeks ago. I saw your triskelion in the ice house. It wasn't quite like your usual symbol, I wondered if someone else had carved it there for a joke.

There was a long break, and then Jack's answer appeared. *It was a long time ago, I was just a kid. I hadn't embraced the ethos. It was the first and last time I ever left a tag.*

Why there?

Another long break. *My father was a property developer. He bought it, but his plans were turned down. We lived there for a while, but it all went badly wrong.*

Stella stared at the words for a long time. Then she typed, *Does he still own it?*

I suppose. He's in America now, making a fortune. I should think the Manor is the last thing on his dollar-driven mind. Then, before she could type again, he wrote, *I'm tired. Speak tomorrow.*

She sat looking at the screen saver. She wondered how long it would be before he let her visit again. She desperately wanted to tell him about her idea. It could be so good for them both.

She sighed. Jack could be like this for an eternity, and then her project would never get off the ground. She would be left in limbo, waiting for him to say the word.

She would set it all out in writing and send it to him. At least he could give it some thought, and then she would know where she stood.

Part of her wanted to wait until Michael was back, but he had told her she needed to move forward on her own. Today would be her starting point.

She kept it succinct, and told him he need not reply. There was no rush for an answer, but other urbexers had encouraged her to go ahead. *"Speak tomorrow. S. x."* She shook her head and deleted the 'x'.

So, Jackhammer, the ball is now in your court.

* * *

Frida retained her composure until Michael left. They agreed not to tell Helmut until his brother Kurt returned home in a day or so. Then the family would discuss it.

She would join him in the town the following morning and get the paperwork started. 'The sooner the better,' she had stated shortly. 'I'll drive down tomorrow as soon as I've sorted out the children. I should be there by ten. We can go to the solicitor and then the estate agents.' Then she gave him a distant look and added, 'I can attend to the viewings. I'm sure you want to get back to England as soon as possible.'

Michael gritted his teeth. 'I will stay for as long as it takes. Although I hadn't allowed time to organise the sale of our family home.' That part had yet to sink in. The house was a listed building, and had been in the family for generations. He had always expected to pass it on to his sons. 'You are sure about that, are you?'

'Perfectly. No ties with the past, Michael. It will be easier in the end, I promise you.'

There was nothing left to say.

It was like a bad dream. He felt as if he'd wandered into someone else's life. He was being swept along in the current, and in the distance he could hear the roar of the falls.

He stood on his son's doorstep, hesitating. The mountains had disappeared into the night. 'I'll see you in the morning, Frida.' He wanted to hold her, to say that this wasn't what he had intended, that he was sorry. She stepped back.

'Yes, tomorrow around ten.' The door closed.

With a heavy heart, he eased himself behind the wheel of his car, and set off back down the mountain.

He turned the key in the lock. It has always been a little stiff, he thought, and this made him terribly sad. He took off his coat and went into the dining room, where he poured himself a large whisky. He carried it to the lounge and sat down heavily on the couch. He thought about phoning Beth, but it was late and he was far too upset.

The silence in the room was mocking. 'Where are you, Frisbee?' he whispered.

He finished his drink, and poured himself another.

What a fool. He raised his glass. 'To Michael Lindenfeld, supreme idiot.'

Why hadn't he and Beth simply followed their hearts? All their good intentions had been for nothing. Frida had known from the very start! By staying with her he had sentenced her to a lifetime of waiting for the hammer to fall. She had spent their whole married life knowing that one day he would leave her. She must have been in purgatory.

Never again would he sacrifice anything for the sake of "doing the right thing."

How could he tell Beth? Sorry, but all those years ago we made a terrible mistake. No, he couldn't. He would never tell her what Frida had said.

He walked to the window and opened the curtains. The house looked out onto a wide avenue lined with trees. The frost glistened on their branches. He had walked the boys along this street on little leather reins. He had waved from this window when Helmut went off to propose to his sweetheart. The funeral cortege for his father and then his mother had started from this house. Soon a board saying *Zu verkaufen* would be attached to the front wall. For Sale. The end.

He drew the curtains tightly shut. Why hadn't he had the courage of Stella and Edward? Stella had said their case was different, because no one else was involved. Still, they could have hung on and "done the right thing" for each other's sake. But they had recognised their mistake and moved on. Now Edward had a wonderful wife and child, and he was sure Stella would one day have a family. But what did he and Beth have? They would have each other and freedom at last, but old age loomed before them, with its accompanying loss of dignity. He thought of all the various ailments that later life had in store, and then stopped. The whisky was making him sentimental and stupid. It wasn't just old age that brought ill-health! Look at what Stella had suffered and now Edward, with an incurable disease. By comparison, he and Beth were fighting fit and bloody lucky!

Michael sighed. The house was only bricks and mortar after all, and actually he'd always considered it rather austere. Maybe Frida was right. She was certainly making it easy for him. He was at peace in Coggles Barn, with the dog asleep on his lap and Beth sitting close by. He'd never truly felt that way in Germany. He placed his unfinished whisky on the table. Tomorrow would bring some clarity. He just hoped that some small part of the old Frida would show itself before his final departure from her life.

CHAPTER TWENTY-FIVE

Jack glanced at the digital clock. It was approaching three in the morning. He was exhausted, and racked with pain. But at least he had something other than himself to think about.

Stella had ideas. Brilliant, forward-thinking ideas that could certainly work if implemented correctly. There was only one snag. They involved him.

He read and re-read her message. After the first reading she was almost consigned to the trash bin. The second time he muttered that no one wanted such rubbish. Then he looked at it again. It might just be possible.

Finally he began to put his own thoughts into it.

Now, five hours and six mugs of coffee later, he had the skeleton of a business plan which would use their combined images to maximise their potential. His father had known nothing about being a good dad, but he did know how to make money. His only son carried his financial acumen in his genes. Jack yawned. For the first time since the accident, he had something he really wanted to achieve. It felt weird, but not unpleasant.

He dashed off several emails. One or two of the recipients would probably think they were getting messages from beyond the grave! The thought amused him. Time to call in some favours.

The last email was the difficult one. Finally he sat back, satisfied with his night's work, and pressed Send.

"Stella – don't hassle me on this – leave contact until you hear from me - I've taken on board everything you said and it's a brilliant idea. Not only that - I think I know a way to help you. Jack."

* * *

Stella woke early and took Frisbee for a walk to her house.

She opened her mail, while the spaniel happily sniffed his way around this exciting place full of new smells, including the delicious aroma of pizza.

She opened Jack's message and stared at it. He wasn't mad at her. She had been unable to sleep, wondering what his reaction to her idea would be. He was going to help!

She had to stop herself tapping out a reply. She would do as he said, and wait. He was on board, that was the main thing. With his help, this project would be the next chapter in her life.

Frisbee stuck his nose around the door and wagged his tail.

'Come on in, fur-face! We've just had good news!'

The dog trotted across and laid his chin on her lap, staring up at her. She stroked the velvety fur on either side of his face and said, 'I think it's going to be a good day.'

Frisbee wagged his tail. He clearly agreed, but then pretty much every day was good in Frisbee's life. With a contented sigh he wound himself around her legs, and fell asleep across her feet.

'Next time around, I'm coming back as a dog.'

* * *

Tom smiled at his mother across the breakfast table. Between them was a giant brown pot of strong tea. His brothers had gone out.

'How do you feel about it then?' he asked.

She nodded. 'I think you're doing the right thing, son.'

'You're not just saying that?'

'I'm not daft, Tom. I know that Bill and Clive aren't pulling their weight. Their heart is not in the land, not like you and your father, bless him.' She poured more tea. 'And, Paul, well I think he'll do so much better without the other two influencing him.'

'Paul has a feel for farming, I can sense that. You're right, and I'll support him if he wants to make this place his life.' He grinned. 'I'm going to need a good manager if we're bringing in outside labour, and I'd prefer to keep it in the family.'

'Well, if that doesn't give the lad an incentive, me duck, nothing will!'

They sat in silence for a while, both thinking about the major changes that Tom was about to introduce. It was a gamble, but things could not go on as they were. The only thing Bill loved about the farm was the machinery. A local engineering company had made several offers of employment, and now he was off to see the managing director. Tom was sure that he would return with a healthy contract in his hand.

Clive was different again. Their mother said he was a throwback to his great grandfather, who had been a war artist. There was a painting that had hung on the kitchen wall since long before Tom was born. It showed a group of Second World War soldiers with filthy, haggard faces returning bloodied and weary from a battle. His great grandfather had had an extraordinary talent, and young Clive had inherited something of that, although his artwork was related to technology and advertising design. He'd already enrolled on an intensive course, and there was apparently the chance of an apprenticeship later.

'We can manage, Mum.' Tom took her hand across the table. 'I've done the maths, and spoken to the bank. This *will* pay, maybe not this year, but it will.'

'And Bill will be putting something in the pot for the first time!'

They laughed together. It felt right, not a gamble at all. He'd simply seen the light before it was too late.

* * *

Michael was writing a new set of lists. There was now far more to do than he had expected.

Firstly, he had to tell his partners at the clinic. They would be shocked he was sure, although since Frida's revelation he was no longer absolutely sure of anything. Whatever their reaction, there would be a massive machine to set in motion — decisions to make and countless legalities to formalise. It was daunting, but not as daunting as the things he needed to sort out with Frida.

For the first time ever, he dreaded seeing his wife.

He ate a miserable breakfast of stale cornflakes, longing to be back in the kitchen at Coggles Barn, sneaking bits of toast crust down to Frisbee waiting patiently under the table. Michael was putting off calling Beth. He felt he should get the morning out of the way first, and then he would be able to relax.

Frida would be with him in an hour or so, and he had already primed the solicitor. At least *someone* had been shocked to hear the news.

To pass the time he checked out the names and addresses of estate agents and picked a couple of likely candidates. Whoever took on the task of selling this property would be lucky. It was in very good repair, and located in a highly sought after area. He wondered if Frida would tell the boys that this had been *her* idea. Both Helmut and Kurt had expected to inherit one day, and Michael could foresee fierce arguments arising between them and their two disgruntled sons.

But what did he know? Maybe the boys had been expecting him to leave too? They were both very close to their mother, so they could have guessed that something was amiss. Whatever direction their "family discussion" took, he was pretty certain to emerge as the villain.

Michael tipped the leftover cornflakes into the bin, counting the days until his one-way flight to Heathrow.

CHAPTER TWENTY-SIX

Four days had passed, and Coggles Barn hummed with nervous energy.

Beth was on tenterhooks, wondering what was happening with Michael, and Stella had tracked back and forth between her house and the barn, checking for emails that never arrived. She was beginning to wonder if Jack's enthusiasm had wavered. And now she was receiving almost daily texts from Tom and his crew, urging her not to let her ideas fester. They were clearly ready and willing to pitch in and help, and probably believed that she was just procrastinating. She had even gone back to the gym, both to appease her nagging Gran and to control her frayed nerves.

Stella swam towards the steps of the pool. She had done fifty lengths and was feeling pretty tired. Five minutes in the steam room and she would go and change.

She breathed in the steam that always smelled of eucalyptus, and rested against the tiles. The door opened, and there was the last person she had expected to see. Robbie.

'I thought you were in Cornwall!'

'Back last night. It was great. My aunt and me got rat-arsed together.'

Robbie looked better than he had in years.

'She sounds really nice.'

'She is, and she's asked me to tell you that you and Beth have an open-ended invite to go and stay in Trewellard whenever you like.' Robbie's face creased into a smile. 'She's the best thing about my family. In fact, she's the only good thing — nothing like the rest of them! She's talented and she's got a wicked sense of humour, especially with a glass in her hand. And she believes that life is for enjoying, not just making money and brown-nosing "influential" people.'

'It sounds like she was just what you needed.'

'Dead right. Now I can't wait to get back to work.'

'It's still on track?'

'Confirmed, Stel, and all thanks to you.' He looked down at her earnestly. 'If there is ever anything I can do for you, absolutely anything, just ask. Okay?'

'Soppy sod! You go enjoy your new team, and you owe me nothing.'

'We'll fight over that one later, because I'm actually here for another reason. I rang Beth and she said you were swimming this morning.' His eyes lit up. 'You will *never* believe what I'm going to tell you.'

'Well, spit it out.'

'Superintendent Croxforth is moving on! Well, *being* moved on is more like it.'

Stella gasped. 'You're kidding me!'

'No. I had a call late last night from my mate, Kyle, who works in custody. He said it's all over the station. She's telling everyone that she's been given the task of getting a failing division up and running. In fact she's been hauled over the coals and reassigned.'

'Why?'

Robbie moved closer. 'This is speculation, but I think DI Jackman, my new boss, has asked some questions in high places. He was appalled by her treatment of you, after the force had promised to support you. He considers her conduct both unprofessional and unacceptable.'

'Rowan Jackman said that?'

'Marie said so, and she wouldn't make it up.'

'No, she wouldn't.'

'So, expect a call or a visit from someone wearing lots of gold braid. I think you are in line for an apology.'

Stella narrowed her eyes. 'And how exactly did Jackman get to know about the way Croxforth behaved?'

Robbie looked heavenward. 'Well, he did ask me to be candid about my reasons for transferring, and I could hardly lie to a senior officer during an interview, could I?'

'You little stirrer! Remind me never to upset you!'

'Stella, you have no idea how callous that dreadful woman was, especially about you. And since you were good enough to rescue me from myself, I thought I might turn the tables.'

'And didn't it work well!'

'Better than I'd hoped.'

Stella stood up and kissed him on the cheek. 'Frankly, it couldn't happen to a more deserving woman! Robbie, I'm overheating, and with my problems I'm not supposed to stay in here for longer than five minutes. So, I'll see you soon. Promise to let me know how you get on?'

'I promise. Take care, Stella.'

* * *

Jack had expected some fairly swift responses to his requests, but the phone had been ringing all day and the emails had poured in.

He hated talking on the telephone and kept his conversations businesslike, even when his father rang from the States. They rarely contacted each other. Even when he had his accident, his father and stepmother had only managed a single fleeting visit. After all, they had important things to do, like dining with the accountant and sweet-talking the tax man.

Jack checked the fridge. He'd been so engrossed in his new project that he'd completely forgotten to order any food. He pulled a pot noodle from the cupboard, checked the sell by date and boiled a kettle. A month out of date, but it probably wouldn't kill him. That and Weetabix should keep him going until Tesco arrived the next day. Food was not a high priority at present. He scribbled a shopping list, added a few treats — like a bottle of vodka and a giant bar of Toblerone, and began on the pot noodles.

Back in the office and feeling slightly nauseous, he went back into his inbox and saw that another six emails had arrived.

He read one of them twice, and picked up the phone.

'I appreciate your efficiency. So all you need at this stage is my witnessed signature on the original paperwork?'

The secretary assured him that would be fine, and then matters could be fast-tracked as he had requested.

'Perfect. Can you courier them to me, please? And ensure that the company send two employees that can act as witnesses. As you know, I am disabled. I live in a remote spot and cannot get into town. Just charge this extra service to my account.'

He replaced the receiver and saw a new message. Wonders would never cease. His father had actually done as he'd asked! Jack switched on the printer and heaved a happy sigh. Oh yes! Things were finally moving. His persistent friend Starburst was about to get one hell of a surprise. He just needed to check one last point before he proceeded. It could make a considerable difference to his cost estimates.

He typed. *'Stella, if the business takes off, and I see no reason why it shouldn't (with all the right equipment and know how), were you serious about extending to premises suitable for a gallery and a studio/print workshop?'*

He waited but there was no reply. No matter. She would see it soon. Jack let out a long, low whistle. He could hardly believe he was doing this. Stella had burst back into his life and shown him a way out of his hell.

It felt unbelievably good to be in charge of his destiny again.

* * *

When the phone rang, Stella half expected it to be Jack. She was still shocked that he was showing such an interest in her plans for the image library and the book. In his last email he had been asking about her commitment to a gallery as well! She desperately wanted to talk to him, but he was still asking her to wait.

'Stella? Is Beth there, please?'

'Michael! No, sorry, she's taken the dog out for a late stroll. Can I get her to ring you when she gets back?'

'It's nothing important. I just needed to hear a friendly voice and yours will do nicely. How are you coping without me?'

Stella thought he sounded terribly tired.

'I'm on a high at present. The plans for my photographs are really coming together.' She wanted to say more, but it could wait until his return.

'Splendid. Things are coming together here too. Much slower than I hoped, but the end is in sight.'

'We miss you, Michael. Even the dog keeps checking the door each time he hears a noise.'

'No more than I miss you all, I can assure you.'

Stella felt a rush of affection for him. 'What did your partners say about you moving here?'

'Let's say it's been harrowing *and* complicated. I was very much the lead singer of the group, if you get my meaning, and also co-owner of the premises that houses the clinic. I've spent days unravelling a whole tapestry of deeds and documents.' He gave a short laugh. 'But I feel freer with each day, and closer to getting home to England.'

'I wish we could help you.'

'You are, by being there and listening to my ramblings!'

Stella laughed. 'Well, you've listened to enough of mine! Have you decided what you are going to do when you get back?'

'Absolutely. I've already contacted the university and told them that I'll accept the post, working three days a week, and then Field-Latimer and I can concentrate on getting the new clinic up and running. At least when my affairs here are concluded, I will have some ready money to put into finding a suitable place for it.'

'Phew! No pipe and slippers for you. But I suppose academics never retire, do they?'

'Not while there are things to discover and improve on. Science never rests.' He paused. 'But I should. I've got an early start tomorrow, and hopefully I'll be heading for the airport by the evening. Nothing certain, but there comes a point where you have done all you can. I will have to come back of course, but I can do a lot online.'

He yawned. 'Tell Beth that I will ring as soon as I know my flight time. Until then, you both take care — oh, and give my little friend Fris a hug from me.'

Stella hung up, thinking that it was a bit like having a father again, or maybe a grandfather. She felt as if she had known Michael all her life.

CHAPTER TWENTY-SEVEN

By the middle of the next day everything was in place. Jack finally trusted that he was doing the right thing.

His legal advisor had brought the papers personally, along with one of the office juniors so they could witness his signature. Jack had done the unprecedented, asked them in and offered tea or coffee.

Jack gave them copies of all the documents his father had sent from the USA and when they left, he felt he'd done all he could. Jack felt pretty pleased with himself.

Back in the kitchen he opened the bottle of vodka and took a carton of juice from the fridge. Passion-orange-guava juice was perfect with vodka.

Jack didn't normally drink — he was on too many medications. Now he sniffed the fruit juice and it smelled like Hawaii.

He raised his glass.

* * *

'Me again!' Michael sounded much brighter this time.

'What a shame! You've missed Beth *again*.'

'I tried her mobile but it's switched off.'

'She's running, Michael. She doesn't like interruptions when she's doing a time trial.'

'What a woman!'

'Yup. She reckons that by next week she'll be ready to take on a half marathon.'

'Amazing!' He laughed. 'Look, when she gets back, tell her I'm coming home. Just that, tell her Michael is coming home. Okay?'

Stella beamed at the phone. 'I certainly will. Are you sure there isn't anything else I can add to that?'

'Not at present. Some things need to be said in person.' He chuckled. 'I've got a seat on the last flight out tonight. My hire car will be waiting for me at Heathrow, and I'll come directly to you. It will be late, but I've got a lot to tell Beth.'

'I bet you have!'

'I'll see you later.'

'Oh no you won't. I'm going to be safely in my room with the door shut and some heavy metal playing through my earphones! Have a safe journey, Michael, and I'll see you tomorrow.'

Stella hung up and realised that her headache had disappeared.

* * *

Beth checked her watch, and made sure her body was coping with the long distance and uneven ground. Running on the fen lanes was pretty unpredictable with their potholes and badly patched sections. She did the best she could to keep safe and kept on top of her equipment, replacing her running shoes every 500 miles and always wearing suitable clothing.

Some idiots used the fen lanes as race tracks, and in summer especially, the grasses and crops were too high to see around the bends. Winter was better, although the nights drew in early, and even now the dead, dry rushes on either side of the ditches formed a thick curtain that made visibility difficult.

She was ahead of her schedule and slowed her pace a little. The stretch that she was approaching, a winding lane around the peripheries of three big fields, could be a bit dicey, but at least she wasn't stupid enough to wear headphones when she ran. The wind was blowing in her face, carrying the salty ozone smell from the distant marshes.

Beth heard the whistling wind, but she didn't hear the engine of the big Nissan vehicle that came up the lane behind her. Then a horn blasted, followed by an ear-splitting squeal of brakes, but all Beth saw were black reeds and the dark water in the deep ditch rushing towards her.

* * *

Stella didn't recognise the big navy-blue 4x4 that drew up outside Coggles Barn. She didn't know the white-faced man who stood nervously on the doorstep.

'Miss Stella North?'

Fear trickled down her spine in an icy dribble. How many times had she asked that very question when she was a copper?

'It's your grandmother.'

Stella realised that she had stopped breathing and took in a gasping breath.

'I just never saw her.'

The fear turned to terror.

'I'm so sorry. But could you come and help me get her out of the car? She's twisted her ankle rather badly. I've offered to take her to the hospital, but she insisted that I get her home. Oh, I'm Roy Ainsley, Miss North. I live out on the fen lane.'

'Oh, yes, of course I will. You look pretty shaken up yourself.'

The man shook his head, 'I've been driving that lane for years. I've even seen Beth running out there, but this afternoon, well, the high reeds completely hid her.'

They hurried to the vehicle, where Beth was struggling to get out of the passenger seat.

'Oh, Gran!'

'Don't fuss, girl! You're as bad as he is! For heaven's sake, Roy, you never even hit me. It's just a sprain. Some ice and a couple of anti-inflammatory pills will have it sorted in no time.'

Inside, Stella took a look at the ankle. At least it wasn't broken.

'The wind was blowing in the wrong direction, and I wouldn't have heard a Formula One McLaren. It's me that should be apologising. You were hardly speeding. Now go home and forget all about it. And thank you for the lift. Even I will admit that walking back would have been rather painful.'

After the man had gone, Beth accepted a large cup of tea with a dash of whisky in it. She sipped it and laughed. 'He must have wondered what was happening! The second I heard the horn I threw myself into the ditch. I did a perfect parachute landing fall. Poor Roy thought he'd knocked me into the middle of next week. I hurt my ankle when I slipped getting out of the bloody ditch!'

Stella laughed. 'Parachute landing fall? What on earth do you know about those?'

'If I told you I'd have to kill you after.'

'You never cease to amaze me, Gran.'

'And long may it continue.' Beth looked askance at Stella, and said, 'Please don't laugh, but I've decided to write a memoir about my life. I don't mean for publication, it will be just for you. When I'm gone you can have a giggle at my expense.'

'That's a fantastic idea, although I have no intention of waiting until you pop your clogs to read it. You could start it while you are waiting for that ankle to heal.'

'Rubbish! I'll be back out in no time.'

Stella didn't doubt it for a second. Then she remembered Michael's message.

'He said, "Tell Beth, Michael is coming home." Nothing else, just that. But you will be delighted to know that he is on the last flight out of Dusseldorf tonight and he's got lots to tell you.'

Swollen ankle or not, Stella had never seen her gran look so happy.

CHAPTER TWENTY-EIGHT

Michael had been back in the country for three days when Beth declared that she wanted to throw a party.

'I would call it a family get-together, but as our family is somewhat small, we had better invite our friends too.' She looked hopefully at Stella.

'Sounds great. Any particular reason?'

She nodded. 'I want to get everyone together so that they can meet Michael properly. Plus it would be really nice to be all under one roof for once without some sort of catastrophe raging around our ears.'

'So, no special celebration then?' Stella was smirking at her.

'No, but Michael will be here much more from now on, and I think I'd like to explain why.' She tilted her head to one side. 'Do you think you'll be up to it, sweetheart? A lot of people all milling around? Will it be too much for you?'

'I'm fine with it, Gran. I think it's a great idea. Who are you going to ask?'

Beth counted them off on her fingers. 'Well, Edward, Lexi and little Ethan, of course. The neighbours, because I don't really see enough of them and they are awfully nice people. Dr Field-Latimer and his wife, now that he and Michael are going to be colleagues. Robbie, if he'd like to join us. A couple of friends from the gym . . . oh, and Tom, and why not ask your new urbex friends, the ones with the funny names? If you think they wouldn't mind spending the evening with a bunch of old fogies.'

'Why not? I'll ask them.' Stella grinned. 'If there's drink flowing I'm willing to bet that Emily would love to come.'

'Anyone else that you can think of?'

Stella shook her head. 'No, I think that's everyone.'

'What about your Jack? I know he's disabled, but we could get him picked up. Our taxi company does have a people carrier that's adapted for wheelchairs.'

Stella pulled a face. 'I don't think so. In fact, he'd probably rather stick pins in his eyes. No offence, Gran, but he's a complicated man, and he's always been a loner. Now he's the way he is, it's a hundred times worse.'

'Would it hurt to ask? Even if you know he'll refuse, it's sometimes enough just to know that someone wants you there.'

'I'll think about that one, Gran. I haven't heard from him for a few days, so if he contacts me, I suppose I could mention it.'

'I think you should.' Beth had very strong feelings about Jack Hammond. She had never met him, but she had a feeling that he would always be connected to her lovely granddaughter in some way.

'So when is it going to happen? And what kind of party is it?'

'No time like the present, so just as soon as we can get it all organised. What about next Friday evening? That's if everyone can make it at such short notice. And it's definitely *not* posh clothes, just a nice buffet and plenty of vino.'

'Perfect. What can I do to help?'

'You're busy with sorting your photographs. Leave it to Michael and me. If you could just ask your friends and let me know who is coming, we'll do the rest.'

'I'm on it.' Stella paused. 'Actually, can I add another name? If she's free, I'd like to ask Marie, the DS from Saltern-le-Fen. Apart from being a good friend, it would give her and Robbie a chance to get to know each other without being surrounded by a dozen other plods.'

Beth smiled. 'Wonderful. I'm really looking forward to this.'

That afternoon, amid torrential rain, Stella had a call from Tom.

'I've found those diaries, Stel, from our old exploits. I'm well rained off on the farm and I've finished the interviews for our new manpower, so shall I bring them over and we could spend an hour or so collating my notes with your photographs?'

'I'll meet you at my place in half an hour. Oh, and Tom, Beth wants to invite you to a party here at Coggles Barn on Friday evening. Can you make it?'

'Try and stop me. Say thanks for me. See you soon.'

The weather was so atrocious that Stella drove home. She decided that the time really had come to move back. Beth and Michael would need space. Michael had not said anything, but Stella had the feeling that things in Germany had not been easy.

She unlocked the door and went inside. It would be a big move for her, and scary, but it felt right. She'd tell Tom and see what he thought. *And,* she thought rather apprehensively, she would also tell him about her visit to Jack Hammond, and the possibility of his joining her new venture. Somehow she didn't think this would go down too well.

They spent an hour happily lost in the past, before Stella broached the subject of her visit to Jack. 'The place was like a fenland version of Guantanamo Bay! I swear it had more cameras and security features than a psychiatric secure unit.'

'I can't think why you went without telling me. I'd have driven you, you know that.'

'When I contacted him he was really weird. I think he'd have left me on the doorstep if he'd seen anyone else there.'

'And the bastard still threw you out,' growled Tom. 'What a prize shit! And how self-bloody-centred can you get! It was really brave of you to go to him, and then he treats you like that.'

'You didn't see him, Tom. He was such a legend, now he's stuck in a wheelchair, and he's clearly in constant pain. I saw shelves full of different medicines in his office.' She smiled at Tom's fierce expression. 'And he *has* said sorry. It was just all too much for him. I mean, you know how long he's been hiding under a rock. He freaked out, that's all.'

'I wish I'd never mentioned him to you. It would have been better if he'd stayed under his rock.' He exhaled. 'But you won't go alone again, will you? Even if he begs you to?'

Stella wasn't sure. She did want to see Jack again, very much. But maybe she'd keep that to herself.

'Don't worry. Once bitten and all that, but I *am* interested in his photos and his ideas. I wish you could have seen them, they were powerful stuff. And if it helps him to get even a little bit of his old confidence back, we can't abandon him, can we? He was our hero, back then.' She waved a hand at the boxes of pictures.

Tom looked mutinous, but shrugged. 'I guess not. But be careful. And don't take everything he says as gospel. He sounds a bit unhinged to me.'

'He said he can help, and I believe him. He has the expertise and you should see his computer. It's like something that NASA would use.'

'Well, just be careful.'

She decided to change the subject, and asked Tom what he thought about her moving back home.

He approved wholeheartedly, saying that Beth was only minutes away in an emergency, and if Stella needed anything, his phone was always in his pocket.

'That makes me feel so much better.' She really did. Stella knew that Tom was solid, and meant what he said.

'Day or night, Stel. Even if you get an attack of the heebie-jeebies, just ring and we'll talk it through, understand?'

'Yes, skipper!' She saluted.

'So when is it going to happen?'

'After the party, I think. I haven't talked to Beth yet, but I'll aim to pack up the next day and ferry my stuff home.'

'Want a hand?'

'Let's see, shall we? In a funny kind of way I want to do it by myself, just to prove that I can. But if I fall apart, I'll yell, I promise.'

After Tom had gone, Stella rang Robbie, who jumped at the chance of an evening in their company. Marie said she'd love to come and it would be an excellent idea to meet with Robbie outside the shop.

'Going well,' Stella said to herself. Beth had wanted to ask Lexi and Edward herself, and Tom had already sent texts to Razor and Butterwitch, who had both given the thumbs up. So Stella was left with the big question. Should she ask Jack?

Her brain said no. Her heart said yes.

She walked slowly up the stairs to her office and sat at the computer. He was still insisting that she wait for him to contact her, but this was not about the photo gallery. It was a simple invite to a party. She sighed. She knew he would never agree.

Jack — Beth has asked me to tell you that she is having a small party next Friday. I know it's not your thing, but she said to ask you anyway. You would be very welcome and she'd arrange transport. No pressure, but it would be great to see you. There will also be a couple of next generation urbexers there who would love to meet you. (Nice to know that the baton is still being carried forward, huh?) Hope you are okay, Stella.'

She read it through several times, then stabbed the Send button. If it was a mistake, sod it, she had meant well.

She sat for a while, wondering if she'd hear from him, then got up and wandered back down the stairs. She had better get back to Coggles Barn and tell Beth that she had a full complement of takers for the party.

And break it to her that the time had come to move back home.

The phone made her jump, but the person at the other end was even more of a surprise.

'That was sweet of you, Stella. I appreciate the thought.'

The voice was full of quiet emotion. It made Stella's heart lurch, because when they had met it had been full of bitterness and desolation. He had been like a house with no lights at the windows. She could relate to his anger, that was a natural reaction, but his utter hopelessness had been hard to swallow. She wondered if she had given off the same signals in the throes of one of her depressive episodes. She hoped not, because seeing Jack like that was horrible.

Now he sounded like a different man. Michael had said that sometimes a small thing, one simple action, could kick start a whole series of positive reactions. Was this new venture that thing?

She realised that she hadn't answered him. 'But you aren't coming, are you?'

'I don't think I'd be very good company, do you?' He laughed. 'Come to think of it, I never was.'

'I think you were pretty good.' Stella smiled to herself.

'Starburst! Not on the phone.'

Was this the same man that just days ago had almost thrown her out of his house?

'I would come, Stella, but going to a party isn't exactly what I'd planned for my first trip out.'

'So you do intend to come back into the world?'

'I do, but on my own terms. I've been sunk in apathy for too long. Now I've woken up. Now I have something to work towards, but it has to happen as and when I can deal with it. Do you understand what I mean?'

'One step at a time. I had to do everything like that after my injuries, and the shock of my whole life changing.'

'Now look at you, you are galloping!'

'Trotting, maybe. But it's still a lot better than sitting in my stable feeling sorry for myself.'

There was a silence and Stella wondered if she'd gone too far.

But then he said, 'Look, even though I probably won't make it to the party, please tell those youngsters to keep urbexing alive. Tell them I said this . . . they *must* ignore those "Keep Out" signs. Tell them to be trailblazers, walk off the beaten track and keep history alive. And pass it on, Stella. Our photographs will speak to those who can't crawl down storm drains and slip across rooftops.'

'Jack! You're making me want to rush out and explore an abandoned building.'

He laughed. 'Good. That was the idea. Now, please thank your grandmother for my invite. And all the work I've been doing for the online image gallery and the rest of it will be with you very soon. Now enjoy yourself.' There was a pause. 'And thank you, Stella.'

Then he was gone.

It took her a while to take it all in. She and Jack had just had a proper, relaxed conversation.

Stella shook her head. It was a miracle. The curtain was coming up on the next stage of her life.

CHAPTER TWENTY-NINE

Friday evening came, and Coggles Barn was alive with music and colour. Michael had taken over the catering and had produced an amazing array of dishes. Beth had filled several clear glass vases with hyacinth stems and bunches of bright yellow narcissi. The flowers made Stella think of spring.

She had got Robbie to download an assortment of tracks from the sixties and seventies. Lexi danced happily to the Supremes, while Edward and Ethan looked on, bemused.

Robbie grinned broadly at Stella. 'You were right about the music. It's going down a treat.'

'It's a great evening, isn't it? Nothing like this has happened here for a very long time. It's so nice to see everyone just having a good time.' She sipped her wine. 'You'd better go and have a word with your new DS, hadn't you?'

Robbie nodded and looked over to where Marie stood talking to Donald Field-Latimer. 'She's very impressive, isn't she?'

'Don't be fooled by the Lara Croft exterior. She's a diamond of an officer. You are so lucky, kiddo!'

His smile widened. 'And don't I know it.' He clinked glasses with her and headed off in Marie's direction.

Tom ambled over with two plates of food. 'Here, Stel, you have to try this, whatever it is. It's fantastic! Michael is obviously in the wrong job.'

'He's been cooking all day and the only one allowed in the kitchen was Frisbee!'

'What's the score between him and Beth?' Tom looked across to where they were chatting with some of Beth's running buddies.

'All will be revealed, hence this party.'

Tom nodded sagely. 'Ah. I see.'

Emily and Ray appeared. 'Hi, you two!'

Stella drew the three of them into the empty kitchen. 'I have a message for Butterwitch and Razor. It's from Jackhammer.'

Their mouths dropped. 'For us?' they said in unison.

Stella repeated Jack's words, adding, 'I think a little bit of him wanted to come tonight. He is making terrific headway, but it's too soon right now.' She noticed Tom looking sceptical. 'He is definitely going to help with getting the gallery set up,' she said.

Tom continued to look unconvinced.

'Awesome,' sighed Emily, and took a long gulp of wine.

'Absolutely,' agreed Ray, sipping at his.

Michael's deep voice called from the lounge. 'Okay, everyone, may I have your attention please! Beth wants to say something.'

Robbie turned down the volume and everyone fell silent.

Beth said how lovely it was to see them all together enjoying themselves, and then she reached out and took Michael's hand. 'As you all now know, this is Michael Lindenfeld. Michael and I knew each other many years ago. If things had been different, you might well have been gathered here tonight to celebrate our ruby wedding anniversary. But that wasn't to be, and we both went in different directions.' She glanced across to Stella and smiled. 'Even though we never forgot each other, we did have full and rich lives with no regrets. My lovely granddaughter is proof of that. But things have now come full circle, and I want you to welcome Michael back home to England. You will be seeing a lot more of him around the village, and to all those who told me to give up Coggles Barn because it was much too big for one — well, you were wrong!'

The room resounded with laughter and shouts of "Cheers!" and "Congratulations!"

'So, are you going to start holding cookery courses, Michael?' asked Donald. 'Your food is delicious.'

'If he is, then I'm going to send Lexi along,' said Edward.

Lexi laughed. 'It's back to gruel for *you* tomorrow!'

Stella raised her glass and toasted Beth and Michael.

Had she imagined that tiny flicker of sadness in Michael's expression when Beth had said "*lives with no regrets?*" She needed to talk to him. If something was wrong, she wanted to help him if she could.

'Got a moment?' Marie touched her arm.

'Of course.'

'I'm not sure how you will feel about this, but DI Jackman has asked me to speak to you about something.'

Stella tilted her head. 'Jackman?'

'He said that he wants you to know that there are ways to get you back on the job. He said to tell you that when you are feeling stronger, you should go and see him. He thinks it would be criminal to lose you.' Marie pursed her lips. 'And he's not the only one. We know you've got a way to go yet, but Jackman said it's important that you know we all want you back.'

Stella was dumbfounded. She managed a croaky, 'Thank you, Marie. Thank you so very much.'

Robbie came up beside them. 'There's someone at the door asking for you.'

Her heart leapt. He'd come! Jack had actually found the courage to make it to the party!

She hurried to the front door, and found a courier in motorcycle leathers. 'Parcel for Stella North. It has to be signed for.'

Stella tried to quell her disappointment. She knew Jack was never going to come. She stared at the small package, signed for it and watched the courier stride back to his bike.

Back inside, she tore off the wrapping and found a thick bubble wrap envelope, and a thinner one with her name across the front.

'Presents? Oh Lord, have I missed your birthday?' Tom appeared at her side.

'No, my birthday is the end of March, and I haven't ordered anything.' She opened the thicker envelope.

'It's a portable external hard drive.' Tom looked puzzled.

Stella ripped open the letter and read and re-read the neat script. *"Stella — These are what you need to get started. I wanted you to have them now, as the whole package could take a while to get through. I'll explain in detail later, but in the meantime, thank you for restoring my resolve. Enjoy the party. Jack."*

Tom was looking at her anxiously. 'Is it private?'

She passed him the letter. 'Not really. Read it.'

'What does he mean by *"the whole package?"*'

'I'm not sure, but he was talking about finances and costings, and he wanted to know exactly what I had in mind long term. Should we see what's on this hard drive?'

They prised Beth from a group of friends and asked if they could use her study and her computer for a few minutes.

Soon they were inside with the door closed.

Stella plugged in the USB cable and opened the file.

'My goodness!' Tom stared at the screen.

'It's his photo files! But a whole lot more than he put up on his site. There must be fifteen years' worth of urbexing here! Look!' She pointed to a file named *Bethlehem*. 'Jeez! I never knew he went to those abandoned steelworks in Pennsylvania. It's one of the biggest industrial sites in America's rust belt!'

'Open it!'

She did, and was almost thrown backwards by the immense power of the images that appeared. They both let out whistles of amazement.

Tom stared at her, his mouth slightly open. 'This is unbelievable! What else has he got on here that we didn't know about?'

Stella clicked on a file named Power. The first shot showed a jungle of steel pipes and huge structures inside a massive, derelict power plant. She moved to the next image. This one took the viewer up into the interior of the great cooling tower. He had labelled it, "The Heart of Silence."

'These are stunning! I'm sure that's in Belgium,' she whispered, 'but it isn't the famous IM plant, or that giant gigawatt thermal power station they call the Cloud Factory. So where is it?'

'Is there an index?'

She went back to the menu. 'Yes, but . . .' She closed down the hard drive and shook her head. Coming just after what Marie had told her, her head was buzzing. 'This is too much to take in right now. We need to do it properly, not here, not at a party. It's Beth and Michael's evening, isn't it?'

Tom nodded. 'You are right, but can I just have another look at that letter?'

She passed it to him, then disconnected the device and slipped it back into the bubble wrap pocket. 'I'd better get back out there now. Have you got time tomorrow to look at this with me?'

'You bet! I'll make time.' Stella left him still reading over the letter. She wondered what was bothering him.

She was discussing Superintendent Croxforth's ignominious departure with Marie and Robbie when Tom approached her and whispered in her ear.

'Stella, I'm worried. I've got very bad vibes about Jack Hammond.'

They went back to the study.

'Have you got Jack's telephone number, Stella?'

'Yes, but why? I can't ring him now, it's almost eleven.'

'You said he sleeps badly and sometimes he's up all night on his computer. Please, I want you to ring him.'

Tom was obviously really worried, so she went and got her phone.

'No answer.' She looked at him anxiously. 'Is that good or bad?'

His face said it all, but still she didn't get it. 'It was a simple letter, Tom. What's the problem?'

'Why was Jack so interested in your *long term* vision for this gallery? Why start working out financial projections, for God's sake? Have I got it wrong, or didn't you just suggest that you combine your images with his for an online image library and maybe a publication?'

She nodded. 'Yes, although I did mention that if they generated enough interest, maybe sometime in the future we could have a studio.'

'In the future . . .' Tom chewed the inside of his cheek. 'Stel, is Jack well off?'

'I guess he is, why?'

'What do you know about his family?'

'Tom! What's with the third degree?'

'I hate to sound like one of you coppers, but can you please just answer the question?'

Stella exhaled. 'I don't know much about it but I don't think he gets on with any of them. His father lives in the

States and worships money. He has sisters, two of them I think, but that's all I know.'

'And his accident? Did he get compensation?'

'Of course he did. He was nearly killed by a lorry that was exceeding the speed limit on ice!'

'Stella, I want to go to his place. Now.' Tom looked almost haggard. All his usual cheer had disappeared, and he was deadly serious.

'You're scaring me, Tom! I don't understand what you're saying.'

'The letter. He says the whole package will take longer to get through. All this crap about finances and overviews. I think he's talking about probate. He's making a bequest, Stella. *That's* how he's planning to help you!'

At last it hit her. Hard.

Things he had said, which she had taken to mean positive healing, were anything but. And his message to the kids now sounded like last words. Yes, she had restored his resolve all right, his resolve to take his own life. 'I'm going to get Marie and Robbie,' she whispered. 'We'll be needing their help. And I should have a word with Michael or they will worry.'

'Okay, but let's slip away quietly. We can't ruin Beth's evening.'

They decided to take Tom's vehicle as he had not been drinking. Stella explained their fears to Marie and Robbie, then wondered how they would get inside Jack's fortress. 'It's locked up tight, with security everywhere.'

'Since when has a locked door kept an urbexer out?' said Tom grimly, staring through the windscreen.

'What's an urbexer?' asked Marie.

'Long story. I'll fill you in later, but it's okay, Tom's not a cat burglar. He's just good at climbing and getting into places.'

'If there's even a rat hole, I have a good chance of getting inside.'

'And you are pretty certain that if we just ring the bell, he won't answer?' asked Robbie.

'I've rung his land line and his mobile several times. He's severely disabled, Rob, and because of his crash he doesn't have a car anymore. He's there alright, he's just not picking up. From the wording of that note, we think we know what he's done.'

'Then I hope we are in time.' Robbie's voice was sombre.

Stella sighed. Deep in her heart she knew that Jack had planned this too well for them to be able to steam in and save the day. He had always been meticulous when organising his explorations. He would be just as thorough in planning his departure.

CHAPTER THIRTY

According to the doctor Marie called to the scene, Jack Hammond had been dead for at least two days. The heating had been turned off, and the low winter temperatures made it difficult to be more accurate.

'It's still classified as a suspicious death until we've had the post-mortem results,' Marie explained to Tom. 'But with the amount of evidence pointing to suicide, CID is happy to let uniform deal with it.'

Tom puffed out his cheeks. 'At least he made quite certain that no one else should be held accountable. He's left letters for his father, his friend, Walt, his solicitor and for Stella. Plus a note of apology to whoever found him.'

'Along with enough empty packets of drugs to kill a rhino, an empty bottle of vodka and a house locked from the inside.' She frowned at him. 'And by the way, I'm not sure I want to know how you managed to get inside so quickly.'

He grinned at her. 'Yeah, best not to ask, huh?'

Stella sat with Robbie and watched as the black undertaker's vehicle drew into the parking area. Jack would be getting outside at last.

'I hope he's at peace now,' she whispered.

'Well, one thing's for sure, he's no longer trapped inside that dreadful house or his broken body. He's free now.' Robbie put his arm around her. 'Stella, with or without you, he would have done this at some point. From what you've told me about him, he's been heading towards it from the second that lorry hit him.'

All her energy had gone, her batteries were suddenly drained.

'It's too soon to try to understand anything, Rob, but I know I pushed him too hard. I should have read between the lines, and now I feel so guilty.'

'Then don't!' Robbie was stern. 'It's not your fault that he didn't have your strength! Everyone is different, Stella. Jack dealt with his problem in his way, end of story.'

'Maybe when you see the letter he left you, you'll feel better about it.' Tom sat down next to her.

Maybe, she thought, but was unconvinced.

'Stella?' Marie joined them. 'Those letters will not be officially released until the post-mortem is completed, but the officer in charge has said that if you want, you can read yours before it's taken away.'

Stella knew it was something she should do on her own. 'I don't think I'm up to it, Marie. The post-mortem will be done either tomorrow or the day after. I'll wait, I think, and get my mind in some sort of order before I listen to a message from the dead.'

'Okay, I understand. I'll tell him.'

Stella felt a sudden urge to get away from this awful place. 'I want to go home.'

'Me too.' Tom stood up. 'And I need to be on the land in four hours' time. Rob, go get hold of your new boss. We've left our details with your buddies and we need to go.'

They said little on the drive back to Coggles Barn. A part of Stella's life had gone for ever. It was small, but it had always been there, like an eternal flame burning in the background.

At Beth's, all the stragglers had left, and only Michael was still up, clearing away and stacking the dishwasher. 'Beth's turned in.' He smiled at them, and then his look turned to one of concern. 'What's happened?'

Stella was relieved that Marie took it upon herself to explain, briefly and concisely.

'You poor things must be frozen. Can I make you some coffee?'

'Thanks, Michael, but we'd better get home.'

'And I need to ring for a cab,' added Rob. 'If I can get one at this time of night.'

'I'll give you a lift if you like.' Marie looked at him. 'I always carry a spare helmet.'

Even Stella was forced to smile at the terror on Robbie's face.

'Or I can drop you off, if the thought of grabbing hold of Marie is too scary.' Tom laughed.

Robbie smiled gratefully. 'I'm not good on bikes. I always lean the wrong way.'

'What an admission!'

Tom hugged Stella. 'You try to get some sleep. We'll talk in the morning, okay?'

She nodded and felt tears welling up in her eyes. 'Ring me?'

'I will. Now get to bed.'

'Tom?'

He stopped and looked back at her.

'Thank you for seeing what Jack meant. It would have been horrible if he hadn't been found for weeks.'

Tom nodded and sighed.

After they had all gone, Michael brought her a hot drink and sat next to her on the sofa. 'Want to talk? Or would you rather take this up to your room?'

'We've ruined your evening.'

'No way. Beth and I had a lovely time. And I certainly won't be telling her about all this tonight.'

'It's such a waste, Michael.'

'These things happen. They are heart-breaking, but sometimes they are inevitable. He must have been desperately unhappy.'

'The funny thing was he seemed so much brighter, so full of enthusiasm.'

'Maybe he just saw a light at the end of his very dark tunnel.'

'He left me a letter. I should have it in a few days.'

'Then wait until you read it before you judge him.' Michael put his arm around her. 'And don't even think about moving out tomorrow. You are very precious to your grandmother *and* to me, so there is no rush about going home.'

'But nothing has really changed, has it, Michael? So as long as I feel up to it, I'll stay on track to get home. I'm still convinced that the time is right.'

'That's fine. But remember, there is no pressure.'

Stella stood up, leant down and kissed his cheek. 'I'm going to bed before I start bawling my eyes out.'

'Nothing wrong with that. I've felt like doing that myself recently.'

Stella stopped. In all the mess of her recent emotions she had forgotten the sad look that she had noticed on Michael's face. 'Something is wrong, isn't it?'

'Nothing is wrong. Nothing at all.'

'You are a rotten liar.'

He gave a short laugh. 'Okay, Miss Marple. I'm just angry with myself, and truth be told, I suppose I feel cheated.'

'Cheated out of all the years that the two of you could have shared?'

'Wouldn't you, if you were our age?'

Stella took a deep breath. 'If you'd asked me that before I got shot, before Edward got ill and maybe even before Jack died, I'd have said a resounding, "Yes!" But not anymore. If you feel angry, you're wasting the time you have left. I think you and Beth should be forever grateful

251

that you are together now, and enjoy every bloody second, don't you?'

'And when exactly did you turn into Karl Jung?'

'Since I started doing your wretched homework, Professor Freud.'

'Point taken, and you are right, of course. Now, as dawn will soon be breaking, I think it's time for bed, don't you?'

Stella agreed and started up the stairs. 'See you in the morn—'

She put out her foot and slipped on a paper napkin that lay unnoticed on a step. She lost her balance and crashed to the bottom, everything happening in slow motion. Stella saw Michael's wide, horror-stricken eyes. Her head hit the bottom step and there was a blinding flash of white light. Then nothing.

CHAPTER THIRTY-ONE

'Stella? Can you hear me? Can you open your eyes for me?'

She'd been here before.

Shadowy figures, men she thought she recognised. Was that her father? He was hazy, wavering in and out of focus, but he was definitely calling to her.

And Jack? Yes, Jack. He stood beside her, but his tall, athletic figure was distorted.

'Stella? Squeeze my hand if you can hear me?'

Why was her father being so persistent? She was happy and safe where she was. Wasn't she? She thought she'd had the same feeling in the past. Then, she had forsaken her warm cocoon. She wondered why.

'Stella.' The voice grew louder as the face came towards hers. She recognised his brown eyes.

'Michael?' she croaked.

'I'm here. And so is Tom.'

She stared at the tall figure and realised it wasn't Jack. Then she remembered that Jack was dead. Wasn't he?

'I don't know what happened.'

'You fell, Stella. You hit your head.'

Okay. People hit their heads all the time.

'You're in the hospital, Stel. You've been unconscious.'

Tom's voice, deep and gentle and full of relief, sounded like honey dribbled over ice cream. 'I'm starving.'

The two men laughed. She had no idea why. Being hungry was no joke.

Then there was another voice, a double-barrelled one. Stella screwed up her face in frustration. That definitely wasn't right. Voices weren't double-barrelled.

'It will pass. The confusion is only temporary. Just try to rest now, Stella. You are back with us, and that's what matters.'

Stella breathed in, and then exhaled slowly. She was aware that a strong hand had taken hers, and she knew she was home again.

* * *

In the waiting room, Beth was dozing fitfully.

'She's awake, Beth. Stella's awake.'

Beth spluttered and sat up. 'Is she . . . ?'

'Confused, but she knew who I was. She's sleeping now.' Michael sat down next to her and put his arm around her shoulders. 'Donald says that the latest scan results show no bleeds on the brain.'

'So why has she taken so long to come round? Two days! I thought . . .' Tears began to course down Beth's face. 'After all she'd been through, everything that she'd overcome after that terrible shooting incident, I thought that I'd lost her over a discarded paper napkin.'

'It was swelling, that's all, around the area of the original bullet wound. Now it's going down. She'll soon be fine again.'

'So, no permanent damage?'

'She'll need to be observed for a while, but I'm sure it was just her brain protecting itself. Basically it put her into hibernation until the inflammation subsided.'

Beth rubbed her tired eyes. 'And is Tom still with her?'

'That boy hasn't left her side since she was brought in. He hasn't slept for more than a few minutes at a time.'

'I have good feelings about Farmer Chalk, Michael.' Beth sighed and wiped her eyes. 'If only Stella would wake up and realise it.'

'We'll see.' Michael yawned. 'We'll see.'

* * *

Tom was sitting in an armchair beside Stella's bed, snoring softly. He was holding her hand. They had had to prise him away from her in the emergency room, and now it seemed he would never let go.

Visitors had come and gone in a steady stream. Beth and Michael had been there off and on all day, Edward and Lexi had brought Ethan to see her, Robbie had dropped in, closely followed by Emily and Ray, and finally Marie had taken time out, with Jackman's blessing, to visit her.

Tonight the room was quiet. Stella had dozed for a while after supper, but now she was fully awake, although she didn't have the heart to disturb the man sleeping beside her. In the dim light of her room, she had time to think.

Everything was crystal clear now. In fact she felt more lucid than she had for months. And not just lucid, she felt a stillness, a sense of peace that hadn't been there prior to cracking her head on the stairs.

Marie had repeated DI Jackman's message about returning to duty, but the more Stella thought about it, the more she realised that it wasn't going to happen.

It had been her dream to get back into the police force. But she had come to understand that her life as a detective was over. She'd done her bit, and got her commendation. Now it was time for her to have a life of her own, and unless she was very much mistaken — she glanced at the sleeping figure of Tom Chalk — she had someone to share it with.

As the minutes ticked by in the silent room, Stella at last allowed herself to think about Jack Hammond.

By freeing himself, he had freed her too.

For years he had cast a long shadow over every one of her relationships. Every man had been compared to the Jackhammer. But what she had had with him had not been real. She knew that now. It was unsustainable out in the real world. Unwittingly, Jack had held her back from committing herself to anyone else. She had been carrying a torch for something that had happened in a fleeting, impossible moment, in an enchanted castle.

Stella sighed and listened to Tom's regular breathing, feeling the pressure of his hand wrapped around hers. This was *real* life. Someone who would be there for her, and who would care more for her than for himself.

In ITU, before she had properly woken up, she had heard him say to Beth, 'I let her down once before, and I've never forgiven myself. I wasn't there for her because I was scared. That will *never* happen again.'

She looked at his sleeping face. There was gentleness and humour in his expression. She had always been comfortable in his company, and she had always known that she could trust him, especially when they went on explorations together. She laughed softly. She'd even trusted him with her virginity!

She squeezed his hand gently, knowing that they would be together. She didn't want dangerous anymore — dangerous men, dangerous hobbies and a dangerous career. She wanted to be safe. She and her family.

And that was another thing. Seeing Edward and Lexi with their son had made having a child seem like a wonderful adventure.

Tom's eyes opened, and he grinned at her. 'Hey! Sorry, I must have dropped off. How are you feeling?'

'You "dropped off" for a whole hour! And I feel really good, all things considered. Apparently my head is not my weakest point.' Though I have doubts about my heart, she thought to herself.

'One more day, then Doc Field-Latimer says you can go home.'

'I can't wait. I really can't.'

'And once you are fighting fit, we are going to go back to that lovely old hotel by the waterfall, and this time you are going to do the walk down into the gorge. No excuses.'

Stella settled back into her pillows. 'That sounds wonderful.'

'It does, doesn't it? And this time it'll be my treat.'

They talked for a while, and then Tom's expression became serious. 'Marie came in earlier, while you were resting. She gave me Jack's letter to give to you. She told me that the post-mortem showed no foul play and cause of death was found to be suicide.'

He placed the envelope on her lap.

Stella nodded slowly. 'Shall we read it together?'

'Surely it's private, Stella?'

'As you once said to me, "Just answer the question."'

'Yes, let's read it.'

'Thank you.'

Dear Stella,

By now you will understand how I saw my involvement in your venture. Please don't be too angry with me, but I made use of your enthusiasm for my own ends.

The thing is, I cannot abide my family. There is not one of them that I would want to leave a brass farthing to. And I've pondered this point for some while. I could have left everything to a donkey sanctuary or some other worthy charity, and in fact there is a considerable sum set aside for something like that. (As there is no Home for Retired urbexers, I chose Water Aid). I just needed something to feel right, and your idea was perfect. It fired my imagination and finally I got off my arse and got my life (and death) sorted. And so you will find some things of interest in my will. Don't worry, Stella, I haven't left you my prison block. I saw your face. But I have managed to retain the ownership of Hall Place Manor from my father, and should you wish to set up a studio/gallery/workshop/gaming den/knocking shop, whatever, it is yours. And to help you get started, my computer system that has all the relevant software and programs for what you need, is also yours. There is also a sum of money, as any new business requires a stable financial platform.

You will already have my photo files and I hope you like them. Maybe give me a posthumous credit when the book gets published?

Now, before I finish, I'm going to run the pictures of the Chateau Sapin Noir, and remember what it was like to be Jackhammer.

Yours,

Jack.

Stella sat for a moment, then passed the letter to Tom.

He read it, then said, 'Well, at least there was no stuff about "*I can't go on!*" You have to admire him. He made his decision and he saw it through.' He looked up in amazement, 'And he's left you Hall Place Manor! Ray will be pig-sick! He adores that place!'

'But it's a wreck. I mean, it's a beautiful wreck, but what on earth can I do with it? I was thinking more of a small unit for a studio, not a manor house in acres of rambling gardens.'

Tom puffed out his cheeks. 'I don't think the manor is that bad actually. Last time we were there, Ray was saying that it is basically very sound, and with so many features undamaged it wouldn't take a fortune to restore.' He looked into the distance. 'Actually, apart from all those lovely grounds, it has enormous potential. And there is something else you should know.' He looked at her, eyebrows raised.

'While you were playing Sleeping Beauty, Michael and Donald Field-Latimer were talking about not being able to find anywhere classy enough for their new clinic. The manor could be perfect for them. And I could be wrong, but I would guess they have a considerable amount of the readies to put up for the renovation. What do you think?'

'I think it's not a bad idea at all.' She grinned. 'And if all goes belly up we can get Razor's dad to buy it for his son.'

'It might happen! That guy is loaded. Hey, Stel! I reckon you've been given a gold mine!' Then the frown returned. 'I don't get what he meant about the Chateau Sapin Noir and being Jackhammer again?'

Stella decided that this part of their history didn't need to be explored. 'It was the place in Belgium where I met him. And I think he's reminding us that he got there first. It was the place we'd all spent years hunting for. He found the "Jewel in the Crown," and that made him the greatest urban explorer.'

'Oh, I see. Well, we can't argue with that, can we?'

'And I *will* give him full credit for those amazing photographs.'

'So you'll go ahead with the project?'

'Oh yes, although I imagine it will take a long time before Jack's affairs are sorted out, what with probate and all the legal stuff.' She lay back and closed her eyes. 'I think I should back off from doing anything just yet. It's time to take stock. And right now I'm going to concentrate on getting strong again, and what better way to do it than to have a few days in Yorkshire, especially as you're paying.'

'Let's make it a week, shall we?'

'Why not? And, Tom, don't waste your money on two rooms. One luxury suite would be perfect.'

Tom's eyes lit up. 'Are you saying what I think you're saying?'

'Well, I've had a bang on the head, haven't I?'

A broad smile spread across his face. 'True. And I would be a real jerk to take advantage of that, wouldn't I?'

'Frankly I think you'd be more of a jerk if you didn't.' Her face became serious. 'Baby steps, Tom. Just for a while, okay?'

He nodded. 'That's fine by me. And we'll do exactly as you said, back off from the world. We'll get you better, have a lovely holiday, take stock, and then we'll do what we always loved best, Starburst.'

'And what's that?'

'There's a beautiful world out there, Stella. I suggest we go explore it . . .' He took her hand.

'Together,' she completed his thought.

THE END

Thank you for reading this book. If you enjoyed it please leave feedback on Amazon or Goodreads, and if there is anything we missed or you have a question about then please get in touch. The author and publishing team appreciate your feedback and time reading this book.

Our email is office@joffebooks.com

www.joffebooks.com